"GET OUT OF MY HOUSE!" JOSH RAGED.

Staring openly, Jaclyn refused to answer.

"Can't you hear me?" he demanded.

"I hear you," she whispered, staring at his broad chest that stirred such a deep longing in her it was hard to tear her eyes away.

"Then get moving," he commanded.

"I have no intention of doing so. Not yet anyway," she added. "I'm here to deliver myself as a gift from your best friend."

"Think again, witch," he snarled. "I'm not interested in you or your wares, so shove off."

CANDLELIGHT ECSTASY SUPREMES

49 COLOR LOVE BLUE, *Diana Blayne*
50 ON ANY TERMS, *Shirley Hart*
51 HORIZON'S GIFT, *Betty Jackson*
52 ONLY THE BEST, *Lori Copeland*
53 AUTUMN RAPTURE, *Emily Elliott*
54 TAMED SPIRIT, *Alison Tyler*
55 MOONSTRUCK, *Prudence Martin*
56 FOR ALL TIME, *Jackie Black*
57 HIDDEN MANEUVERS, *Eleanor Woods*
58 LOVE HAS MANY VOICES, *Linda Randall Wisdom*
59 ALL THE RIGHT MOVES, *JoAnna Brandon*
60 FINDERS KEEPERS, *Candice Adams*
61 FROM THIS DAY FORWARD, *Jackie Black*
62 BOSS LADY, *Blair Cameron*
63 CAUGHT IN THE MIDDLE, *Lily Dayton*
64 BEHIND THE SCENES, *Josephine Charlton Hauber*
65 TENDER REFUGE, *Lee Magner*
66 LOVESTRUCK, *Paula Hamilton*
67 QUEEN OF HEARTS, *Heather Graham*
68 A QUESTION OF HONOR, *Alison Tyler*
69 FLIRTING WITH DANGER, *Joanne Bremer*
70 ALL THE DAYS TO COME, *Jo Calloway*
71 BEST-KEPT SECRETS, *Donna Kimel Vitek*
72 SEASON OF ENCHANTMENT, *Emily Elliott*
73 REACH FOR THE SKY, *Barbara Andrews*
74 LOTUS BLOSSOM, *Hayton Monteith*
75 PRIZED POSSESSION, *Linda Vail*
76 HIGH VOLTAGE, *Lori Copeland*

STOLEN IDYLL

Alice Morgan

A CANDLELIGHT ECSTASY SUPREME

Published by
Dell Publishing Co., Inc.
1 Dag Hammarskjold Plaza
New York, New York 10017

ISBN: 0-440-18335-9

Printed in the United States of America

First printing—June 1985

Stolen Idyll is dedicated to the many wonderful readers who took time to write and ask for an update on Brad and Brandy from my first book:

MASQUERADE OF LOVE

A CANDLELIGHT ECSTASY ROMANCE®
APRIL 1982

Thank you for the letters.

To Our Readers:

Candlelight Ecstasy is delighted to announce the start of a brand-new series—Ecstasy Supremes! Now you can enjoy a romance series unlike all the others—longer and more exciting, filled with more passion, adventure, and intrigue—the stories you've been waiting for.

In months to come we look forward to presenting books by many of your favorite authors and the very finest work from new authors of romantic fiction as well. As always, we are striving to present the unique, absorbing love stories that you enjoy most—the very best love has to offer.

Breathtaking and unforgettable, Ecstasy Supremes will follow in the great romantic tradition you've come to expect *only* from Candlelight Ecstasy.

Your suggestions and comments are always welcome. Please let us hear from you.

Sincerely,

The Editors
Candlelight Romances
1 Dag Hammarskjold Plaza
New York, New York 10017

CHAPTER ONE

"All packed and ready to go," Jaclyn said out loud while giving the guest room a final once-over.

She lifted the receiver, intent on phoning Pan Am to find out if the heavy blanket of coastal fog would delay her upcoming flight. Evidently unnoticed, she listened to her brother greet his best friend.

"Listen close, Josh," he began, "because I've just arranged to send you the finest birthday and early Christmas gift combination any man ever received."

"Knowing how your mind works, Bruce, I presume it will have something to do with women," Josh answered smoothly.

At the sound of Josh's voice Jaclyn felt a tremor run the length of her spine. Quickly sitting down on the edge of the bed, she gripped the receiver in both hands and listened to the man she had loved since she was fourteen years old.

"Am I right?" he continued with obvious boredom.

"I'll say you are," her relative admitted with a suggestive laugh.

"I'm not interested," Josh countered quickly. His reply was blunt and unmistakably meant to stop any further comment on that subject.

Jaclyn's expression softened, changing her eyes from slate to a dreamy dove-gray. She had never outgrown the miracle of physically reacting to Josh's sensual masculinity. It had always been that way when she was in his presence or heard his deep resonant voice. He had filled her mind with unspeakable desires when she was an innocent teen-ager. Now a mature woman nine years older, he still had the power to bring vivid erotic images into her dreams.

"I'm not in the mood for feminine company to-night." Josh interrupted her introspective thoughts with decided firmness.

Unperturbed by the rejection, her brother asked, "And why not? You're beginning to act as dedicated and serious as my little sis. Lord only knows why she chooses to live like a nun in this day and age."

"Still waters run deep, old buddy," Josh responded calmly. "It seems that after all these years you still don't understand my psyche nor Jaclyn's either."

"Maybe not," Bruce conceded, "but I do know you were a hell of a lot more fun in college. We really had some wild times together, didn't we?"

"Agreed, but that was over ten years ago too," Josh reminded.

"Yes, and it wouldn't surprise me if it's been that long since you've had a really hot piece of tail!"

Mutely, Jaclyn strained to hear each word. She couldn't have replaced the receiver if her life depended on it, she was so intent on hearing what Josh would say.

"So?" he answered in a flat voice edged with exasperation. "Who appointed you record keeper of my sex life?"

"No one," Bruce admitted easily. "You told me yourself you can't sleep at night. Nothing cures insomnia quicker than sexual exhaustion if not sexual satisfaction."

"I said I'm not interested. Now forget it!" Josh

commanded with obvious annoyance. "Being blind is all I can handle right now."

"You don't need your eyesight to make love," Bruce teased.

"I don't need a social disease either!" he reminded his friend bluntly.

"Would I send you anything but the best?" Bruce retorted with devilish humor. "This is high-class stuff and cost me a bundle. She's no amateur night tryout, but a professional working girl all gift wrapped and ready to satisfy any of your needs."

"I'm not impressed."

"Didn't you hear me, Josh? I said this chick will do anything. Did you get that?" His voice rose, echoing his own excitement. "Anything you ask . . . she'll do it to you or let you do it to her, for that matter."

"Yeah, me and anybody else who's stupid enough to fork over a twenty-dollar bill."

"Twenty dollars!" her older brother returned in disgust. "I didn't get this broad off the streets. She's guaranteed by the best"—he laughed—"escort service"—he laughed louder—"in the area."

"I'm not now, have not been in the past, or will not be in the future interested in using you as a pimp!"

"I was afraid of that," Bruce complained. "It's too late now to stop her. She's on her way to your house, and it cost me two hundred bucks, so use her, damn it!"

"You use her!" Josh snapped back with rising annoyance. "I don't need you . . . best buddy . . . to procure women for me. I'm not helpless nor am I so damned hard up to get laid I'd use the services of a hooker I can't even see."

"Don't be so stubborn," her brother chastised while mentally going over his plans without thought of change.

"Me stubborn?" Josh argued. "Take her yourself, Bruce. You're between wives now and have always been willing to get it on with anything female since I've known you."

"So were you a decade ago."

"I've matured, thank God, and learned to direct my energies to more productive endeavors."

"What's more productive than a good piece of tail?" Bruce contradicted without animosity. "A clump of cold clay and those bronze statues you create make a damned poor substitute for warm thighs wrapped around a man's hips."

"Get your brains out of your Jockey shorts, friend. I don't want any, so thanks but no thanks."

"Can't you just accept an hour's fun and games without all this psychological bull? I feel guilty enough as it is for ramming your head through the windshield."

"Don't," Josh pointed out truthfully. "The car accident wasn't your fault. I saw my specialist today and he all but guaranteed me I'll be completely healed with normal eyesight in two . . . maybe three months at the most."

"Well, I'm not canceling now," Bruce answered with decided stubbornness.

"Then she'll damned well find my door padlocked!" his friend stormed back with such determination the guest room resounded with his anger.

Jaclyn hung up the phone at the same time Josh slammed down the receiver, knowing she should feel ashamed at listening to the uninhibited conversation between the two men.

Her palms were clammy with fear that Josh would welcome the girl offered. She couldn't bear to know another woman would touch him intimately and be the recipient of his virile body the night before she planned to fly back to Paris.

A frown creased Jaclyn's temples as a sudden idea formed and grew into a plan more daring than her brothers. "It's foolproof," she whispered to the empty room. Her mind reeled with reasons to go ahead with the impetuous scheme. She stood up, tightened the belt of her coat, and stepped forward.

This was a chance in a lifetime and one any high-spirited female would take full advantage of, she thought. Then she prompted herself with fingers crossed just to assure a little added luck.

While Bruce was still involved in the living room, she rushed into the next-door master bedroom. She knew he and Josh had keys to each other's homes and where Josh's was kept. Quick as a thief she pocketed the shiny metal and returned to her room.

Slipping her purse strap over one shoulder, she lifted up her worn duffel bag and a large suitcase crammed full of fashionable seaside boutique purchases. With her chin tilted at a determined angle, she forced herself to walk quietly from the upstairs bedroom.

"After all, it will benefit both of us equally," Jaclyn claimed, trying to rationalize any inner doubts. "At least I hope it will," she admitted with more honesty as she reached the end of the hallway.

She was just in time to hear Bruce willfully give a message service Josh's address, then his own credit card number for the supposed legitimate escort service.

"Have a well-stacked, sexy girl there at eight o'clock sharp and tell her to say Bruce sent me!" he insisted, turning his head as she descended the stairs.

"Oh, hi, sis," Bruce greeted. Ignoring her thoughtful look, he forgot the call and grinned. His smile was as big as his love for his only relative. Taking her luggage, he kissed her brow. "I'll miss you, little one."

"I'll miss you too," Jaclyn returned, nuzzling her brother's strong shoulder. "It was well worth the thirteen-and-a-half-hour flight even if I could only stay a few days."

What a liar I am, she thought. Bruce would die of shock if he knew the main reason she'd flown over was to assure herself Josh was all right. Her heart had almost quit beating when she'd read the long-delayed letter that explained briefly about his serious car accident. And once she had seen him the moment she arrived, she was reassured he would be fine. Bruce would never know the anxiety she had felt when she got the news.

Through the years she'd become an accomplished actress at hiding her inner feelings from family and friends and most of all from the man she loved. "Thanks for the hospitality." She gave his arm an affectionate squeeze. It was always painful to say goodbye.

"What happened to your voice?" he asked, looking at her with curiosity. "You sound like a deep-voiced sex siren instead of my shy, innocent baby sister."

Jaclyn's heavy lashes lowered in protest. "I'm no longer a child, Bruce."

"Honey, with men you're still as sinless as a newborn baby." His laugh was loud at her unexpected display of concern over his remarks.

She momentarily bristled at her brother's refusal to believe she had matured, meeting his glance with a touch of chagrin. "I might be," she admitted, shooting him a frosty glance. "Then again I might not be."

Heaven knows that inside her stomach muscles were still quivering at the expectation her secret fantasies could soon be real. Even Bruce would have to agree those dreams were neither childish or naive.

"Surely you didn't pick up a cold that affected your voice as well as your present mental state in our California sunshine?" he teased. His eyes still twinkled with ready humor at her sudden comeback.

"California wetshine," Jaclyn mocked huskily, deciding it best to ignore any further discussion about her innocence or lack of it. "Fortunately, I'm not sick, only hoarse. As you know, it's rained every day since I've been here."

"All six of them," Bruce scolded back. "You're not mad I can't take you to LAX, are you?"

Jaclyn shook her head no. "You couldn't anyway since I have to return the rental car. Besides, my flight leaves at nine in the morning, and it's more convenient to stay at a hotel that has commuter service direct to the airport terminal."

Giving him an impish smile, she teased, "Who's your new girl?"

Josh was right. Her brother's interest in women was constant, and though never mentioned, was probably the reason for the early breakup of his marriages.

"A gorgeous typist at my toughest competitors'. After tonight she'll probably be begging to be my private secretary."

"I can't keep up with all your women."

"Don't try. Just take care of yourself, sis, and try to stay away from men like me," he pointed out seriously. "Someone in our family has to have a few morals, though I think, despite your brief claim of questionable chastity, you're overdoing the celibacy bit a little too much."

"Is being a little bit celibate anything like being a little bit pregnant?" she countered in an amused voice.

"Touché, sis. You're shocking me tonight." He

kissed her forehead and gave her a long, thoughtful look. "Seriously now, you've never even been interested in the male sex, have you, honey?"

Before Jaclyn could dispute his question he hugged her. Many times in the past she had wished for the right opportunity to tell him her shyness was outward only and that inside she was often torn apart with passion for Josh. She knew her deep yearning for his best friend was equal to any woman's.

"You're the only family I have now," Bruce added tenderly.

"Just me and three ex-wives," she reminded him as they walked from his luxurious condo to the underground garage.

"Don't mention them," he grimaced, placing the luggage effortlessly in the trunk of her rented Ford. "See you in six months."

"Three months and fourteen days to be exact, big brother," Jaclyn corrected. "I'm returning for a gala twenty-fourth birthday party."

"Hosted by anyone I know?" he questioned curiously.

"Your best friend."

"Josh?" Bruce asked aghast. "When did he promise you that?"

"When I was sixteen." Jaclyn snuggled deep into a full-length black leather coat that contrasted vividly with her ash-blond hair. Gracefully sliding behind the steering wheel, she stared upward with complete confidence.

"Forget it, then, as Josh will have. Tell you what I'll do," Bruce promised. "If this new woman doesn't strike sparks like I think she will, I'll fly over and we'll celebrate by driving down to Monaco and trying our luck at the roulette tables."

"No go." Jaclyn gave her brother a sweet smile as

she slipped the key into the ignition. "I've waited eight years for this party, and I guarantee I'm not about to let the man forget it now. Also, I expect each of you to get me a really grand present."

"Will you have a collection ready by then?"

"As promised," Jaclyn answered, letting the motor warm up. "I assured Josh when I first arrived it would be finished and ready to exhibit in his gallery on the day of my party."

"I'm amazed." Bruce shook his head, never quite understanding his sister's serious personality and apparent pleasure in hard work.

"I don't know why. When I was sixteen, I pledged I'd be skilled enough by the time I was twenty-four, and I've been working toward that goal ever since."

She looked up at her brother's handsome features and explained in a voice he had to strain to hear. "At that age Josh was the most talented and important person I knew. He encouraged me and believed I had special artistic talent. He also told me if I studied diligently and continued to show promise, he'd guarantee I'd have the best exhibit he could plan."

"You never told me that before," Bruce said, thinking he'd have to thank Josh when he saw him next. "You've done well, then, considering you spent two years worrying the hell out of me working for the Peace Corps."

"Those years are what has made my art so important now. Improved it too," Jaclyn pointed out. Impatient to leave, she urged, "The fog's getting thicker. I'd better go soon, or I won't get checked into my room until midnight."

"Drive carefully and keep safe, little one," Bruce said, giving her a quick kiss on her smooth brow.

"You, too, brother mine," she added, unashamed that emotional tears shimmered in her eyes.

With a wave she turned her attention to driving and backed out of the garage in preparation for the winding trip down the hillside.

Arriving at the main highway, Jaclyn turned south instead of going north toward Los Angeles. From the moment Bruce called the escort service she had become preoccupied with an idea that would leave her brother aghast with her intent.

"One phone call coming up," she spoke to the darkened interior of her car. Stopping in front of a gas station phone booth, she grabbed a handful of change and walked into the glass enclosure.

Pleased to get the reservation clerk on the first try, Jaclyn identified herself. "Something unexpected came up and I have to cancel my seat on overseas flight number one-sixteen to Paris. I'll rebook when I arrive in Los Angeles tomorrow."

In the car she smiled. Now that was what was meant by burning your bridges behind you. She intended to be such a thoroughly exciting temptress Josh wouldn't let her leave one second before his hour was up.

She drove toward the next corner with a determined smile lighting her expressive face. After all their heavy lovemaking, she continued thinking, she'd undoubtedly have to rent a motel nearby as she intended to be so sexually satiated she wouldn't be up to driving to LA until the next afternoon!

With outward confidence belying her churning abdomen she pulled onto a paved street bordering Josh's oceanside gallery. On the rare opportunities she had browsed inside she was always filled with awe over works that inspired her constant need to excel.

The foggy darkness acted as protective covering as she eased into a tree-shrouded parking space and waited for the woman her brother procured.

"Right on time," she whispered, checking her watch in the faint glow of the gallery's display lighting when a car slowed down as if the driver were checking addresses. The well-lit numbers of the gallery were clearly visible, and as expected, the unseen driver stopped.

Jaclyn took a deep breath, stepped from her car, and intercepted a tall woman whose unbuttoned mink-dyed rabbit fur jacket exposed a thigh-length, skin-tight red dress. She looked barely legal age but even the dim light couldn't hide the street-wise experience visible in her dark-rimmed eyes.

"You are from the escort service, aren't you?" Jaclyn questioned gravely, standing face to face with her adversary.

"Maybe. Maybe not. Why are you here?" the woman demanded, hitching a gigantic shoulder bag over one shoulder. She looked her interloper up and down as thoroughly as she had just been inspected.

"To see your customer," Jaclyn replied softly. "Bruce sent me."

"You too? It's gonna cost another hundred then," the woman demanded boldly, completely misunderstanding Jaclyn's presence. "They didn't tell me this would be a three-way swing."

"It isn't," Jaclyn confirmed, trying hard not to act shocked. "Your, er, services won't be needed tonight."

"Don't give me that crap," the pouting crimson lips shot back. With a toss of her tightly permed red curls, she snapped, "I've got the right address, the trick's house is supposed to be in back, and since I don't want my old man kicking my ass black-and-blue, I'll earn every dollar as quick as possible. This isn't my first or last trick for the night, you know?"

"I didn't think it was," Jaclyn answered matter-of-factly. The woman was quite striking in a voluptuous, heavily made-up manner. She presumed most men would think her hardness sensual. She knew her brother would think her extremely erotic.

Prepared ahead of time for this situation, Jaclyn thrust a bill into the woman's outstretched hand. "Here's another hundred." She watched as the money was hurriedly crammed into the cleavage of a low-necked dress. "No one will ever know you didn't, er, service"—she almost choked over that word—"the, er, trick," another unfamiliar term, "inside."

"Be my guest," the woman tossed back, rushing to her car. "He must be some special john if you want him so bad you'll pay me extra just so you can have him all to yourself."

"He is," Jaclyn whispered into the dampened air as the woman sped down the road toward the main highway. "Dear God, how very special he is."

Jaclyn locked the car, gripped her purse with icy fingers, and turned toward a bricked path that edged around the side of the gallery. She shivered in the cold damp air despite the warmth of her coat. The brief interchange was sordid but necessary. She had to intercept the woman in order to complete her own hastily arranged plans. So far Josh's seduction couldn't have worked out smoother if she'd planned it for weeks.

"Chin up, shoulders back, and prepare yourself to give an academy-award performance," Jaclyn expelled into the alarming mist.

She couldn't believe that less than one hour ago her only thought was returning to Paris and completing a series of paintings she had been working on for months.

Darn! Why was it so dark tonight? It was an effort just to keep from falling down. She took another cautious step ahead with one hand outstretched for balance. She could hardly see a foot in front of her face.

The switch in plans was uncanny. A chance phone conversation overheard. A sudden impulse, and here she was tiptoeing to seduce her brother's best friend as if she didn't have a qualm in the world. Thank gosh, Bruce would never know, she thought with some relief, glad he thought her safely en route on the first part of her journey to France. Fortunately, he never kept close tabs on her and wouldn't expect to receive a call or letter for at least a month.

Moisture on her coat and hair collected in a damp film and dripped from the overhanging eucalyptus leaves. The thick swirling fog added to her heightened sense of entering a forbidden area.

She should be glad. Without the long stretch of unexpected bad weather she wouldn't have a catch in her throat that made her voice unrecognizable to her own relative. Josh, whom she had only seen for an hour or two the first day she arrived, would never be aware who she was. The aloof beast probably didn't even know she was still in Laguna Beach, she reflected morosely.

Curls from her newly styled hair brushed her cheeks adding to the sense of unreality. Instead of being confined in a long single braid or upsweep as she had worn it for years, the thick waves swung free across her shoulder blades. It was a decidedly more attractive hair style, she acknowledged without vanity.

Even her coat was new and high fashion. Quite unlike the casual khaki raincoat she'd arrived with.

She stopped at the tall gate, searched for the concealed latch, and pushed it back, thinking how out of character her actions were. Lerisa wouldn't believe this even if she gave her the intimate details, Jaclyn realized. Her closest friend would never dream the serious art student who rarely talked about men could suddenly change into a resolute woman intent on convincing an experienced male eight years older that she was equal to him in sexual sophistication.

"Oh, Lord, I must be crazy."

Shutting the gate behind her, Jaclyn peered into the gloom, not certain which was louder . . . the pounding of her heart or the ocean.

None of this would be happening if Josh weren't blind, she thought, as if trying to convince herself he had to share some of the responsibility for her personality change. Since Josh couldn't see to identify her as the woman he made love to, that was the ultimate . . . the only reason . . . she'd embarked on the most preposterous scheme of her entire life.

She swallowed twice, placed her foot hesitantly on the first broad step, and whispered into the gloomy night, "Shoulders back, Ms. Howard. You're soon to be a more typical modern twenty-three-year-old. Experienced, mature, and for once in your busy, serious life-style . . . sexually enlightened!"

There were no lights on in the massive stone house that overlooked the raging Pacific Ocean. Why should there be? she speculated, walking up the low stairs and onto the wide deck. Josh certainly wouldn't be able to tell one way or the other.

"Mr. Kingman, you are about to be had," Jaclyn announced under the cover of a loud knock.

Repeated until her knuckles hurt, she felt her heart beat erratically. It was just as she suspected. Josh had told her brother he wasn't going to answer his door and meant it.

Prepared, Jaclyn reached in her coat pocket for Bruce's key. Just to double-check she felt along the damp edge just inside the north porch light. It was there! She knew one thing no hired seductress did and that was exactly where Josh kept his spare key. Taking her brother's key had been to ensure positive entry if the spare had been moved. She wanted no setback tonight.

With fingers that shook, equally from cold and nervousness, she inserted the key into the heavy wrought-iron knob. Opening the door, she pushed it back and switched on a light that lit the comfortably warm room with startling brightness. Taking a deep breath she stared with darkened gray eyes while praying her knees wouldn't buckle before she finished surveying the room in search of Josh.

"Good heavens, I'm going to faint," she whispered, fighting a sudden bout of nausea.

CHAPTER TWO

"Not in my house, you're not!" Josh raged. He spun a large wingback swivel rocker around and looked directly at her as if his bandaged eyes equaled her wide-eyed stare.

"Get out of my house now and don't dare set foot in it again, or I'll call the police and have you thrown in jail."

Jaclyn ignored his anger. Her heart was torn with sympathy to see the man she loved deprived of sight. It had to be a terrible setback in his heavy work schedule of creating magnificent sculpture with such stunning realism that he was already world renowned. It would be an impossible task since the accident. His heavily commissioned skills would necessitate the use of both eyes and hands to match the previous perfection.

"Get out, damn you!" he threatened in a low voice that would have filled her heart with terror if she were a stranger.

Staring openly, she refused to answer. Despite the trauma, he looked fit and virile sitting with his head raised arrogantly upward and pointed in her exact direction. His widespread fingers clenched the chair arms in a way that suggested he wished they were encircling her throat.

"Can't you hear me?" he demanded.

"I hear you," she whispered, staring at his broad hair-covered chest exposed beneath an unbuttoned white dress shirt. It stirred such a deep longing in her it was hard to tear her eyes away from the sculpted muscles of his athletic torso.

Slowly surveying his lower body, she admired the way his black form-fitting jeans emphasized the power in his long legs. His bare feet were as tanned as his chest and large, yet perfectly proportioned, like the rest of his tall frame.

"Then get moving," he commanded rudely.

"I have no intention of doing so." Amazed at how courageous she felt, knowing he couldn't see her, Jaclyn closed the door, boldly locked it, and set down her purse. Draping her coat over a side table, she casually walked forward and stopped directly in front of him.

"Not yet anyway," she added, hoping her uncommon bravado would see her through the hour ahead. "I'm here to deliver myself as a gift from your best friend."

"Think again, witch," he snarled, tightening his grip on the chair arm until his knuckles whitened and the muscles in his body tensed. "I'm not interested in you or your wares, so shove off."

"Your verbal threats don't bother me in the least," she exclaimed throatily. That was a blatant lie. He looked perfectly capable of carrying out any order he issued.

"They damn well should," Josh advised in a steely voice.

Without warning he lurched up out of the chair and clasped her slender shoulders with uncanny accuracy.

Before she could avoid his touch, she was held securely in the grip of his strong hands.

"If my words don't scare you, then maybe my

strength will," he threatened, pressing his thumbs into her collarbone until she flinched.

She stared with shimmering, tear-filled eyes, refusing to utter a sound of protest though her heart was beating like a wild animal. Nothing she could possibly endure at his hands would equal his traumatic injury.

"What does frighten you?" he demanded when she didn't cry out. "I know damned well the pressure on your fragile bones has to be painful. You're not a masochist too, are you?"

"Maybe." Jaclyn lowered her head to murmur inaudibly, "Maybe I am." It was true she had suffered years of agony over wanting the man who held her. Nearly a decade of deep physical yearning had elapsed because of her inability to express her feelings openly like all her girl friends did.

She raised her eyes to scrutinize Josh's face. It was marvelous and never failed to move her. He was intelligent, ruggedly handsome, and so appealing she'd been unmoved by any other male from the moment they met.

"You're wasting your time here," Josh informed her brusquely. "Hookers don't interest me in the least."

"Why not? I'm free," Jaclyn flared back with equal audacity. "Nothing I do will cost you a cent."

"Which is probably just what you're worth." His voice with heavy with sarcasm.

"You won't know unless you try me," she taunted, continuing her scrutiny unperturbed.

His skin was deeply bronzed, the mustache thick but neatly trimmed. Rough-cut wavy hair crowned his proud head in vibrant chestnut-brown waves. He was so sensual-looking she wanted to burrow her face into his chest and confess she had loved him since she was a teen-ager.

"Try you, hell, you smart-mouthed bitch!" he raged.

"The only thing I'll do to you is throw you out my door."

Despite his indignation tears blurred her vision, blotting out his features as she blinked to clear them away. It was agony to know his keen indigo-blue eyes were painfully injured beneath their narrow strip of bandage.

"Your anger doesn't bother me in the least," she boldly informed him in a husky whisper.

"What does, then?" he insisted coldly, breaking into her deep introspection with spine-tingling wrath.

"Going back to my old man before your time's up," she snapped, imitating the call girl's abrupt words. It was time to forget how maudlin she felt and resume her duplicity. "I have to stay here for an hour at least."

"Why?"

"If I go back early, I'll get beat," Jaclyn lied, remembering the redhead's tart remark. She was fast beginning to think that prostitution was more a crime of violence than of sex.

"I thought you were a high-priced call girl, not some street hooker with a mean pimp."

"Er, ah, I am, but my, er, financial overseer still manages me. He won't allow any of his women to pass up a chance to earn money." Would the questions ever stop?

"You've already been paid for your time, and I know for a fact you were paid well."

"Sure, but my man will think you weren't satisfied when the escort service tells him I came back early."

"Do you think I care what your cheap pimp thinks?" Josh growled low in his throat. "Go hustle on a corner or work a bar. Just get your butt out of here."

Giving her a fierce shake, he challenged with increasing fury, "How the hell did you get inside my house anyway?"

"When you didn't answer my knock, I looked until I found a key," Jaclyn answered back just as forcefully. "People always leave them in obvious places."

"Mine wasn't," Josh contradicted. His expression changed immediately, mouth thinned and motionless in deep contemplation. Still holding her firmly, he inhaled deeply as his dark brows drew together in a deep frown.

"I found it on the first try," Jaclyn bragged, hoping she sounded far tougher than she felt with his body so close to her own. Even with his grip rough on her sensitive skin she gloried in his touch. It was the longest he'd held her since her sixteenth birthday.

"Are you a burglar too?" Josh asked in disgust.

"Not me. It's all I can do to keep up with the demand for my body." Her voice was so saccharine, the words so out of character she nearly gagged. Never in his wildest dreams would he guess who he was holding.

"Damn," he cursed. Shaking his head, he took a deep breath to inhale her scent again. His fingers began to explore her shoulders with slow rhythmic motions as if trying to visualize her image. "If I could only see!"

If you could, I wouldn't be enjoying this, Jaclyn mused, running her hands up Josh's smooth cotton shirt. She made certain to avoid the enticing dark hair covering his hard chest. That she would tackle later.

Heady with thoughts of what lay ahead, she took advantage of his silent acceptance and deliberately brushed his chin with her scented hair. Her fingers came to a rest on the width of his strong shoulders.

So far so good, she exulted, pushing her hips forward. Deliberately brushing the tips of her full breasts against his naked chest, she cautiously eased one leg between his. Thank gosh for all the explicit French films she'd seen on TV during the last few months. Without them she'd probably be standing tongue-tied and motionless or already well on her way out his door.

"You're wasting time, lover," she reminded him in a low drawl which she hoped sounded sexy and sophisticated. "You only get my talents for an hour, then I'm off to my next, er . . . trick . . . and you'll never see me again."

"That's the first good news I've had tonight," Josh said with sarcasm. He had strength in his voice as well as his body. Even in his bare feet, and her wearing her highest-heeled shoes, he towered over her.

Despite his harsh words she was elated by the progress thus far. His sudden intake of breath and taut muscles proved he wasn't totally indifferent to her advances. The fact that she was still in his house was a major victory.

"Are you leaving of your own accord or do I throw you out?"

"Right now neither sounds good," she admitted, which was the first honest thing she'd said since she'd been inside his house.

Leaning her face forward, she was eager to try her rapidly increasing skills of seduction. She touched the tip of her tongue to the base of his taut throat. Oh, Lord, he tasted good! Did he taste that way all over?

"You could always call the answering service tomorrow." She nuzzled his shoulder blade, then pulled back. "Like all my other johns, I guarantee you'll request another, er . . . bout in the bedroom," she crooned in her new husky voice.

Jaclyn watched Josh's anger mount, felt the force of

his grip tighten, before his fingers trailed toward her throat.

"Got any preferences tonight?" she asked with far more courage that she thought possible. She never imagined he'd just stand listening to her as if he couldn't believe what he was hearing. Apparently her calling was in the theater rather than art, as she'd always been told.

"Yes," Josh broke in on her thoughts with the gruff reply. "That you leave this instant."

"It will be rather hard to insist, since you can't see to throw me out?"

Slipping free of his arms, Jaclyn raised her chin triumphantly, pleased he couldn't see her smug look.

"The hell I can't!" Josh reached out so fast he had her back in his control before she had time to protest or draw away. Starting forward, he propelled her toward his front door, making good his threat with effortless ease.

"You're wasting time," Jaclyn cried out foolishly. Desperate to stop him before she found herself out in the cold with her mission a hopeless failure, she flung over her shoulder, "Most of my, er, tricks have me on my back in fifteen seconds flat."

"I'm not interested in joining your fan club or being last in a long line of nightly customers," Josh snapped back with equal flippancy. Still gripping her arm with overpowering strength, he pushed her forward.

"Believe you're the first, then. It's all right with me," she blurted out, tossing her head defiantly.

Jaclyn couldn't believe her actions or the words that continued to spill from her mouth. She'd never talked like this in her life or heard anyone else who did, and she'd certainly never acted this way before. Once started she just couldn't seem to stop. "I'm really good, you know?" she taunted, well aware she was flirting with danger over that remark.

Abruptly enfolded in Josh's arms again she could feel his grasp tighten before he released her to trail his fingers to her vulnerable throat. She watched his forehead furrow as he gripped her neck, sensing his quandary and delighting in the sudden trembling of his hands as his hold lessened and became almost gentle.

"Good, are you?" he questioned hoarsely.

Jaclyn swallowed nervously, praying he'd never be able to tell the difference between knowledge gained from watching foreign films and reading her girl friend's erotic advice books rather than actual experience.

"V-v-very," she stuttered.

With her neck held in his strong hands, Josh raised her face upward with the faintest touch of his thumbs beneath her chin.

"Maybe good just isn't good enough for me," he challenged with open sarcasm.

Jaclyn squirmed, intentionally rubbing her lower abdomen back and forth until she felt him shudder at the continuous contact. It was a heady experience to bring such a sophisticated man to a state of instant arousal despite his anger. She could feel his heated flesh straining the cloth of his tight jeans and was intrigued by the hard pressure against her softness.

"Lover," she said with a smile, wanting to take advantage of his sudden susceptibility. "I can guarantee you that my kind of good is the best you will ever have had. It comes from constant practice and the unending desire to please."

Josh's eyebrows rose in disbelief. "In that case, then . . . before I kick you out the door . . . I'll see just what my old buddy sent me."

"But you can't see!" Jaclyn exclaimed foolishly, forgetting her bold act.

"Not with my eyes," Josh informed her. His face descended, stopping a brief fraction from her forehead. "But with my hands I should be able to get a general idea of how much my present is worth."

Jaclyn froze, her eyes wide with anxiety. She couldn't move if she tried as Josh began a lazy investigation. Why had she bragged about her sexual prowess when she'd never even felt a man's hand on her body before? All of a sudden her blatant speech and daring conduct seemed like the most foolish idea of her life.

One well-kept hand slid down her spine. "You have a perfectly-shaped back . . ." he broke off, splaying it boldly over her bottom with the fingers curving to cradle her feminine shape. He moved slowly over the curvaceous swell, stroking each rounded inch with detailed precision.

"Your buttocks are soft and extremely desirable," he continued. "Not flat or confined in a tight girdle. Quite enjoyable to handle, in fact."

A shiver ran through her body as he caressed the outside of her thighs before gliding forward to rest his palm on the soft mound of silky feminine hair where they joined. "Ahh," he shuddered. "A perfect pillow of love. Too bad so many heads have rested there before mine was invited to do the same."

Jaclyn gulped, swallowing back an instinctive denial of his gross misconception. His touch was making it nearly impossible to remain still. The thin silk of her dress and fragile underwear were no barrier at all and she found the intimacy decidedly pleasurable.

"You're tall and slender, too, with legs long enough to enfold a man. Lengthy limbs able to cling to his hips until he forgets you're for rent to any man with the right amount of money."

"It doesn't matter in the least what you think of my profession as long as you get on with it," Jaclyn shot back. She refused to accept his verbal put-down without a comeback even if her words were all a lie. "I—I only have an hour and I'm in a hurry."

"You're forgetting I'm in control here," Josh warned. "Now stand still!"

He continued upward slowly, skimming her quivering midriff from side to side. "Hmm," he acknowledged in a low voice. "Shapely hips curving into a tiny waist. Very nice indeed, but the lush curves you dared thrust against my chest earlier draw my attention more."

Completely ignoring Jaclyn's sharp intake of breath, Josh continued higher until his palm cupped one full breast. He hesitated a moment as if expecting her to stop him before cupping his fingers around the soft flesh just as though he never intended to let go.

"Exquisite!" he exclaimed hoarsely. "Plump and flawless like a Michelangelo or Botticelli." His long fingers fondled the voluptuous curves through the sheer material of her dress, seeking first one breast then the other. Enjoying the heavy weight overflowing his palm, his thumb tantalized each tip until the nipple hardened and thrust forward.

"My God, woman, your breasts are an artist's dream. Absolute erotic perfection!"

Unable to answer his bold outburst, Jaclyn's heart nearly stopped. The emotional power of his intimate touch sent shock waves throughout her body. She was filled with a sudden urge to hold his fingers over her breasts and never let go. A wave of disappointment surged through her when his trembling hands circled her neck.

Her breath caught in her throat and held when his fingers reached out to touch the shimmering strands of hair sweeping her shoulders.

"Your hair is like spun silk. Soft and sensuous in my hands," he said quietly. "What color is it?"

"Red," she lied, exhaling a shallow wisp of air between her teeth as he moved his sensitive fingertips. With continued determination she allowed him to inspect each feature of her face.

"Your hair is red?" he questioned. "Somehow I picture you a silvery sensual blonde."

"B-bright red," she lied again. No way would she tell him her true coloring.

He outlined her eyes, traced the arch of her brow. "You have excellent bone structure," he whispered, more to himself than to her. "Perfectly set eyes, fine-arched brows."

He ran a fingertip along the bridge of her nose. "Dainty nose, high cheekbones, firm little chin. What color are your eyes?"

"Brown."

"Not blue or green or . . . ?"

"Brown," she interrupted.

"Or, as I started to ask, a color even more to my liking such as shadowy gray with obsidian overtones?"

"Sorry, but they're plain brown."

"Hmm . . . I wonder," he continued, retracing every inherent highlight but her pulsating lips.

She could feel his breath waft against her clear sensitive skin as he inhaled, hesitated, then buried his nose behind the dainty curve of her ear. Slowly and erotically he breathed deep, luxuriating in the sweet fragrance of her favorite gardenia shampoo.

"Excellent, indeed, though I expected you to wear a cloying perfume . . . if only to cover up the scent of your other customers," he commented with blunt emphasis. "No makeup either. Is there lipstick?"

"Ye-ye-yesss," Jaclyn stammered, aware he fully intended to find out by kissing her with mocking lips that had moved directly over her own.

"The only pleasant result of my accident has been to braille you. When my sight returns, I want you to model nude for me."

"I-I couldn't," Jaclyn responded with a quick, uneasy laugh. When Josh could see again, she'd be safe and anonymous thousands of miles away.

"Why not?" he demanded arrogantly. "This is a business arrangement only. You'll be paid the same as you earn hustling, and the work won't be as demanding on your body."

"I, er, I can't sit still very long. I'm much too nervous." At least being nervous wasn't a lie. She had never felt so uptight in her life.

"We'll talk about it later," he replied under his breath. "Now I want to braille your lips."

One fingertip trailed from her molded cheekbone to sensuously outline the passionate shape of her mouth.

Her treacherous lips betrayed her. Cushiony and soft, they always trembled no matter how brief their contact with Josh's. He had never commented on this response in the past and only held her glance a moment, then smiled mysteriously and pulled away. She prayed he wouldn't remember that tonight.

"You have very beautiful lips," Josh murmured huskily. "Touching them only with my fingertip could never satisfy me now."

"I'm yours to touch anywhere you like," Jaclyn reminded him softly, aching for the moment he would kiss her. It was wonderful to be able to speak with honest conviction and stop the brash, unfamiliar words that were necessary from the moment she entered his home.

Kiss me, my darling. Please kiss me! she beseeched him with a silent outpouring from shimmering tear-filled eyes he couldn't see.

Standing on tiptoe, she clung to his neck with tender hands that had longed to cradle his head during an intimate caress. This would be no platonic greeting like those she felt forced to bestow in the past.

"Can you kiss as good as you claim to make love?" Josh rasped, pulling her up to meet his lowered head.

"Try me and see," Jaclyn challenged in an expectant whisper.

She leaned into him, parting her lips to respond as she had wanted to do for years. Tears brimmed her eyes as her fingers gently threaded through his hair to touch the bandage. Dear God, how she wished it was possible to take his pain into her own soul and give him the use of her eyes.

Their lips met. His tentative and hers quivering and moist in anticipation. For a brief instant he appeared to hold back as if fighting his own desires. Any hesitation ended the moment his mouth possessed hers completely. His hunger was obvious. His excitement an overwhelming pleasure.

The same magic that jolted her to womanhood at sixteen coursed through her veins, searing into her heart with the added potency of maturity. Instead of recoiling like a frightened youth, she met each move head on. Without the need to hold back, her inner yearning surfaced with expressive volatility.

A soft purring sound came involuntarily from Jaclyn's throat as Josh alternately toyed and tasted her lips with unhurried thoroughness. She could feel her heart beat erratically when the caress became more urgent and he sought a greater response in return.

Still not satisfied, he demanded more until she clung to his neck for balance while trying to handle the inner tumult that threatened to buckle her knees. Every nerve ending in her supple, sensitive body was ecstatically alive, responding to the feel of Josh's mouth closed over her own as if he had been too long denied and intended to savor the contact forever.

His tongue started to explore, found hers, then pulled back to free her mouth when she squirmed closer. "Your response is staggering," Josh acknowledged, taking a deep breath. "You also taste delicious, erotic as hell, and very very much to my liking."

"In that case don't stop," Jaclyn mouthed a silent plea for another kiss. She squirmed, instinctively placing her body as close as possible to the confined pressure of his arousal. With their bodies pressed intimately close it was impossible to ignore the stirring of his maleness. It was a rock-hard intrusion that expressed more than words that if he'd permit her to stay the seduction was assured.

Biting back a moan of protest when Josh's strong arms relinquished their hold on her shoulders, she realized he was folding her into his heaving chest. Cradled tight, she could feel the imprint of his lithe form from chest to thigh.

A strange yearning flowed through her. She experienced a sudden urge to yield to him and to feel the warmth and protection of his arms. Carefully eased a fraction of a distance away Jaclyn's sensual lassitude was jolted back to harsh reality with Josh's declaration.

"I owe my buddy a big favor for sending you to me. It's been years since I've desired a woman this much." He nibbled the dainty gold heart on her earlobe, adding with passionate huskiness, "I can't believe now that I actually told him I didn't want a female tonight."

"You told me the same thing," she accused.

His hands pushed her back, his bandaged eyes facing her apprehensive stare. "Forget that!" he demanded. "Now I want to take your body in every way possible for a man to take a woman."

Panic over her naivete started to rise in Jaclyn's breast at his blunt declaration. What he thought was nothing but a paid sexual act from an experienced call girl would be the first intimate encounter of her life. And she prayed that her past gynecological examinations would prevent his discovering her virginity.

Nervous and uncertain about what to do next, Jaclyn glanced toward the front door. Was she subconsciously seeking a way to escape?

Intimate pictures of what lay ahead filled her mind. How could she ever hope to convince this man she was experienced? Why had she dared brag about her skills? *Instinct, help me now!* she cried helplessly.

"Why so silent?" Josh asked with a touch of mockery. "Did you doubt your well-practiced services would satisfy me?"

"No, er, no," Jaclyn stuttered foolishly.

"Then let's get to it." He exhaled his warm breath into her ear, letting the tip of his tongue gently probe before slowly circling. "I'm eager to see just how talented you are."

"I'm eager to show you," she returned in a strained voice.

"Move it then, my unseen mistress," Josh commanded. "I've definitely decided your prowess will be welcome in my bed tonight." Josh nibbled his way up and down the side of her neck. "You really are a tasty treat." He licked the hollow of her collarbone, then returned to her ear, exclaiming in a ragged voice, "I also think it only fair to warn you before we begin that I have a very large appetite."

"I can easily handle that," Jaclyn assured him with forced certainty. One more second with his moist tongue seeking to map the interior of her ear and she'd collapse at his bare feet in complete supplication.

Sex shouldn't be much different from dancing, she figured. She'd just let him make all the advances and follow his lead. That way he'd never suspect she was a complete novice. After all, it was the most natural act in the world.

"I think I'll let you make love to me the first time," Josh told her with the ease of a man accustomed to being obeyed.

"Lord help me," Jaclyn prayed with bowed head. Every time she had a spurt of confidence Josh's next words always destroyed it completely. Now he expected her to make love to him! It was fortunate he couldn't see the sudden uncertainty reflected in her face or hear the wild pounding of her heart caused by his unexpected declaration.

"What did you say?" Josh demanded. "I didn't hear that soft little entreaty."

"Lord, how nice," she lied.

"It damned well better be!" he warned, throwing his head back with a touch of inherent arrogance. "Let's get to it, my nameless beauty. The first will be for my birthday and the second an early gift from Santa Claus."

His previous anger was gone, replaced by a dark intensity that shook her to the depth of her soul with its sensual implication.

One hand rose to lie over her breast with the thumb outstretched to rest on the erratic pulse beating beneath her sensitive skin.

"I'm becoming tired of all this conversation and damned impatient to open my presents."

Well aware of the double innuendo of his words, Jaclyn shifted uneasily, not certain what a call girl would do next. She doubted very much if the tall red-head she had intercepted earlier had a heart that skipped beats as she prepared to service just one in a long line of nightly customers.

Unhampered by lack of sight in his own home, Josh reached down to cup Jaclyn's hand in a firm grip before stepping forward. "The master bedroom's this way," he pointed out unncessarily, dragging her in tow. "As aroused as I am now, you'll have enough time before your next trick to give me a sack full of goodies!"

CHAPTER THREE

Jaclyn barely had time to question the stupidity of her scheme before Josh had reached the end of his living-room area and she found herself propelled to a set of broad carpeted stairs.

Striding upward with sure-footed accuracy comparable to any sighted person, he held her palm firmly in his tightened grip.

"The blind leading the blind," she mumbled beneath her breath, thinking one couldn't see and one was too foolish to retreat from the bold promises made minutes earlier.

"Quit tugging on my hand," he scolded without slowing down his ascent. "You're the one with limited time, not me."

Jaclyn followed, counting each step while trying to match his longer stride. Her free hand slid helplessly along the sleek wood banister on her journey to his darkened bedroom.

"Oh, Lord, thirteen steps," Jaclyn moaned beneath her breath when Josh reached the top and stopped. Another omen telling her that she should plead temporary insanity and flee before he found out she not only lied about her occupation but her experience as well.

"Not only thirteen steps up to my room but thirteen

feet across to my bed," Josh announced, overhearing her derisive comment.

One thumb flipped on a light switch that filled their side of the vast room with a soft golden glow. He turned his head, his lips thinned with irritation over his inability to see.

"The damned light's of no use to me, since I can't even enjoy watching you undress, but you'll probably feel more at ease in an unfamiliar room that isn't totally dark."

"Y-yes," Jaclyn stammered, knowing that a pitch-black room was the last worry on her mind.

She barely had time to give the room a cursory search when Josh abruptly brought her thoughts back to her only reason for being there. "Since it's my desire that you make love to me the first time, I'll get myself comfortable on the bed while you slip out of your clothes. There's no need to offer you my help since you're obviously much more experienced at quick changes than I am."

Jaclyn's lashes fluttered, highlighting the sudden pallor of her face. She swallowed to ease her dry throat then looked around as Josh released his grip on her cramped fingers and boldly walked to his massive bed.

It was an intriguing bed with smooth, uncluttered lines, raised on a solid wood platform, and joined to a bookshelf-style headboard containing assorted pieces of sculpture and neatly stacked books.

The unmade bed had soft earth-toned sheets that were rumpled like the oversized pillows. The top sheet and heavy spread were tossed carelessly back, indicating Bruce's assumption that Josh had a difficult time sleeping was correct.

"For God's sake, get over here," Josh ordered. "My ears are extremely sensitive now, and I can tell you haven't moved a muscle to either undress or come give me the expert satisfaction that you claim all your tricks return a second time for."

"I was, er," Jaclyn hesitated, purposely stalling for added composure.

She glanced across his bedroom into the adjoining studio with its two walls of glass. They were angled like the bow of a ship to reach the cantilevered ceiling jutting high above the Pacific coast. She studied her surroundings a moment then started to speak again.

"I was admiring your room. I've never seen one quite like it before."

"You weren't paid for your interest in architecture, and to put it bluntly, my meter's running now as well as yours, so let's get to it."

With Josh's emphatic statement still ringing in her ears, she watched as he stripped his unbuttoned shirt off in one shrug, dropped it, then reached for the waistband of his unbelted slacks. He glanced back over one bronzed shoulder and firmly announced, "Since we only have about thirty or so minutes left, why don't you do what most hookers prefer."

"Oh?" Jaclyn expressed surprise in a stilted inquiry. She hadn't anticipated Josh would ask so many technical questions. It was obvious she'd better start acting more poised or he'd begin to think she was the dumbest call girl alive.

"What did you say?" Josh's query was deliberately drawn out and asked with irritating feigned innocence.

His continuous interrogation was becoming more infuriating all the time. She knew darned well he heard everything she said with explicit clarity.

"I said okay!" Jaclyn lied with husky emphasis. Her subterfuge was getting more difficult by the minute. The last thing in the world she'd have any knowledge of was the average prostitute's sexual specialty.

"I thought so," Josh returned smugly. "It's not only quick and effective but saves wear and tear on your body as well. Right?" he added with a hint of mischief, refusing to let the subject drop despite her unmistakable discomfort.

"Of course," Jaclyn lied again. Josh was getting much too inquisitive about her life as a call girl. In fact, she intended to ask her brother as soon as possible just how he became such an authority on that profession's preferences in the first place.

"Shouldn't we have a drink first?" She spotted a bar near one corner and the thought of a cool glass of water suddenly sounded like an excellent diversion.

"This isn't a social call. It's purely business and for my satisfaction only. Afterward you can set your fanny on a bar stool and drink all night for all I care. If you're as good as you claim, I may even give you a generous tip. But first," he warned firmly, "you give me what's already been paid for."

He turned sideways, undid the top snap on his slacks, and glanced in her direction. "And the quicker the better for both of us."

"I, er, I have to . . ." Jaclyn stuttered.

"Forget it, whatever it is," Josh demanded. "I'm beginning to ache and you know how to ease the pain."

"Er, I, er, okay," she mumbled incoherently as Josh turned away. It was hard to think straight with him so close.

Entranced by the sight of his broad shoulders bathed in the soft radiance of a bedside lamp, Jaclyn stepped forward. Her eyes never left the symmetry of his torso as his muscles rippled and bunched with each movement of his arms.

The sound of his zipper being lowered hissed through the room like an alarm, bringing her to a quick stop. It reminded her of a final warning signal, and she knew the point of no return would soon be reached.

His back was to her as he slid his slacks off one long leg then the other before stepping out of black briefs that did little to hide the contours of his taut buttocks. She stared openly. There was no doubt he had the sexiest bottom of any man she'd seen.

Without the least embarrassment he crawled up onto the middle of his bed and lay flat on his back. Casually placing his arms under his head, he arrogantly rested on the palms of his hands and faced her with complete control of the situation.

"You're naked!" Jaclyn exclaimed, desperately wishing she could take back her most foolish comment yet. Her eyes widened, turning a deep charcoal gray that matched the storm-tossed ocean outside. He was very beautifully naked, she admitted, following each well-defined anatomical curve, protruding and otherwise, with her interested gaze.

"You'd damned well better be too!" he insisted. "As you can see, I'm also ready for my first present. Satisfaction guaranteed, I believe was your claim."

Panic over her naivete started to rise in Jaclyn's breast. She swallowed, wishing she had total recall, as she frantically tried to remember every erotic tidbit she'd read since Lerisa had dumped a library of sexual advice books in her apartment shortly after she moved to Paris.

"You must be the slowest damned hooker in the world," Josh complained as the seconds ticked by and she failed to join him on the bed. He angled his body sideways, one knee drawn up but not enough to cover the obvious state of his arousal.

"I'm coming," Jaclyn retorted.

"Well, I'm not!" Josh shot back boldly. "Not yet anyway."

"Shush!" Jaclyn scolded his blatant chastisement. He was behaving more outrageous by the minute.

Automatically undoing buttons, she slipped off her dress, looked around, and decided to lay it on the seat of a comfortable-looking bedside chair built along the same massive lines as his bed.

She moved forward, clad in a French lace bra and panties so sensual they belied her serious personality. How on earth, she wondered, would an experienced prostitute conduct herself now? She wasn't so naive she didn't realize what Josh expected her to do or so hesitant not to do what he wanted . . . but . . . !

Where did a woman start making love to a man? From his head to, er . . . *it* . . . or toes to . . . *it* . . . or go direct to . . . *it* . . . without any preliminaries at all?

"I swear I can hear your mind going round and round from here," Josh complained. "What are you? Some kind of a weirdo that delights in delaying the act until your trick's driven up the wall with frustration?"

"Of course not," Jaclyn refuted. "My customers are already frustrated before they come to me!" That should prove she could match wits in their verbal interchange.

"Touché," Josh said, and laughed, not the least perturbed by her comeback.

Jaclyn glared, knowing full well he couldn't see, though it didn't matter. He was more irritating by the minute with his forceful actions. Could this sexy brute, demanding she come to his bed, really be the dedicated artist who'd always treated her with gentle consideration?

It was all her fault, she admitted. The plan was stupid, impulsive, and destined to have problems. And what if her doctor's examinations hadn't taken care of the physical problem? But, Lord, she had loved him for so long she couldn't stop now.

Josh's lack of sight gave her the freedom to boldly inspect his rigid body. Lerisa's book explained in explicit detail how to satisfy a man the way Josh expected her to. The author said think of that part of a man as an ice cream cone then take your time and enjoy each lick.

"Oh, dear," she groaned beneath her breath, thinking out loud. "I always pictured a single scoop in my mind."

"You did?" Josh questioned, overhearing and understanding her meaning immediately. His deep laughter filled the room, unknowingly drawing Jaclyn's eyes to his clenching abdomen and the involuntary movement of the topic of their conversation.

"What am I, then?" he teased further, visibly enjoying the current situation more than she was. He rolled onto his back again, completely unashamed of his nudity and the most confident male she had ever known in her life.

"A full triple-decker!" Jaclyn shot back. If he wanted to trade outrageous comments, it was time she showed him she was fully capable of matching his wit.

"You know something, woman?" Josh questioned seriously. "I'm really pleased you're conditioned to . . . should I say? . . . servicing lots of men. In one way that's the only suitable female for me tonight."

"Why's that?" Jaclyn asked, trying hard to hide the chagrin in her voice.

Darned if she would let his sudden wish for a sexual Amazon shatter her intention of bluffing her way through the basic part of their lovemaking. Sheer determination to give him satisfaction should overcome her lack of experience. She'd never left anything unfinished yet and wasn't about to start with Josh's seduction!

"It seems odd you'd want me so bad now when minutes ago you told me hookers didn't interest you in the least?" Jaclyn insisted, annoyed he couldn't see the anger flashing from her eyes.

"They never have before," Josh answered matter-of-factly. "But something about you intrigues me."

This was taking forever. Nearly three fourths of her hour was up and she was still as innocent as when she arrived. The only thing she had learned was a new vocabulary she couldn't use in public and how appealing Josh was in the nude.

"It's probably because I've always had a high libido," Josh interrupted her thoughts. "Or, to put it more bluntly, a strong sex drive which you claim you can easily handle."

If a long, lean muscled body, vibrating with sex appeal was any indication of a man's virility, she was prepared to believe every word he said. Every portion of his anatomy seemed toned to perfect physical fitness and exuded sensual energy held in tight control.

"For years," he continued, unaware of her personal speculation, "I've led a nearly celibate life and—"

"But why?" Jaclyn blurted out, tearing her mind away from the excitement of his being her first lover.

She was filled with curiosity about his current lifestyle, since Bruce used to brag about how the girls clamored to be with both of them in college. Despite her brother's popularity, he often admitted jealousy over the attention Josh's brooding good looks received.

"Why?" Josh answered with a raised eyebrow and abrupt question in return. "That's my business and too personal to discuss with a stranger."

"A stranger sent here for you to have sex with!" Jaclyn snapped, momentarily forgetting her role.

"Which happens to be what call girls do best," Josh pointed out with truthful bluntness.

"Forget it, then," Jaclyn answered peevishly. "I couldn't care less about your monastic life-style."

Trying to understand the man was getting more impossible all the time. He could keep all the secrets he wanted for all she cared.

Laughing at her expressive voice, Josh explained, "Let it suffice to say that since I couldn't make love to the woman I wanted, I decided to channel my energies into my art and . . ."

"The woman you wanted?" Jaclyn interrupted again.

"Yes. Past, present, and future tense! Now, as I was saying, since this affair hurts no one, is strictly business, and will hopefully fulfill a sudden insatiable need for feminine warmth, I'm glad you're in the profession to satisfy male lust."

"I prefer to consider my services a little social work among those with means," Jaclyn sassed, with the beginning of a fine temper that rarely surfaced.

Josh's alternate probing and confiding would try anyone's patience. Despite the deliberate pretense, his continual reference to her as a professional hooker bothered her. After all, it was his sex that was responsible for that occupation in the first place.

"Anyway, my job's a simple case of supply and demand," she exaggerated foolishly. "I wouldn't be in the trade if there weren't always plenty of men willing to pay a premium price for what I sell."

Natural wavy hair brushed her shoulders, glistening silver-blond as she bowed her head over her uncurbed tongue. Heaven help her if anyone else ever heard about the lies she told tonight.

"Whatever you call it, whatever the reason you do it, I'm warning you I have years of frustration to deal with and a strong need. Unless my libido has lessened from lack of use, I'll leave you feeling like you've been serviced by ten lusty servicemen instead of one nearly celibate sculptor."

"Y-you, you will?" Jaclyn gulped hesitantly. Lord, the man sounded like a veritable sex machine.

"Quit stammering like a nervous baby and get in bed," Josh demanded. "A man can't stay aroused forever just talking. You're not only slow but you answer every statement I make with a stupid question."

"I do not!" Jaclyn denied hotly. "Do I?" she asked in a softer voice.

"You're doing it now," Josh shot back. "If I didn't know better, I'd think you'd never even had sex before —much less heard a man talk about it."

"You're crazy," Jaclyn said, laughing uneasily. "Whoever heard of a virtuous hooker?"

"No one. Now shut up and get in this damned bed right now or I'm getting out," Josh threatened. "And if I do, we'll have sex wherever I catch you. . . ."

"Catch me?" Jaclyn scoffed, not the least perturbed. "That's impossible. You can't even see."

"I know every corner of my house, sighted or not. After the chase, which should be rather interesting, and you're in my arms, we'll have sex until I'm satisfied enough to let you go, whether it takes one hour or ten!"

"But what about my, er, manager?" Jaclyn reminded him.

She hadn't planned staying much longer than sixty minutes. As incompetent as she was portraying a worldly sophisticate now, she knew ten hours acting a part would be her undoing.

"And don't forget my answering service either."

"I don't give a damn what your pimp, the escort service, or you say. Get your butt on my bed this instant!"

Josh started to rise in such an intimidating, purposeful manner, Jaclyn knew he meant every word he said and was capable of following through with his threats.

Kicking off her shoes, she quickly did as he asked and mutely eased onto the wide bed. The sheets were the softest percale she had ever touched and as fresh and clean-smelling as their owner. She had dreamed about being with him this way for so many years it seemed impossible that she was actually here.

"That's better," Josh told her, lying back with a satisfied sigh. He gave her a wide smile that went straight to her heart. She was so filled with love for the volatile-tempered, arrogant-acting man beside her that anything he asked of her would be all right.

She kneeled beside him, letting her lingering glance devour him with the heady freedom of knowing she was unobserved in return. It was a wonderful experience to realize she could express her feelings without restraint or embarrassment. Josh would never know who she was, nor would anyone else in the world be aware she stole this one, idyllic moment before returning to Paris.

"Do you realize you haven't said a single thing since you climbed on my bed?"

"I was, er, looking around again," Jaclyn answered softly though her eyes had barely left him since she had entered his room.

Eager to be as close to Josh as possible, she leaned forward to touch his chest at the same moment he reached out to draw her unresisting body down to his.

With uncanny accuracy he caressed the soft skin of her shoulder before moving toward her face. When he touched her bra strap, his fingers hesitated, traced down the scalloped lace cupping her voluptuous breasts, then stopped on the front fastener.

"Get rid of this," he demanded, sliding his hand along her side, past the curve of her waist, and over her hip. He rested his palm on the narrow band of her panties.

"And these too," he added forcefully. "When I make love to a woman, or a woman makes love to me, I want nothing between us but our desire."

Jaclyn's fingers trembled on the bra fastener as she freed her breasts and were even more awkward as she removed her underpants while sitting on the deep-cushioned innerspring mattress. She knew she was flushed, undressing for the first time in front of a man, but he couldn't see, so it made no difference.

Josh's fingertips tracing over her skin had caused her heart to beat at a startling speed. Each touch was magic, and it seemed like an erotic dream to be alongside him with their bodies so close she could feel heat emanate from his tanned flesh to hers.

The charged electricity that blazed to life years ago returned in greater force when Josh rolled her completely into his arms for the first contact with their bodies unclothed.

Jaclyn gave a deep, involuntary moan of delight at the wonder of knowing his flesh intimately against her trembling body. It was nearly impossible to keep from crying out her love as a feeling of tenderness surged through her with such force it brought tears to her eyes.

She pressed a soft kiss into his neck when he hugged her close. Everything would be all right. Her instincts would guide her. Nothing Josh could possibly do to her would be offensive or nothing he asked of her would she hesitate to perform.

"I'm ready to make love to you," she confessed softly into the hollow of his neck.

There was so much to experience and so much to learn, she was dazed with trying to assimilate it all at once. The memory of their bodies touching would keep her in a state of euphoria for weeks after she left. She had never dreamed pressing her naked breasts to Josh's hair-roughened chest could bring such pleasure.

"I'm running short of time," she prompted, eager to give herself fully to him before she left.

"Then don't waste a second," Josh urged in a husky voice that reached out to caress her like a tender kiss. "Start showing me how skillful you are right now."

He inhaled, holding his breath at the shock of Jaclyn's soft curves pressing closer. As she kissed the taut line of his jaw, before trailing her lips along the base of his throat and down to his chest, he knew he'd been too too long without his woman.

His hands trembled on the silky strands of her lustrous hair, his fingers widespread to cradle her head during the slow but thorough exploration of his chest.

Could this actually be happening? he reasoned, raising to press a kiss on her scented hair. What she was doing to him was pure heaven. Expecting another pain-filled night, he was instead experiencing the most sensual pleasure of his life, and she hadn't even finished caressing his upper torso.

"Damn it," he groaned. "Damn it to hell!" he cursed the injury that kept him from seeing her beauty.

"Don't be angry," Jaclyn soothed, reaching up in a rush of compassion to place a fleeting kiss on his brow. "Let me ease all your pain tonight."

Josh lay back, relaxing his head on the pillow while letting each sensation flood into his taut body until it became nearly unbearable to remain the passive partner.

Jaclyn's ministrations were done with such tenderness the nightmare of having continuous headaches was overcome by the enjoyment of experiencing stronger, long-denied emotions. Having her in his bed was the greatest gift he would ever receive.

Unaware Josh's deep need equaled hers, Jaclyn nuzzled her face in the springy hairs beneath her chin. Still awed that she had dared approach him, she inhaled the heady scent of his freshly showered body in bliss. She could feel his heart beat erratically and delighted in watching the rapid rise and fall of his powerful pectoral muscles as he submitted to her touch.

She placed kiss after kiss on his body, releasing years of inhibitions and carefully guarded desires at the same time. From the moment he had taken her in his arms the advice books were forgotten. She was too impatient to follow them anyway. All she wanted to do now was devour him. First with her mouth, then her hands, and finally with the giving of her own body.

More courageous by the moment, Jaclyn's tongue darted out, daring to touch his small dark nipple with lingering strokes.

"Oh, Lord, that's good. So good," his voice broke off as if in agony.

Pleased at Josh's verbal response, while her fingertips massaged the tightly bunched muscles along his side, she became bolder. She nibbled gently at first one erect peak then the other before tracing a complete circle with her tongue and kissing each hard bud until he shuddered and pushed her away.

Unconcerned by his actions, Jaclyn moved lower. There were many more untouched areas to explore. She raised herself up to imprint his masculine beauty on her mind one more time before leaning over. She counted each rib with her lips and tongue before moving to his flat indented navel. It was covered by a line of curly dark hair that went from the thick covering on his chest to end around the rigid protrusion waiting with impatient insistence below.

Wanting to extend her pleasure, as well as his, she nuzzled her way around the enticing sun-tanned flesh of his abdomen until he moaned and moved his hips side to side before gripping her shoulders to stop.

"Enough of that, you teasing witch," Josh warned in a low voice so emotive it was barely recognizable. "I feel like I'm about to explode it's been so damned long."

Jaclyn pulled away, kneeling alongside his lithe, athletic thighs. She surveyed him from head to toe before returning her gaze to his erect flesh.

They were currently painting male nudes in her art class, but Josh made the models look like childish, cherubic statues. Even Michelangelo's sculpture of David, with its oversized feet and hands, looked like he'd just taken an ice-cold swim in comparison to the sexual Adonis portion of Josh's anatomy that he did nothing to hide.

"Quit staring at me," Josh complained, sitting up to grasp her shoulders and pull her close. "I can feel your eyes on my body."

He cradled her face in the hollow of his throat with his chin resting on her tousled hair. "It's killing me not being able to see you in return. Sight is one of our strongest senses and a particularly intense aphrodisiac to a male."

Jaclyn smiled secretly. Little did the man realize what a turn-on looking at his nakedness was for her. Squirming in his arms in order to increase her sense of touch wasn't a bad idea either, she reflected as she softly brushed her breasts against the potent stimulation of his unyielding chest.

"Lie back," she implored, between kisses on his neck. "Let me finish what you requested."

Heady with the success of Josh's vigorous reaction she was impatient to replace each caress. She had complete confidence in her ability to give him what he wanted and trembled with eagerness to continue her newly acquired skills.

Her desires had risen as fast as his and it seemed the most natural thing in the world for her to be the aggressive partner in their lovemaking. Jaclyn reached a hand down and boldly surrounded Josh's arousal with gentle fingers. Her touch was instinctive and she could tell by his body's involuntary response what movement gave him the maximum pleasure.

"Lie down," she urged again. "Let me continue while you relax."

"Relax, hell!" Josh exclaimed hoarsely, clamping his fingers around her hand to still her motions.

It was absolutely necessary to stop her tender exploration the instant she started to stroke his pulsating flesh. He was so near the edge that if her delicate touch continued, he'd find release in an unacceptable manner and with embarrassing speed.

"What's the matter?" She was certain she could give him gratification if he'd let her continue. "Don't you like the way I make love?"

"No, I don't like it." He shuddered. "I love it!"

"Then why did you stop me?" Jaclyn quizzed huskily. Unless she was hurting him, she couldn't understand why he would want her to withdraw.

"My desires have suddenly changed," he told her without releasing her hand.

"Oh, God," he moaned beneath his breath. He'd rather die than remove her hand from his body, but the pleasure was his alone, and she deserved much more from their first lovemaking. So very much more.

Just thinking of being inside her, with her long legs wrapped around his hips while holding her close to his chest, made him shake like a youth waiting for his first sexual experience.

"Do you have anything else in mind?" Jaclyn inquired solicitously.

She gazed with love in her eyes as a light film of perspiration dampened his brow above the bandage. A compassionate smile exposed even white teeth as she waited with his hardness still in her grip. She had known without being told what a difficult time he was having trying to control his emotions.

"Is there anything you want?" she asked in a breathless whisper. She was so entranced by the feel of his velvety skin beneath her fingertips it was hard to keep her thoughts on their conversation.

"Anything at all?"

"Many things," Josh groaned, reluctantly removing her inquisitive hand and placing it by her side. *At least a lifetime's worth,* he thought to himself. "First I think it's time to show you how I act when I'm in charge."

He touched her shoulder and the point of her chin with sensitive fingers. It was impossible to control his need to dominate the relationship. There were many ways to give her pleasure and he ached to try them all.

"But why?" Jaclyn stared with anxious eyes, unaware of the reason for his sudden aggressiveness. Surely he wasn't going to order her out of his house, was he? Not at this point when they were both trembling with unsatiated passion.

"Please. No." She mouthed the words soundlessly.

"Because, you enticing witch—" Josh broke off. He caressed the satiny skin of her back with unsteady fingers. It was impossible to keep his hands still or his thoughts on anything but the relationship ahead.

"Because what?" Jaclyn prompted, leaning into his strength with a wishful sigh.

"For the very good reason I've enjoyed all I can physically endure of your soft hands and sexy mouth freely exploring my body. It's time now for you to learn how I make love!"

Thank you, Lord, she rejoiced in silence, overcome with happiness by his decision.

"Prepare yourself for one hell of a time, woman," Josh moaned against the curve of her neck. "It's been so long I can't guarantee my control is as good as it used to be."

CHAPTER FOUR

With Josh's bold warning ringing in her ears, Jaclyn relaxed, letting him gently ease her onto the bed. She wasn't worried about his control, as hers was lacking also. Besides, she knew instinctively he wouldn't hurt her no matter who he thought she was. That wasn't his style.

Tears blurred her vision, shimmering unseen, as Josh cradled her face within the protective warmth of his palms.

"That feels nice," Jaclyn murmured, enjoying his smallest touch.

Josh lowered his head toward her with the same eagerness she had shown from the moment they first lay side by side.

"Give me your lips, woman," he commanded. "Let me use their sweetness as comparison when I explore the rest of your scented body with my mouth."

Jaclyn's hands lifted, clinging to his nape as she raised her face willingly. It was like a beautiful dream to know he wanted her with such passion. She relaxed indolently, for the first time believing in her heart she was doing the right thing for both of them.

Josh tasted the nectar of her parted lips with unhurried gentleness, though he ached to plunder the warmth inside with the same tempo his body yearned to thrust between her legs.

A damp film of desire beaded his brow as he forced himself to hold back. Each responsive gesture, every tentative touch from the woman beneath him, tested his control to the ultimate. After uncounted months of celibacy, it was agony to slow his heightened emotions to the level that would give her maximum pleasure.

Jaclyn squirmed, pulling Josh closer with surprising strength, until her sensitive breasts were pinned beneath the weight of his chest. She delighted in the unaccustomed pressure of his hard torso against her soft curves, though it received only a fleeting thought. The core of her feelings were centered on the exquisite pleasure experienced as his mouth continued its sensual foray.

"More . . . ooh, more," Jaclyn pleaded as moans of joy escaped her throat when Josh's tongue slipped inside, touched hers, and began a slow dance back and forth, in and out.

She responded with enthusiasm, reveling in the close intimacy. Eagerly imitating each tantalizing gesture with the tip of her tongue, she clasped his shoulders tight. The sudden rippling of Josh's back muscles beneath her wandering fingertips proved she was reciprocating in a way that gave equal pleasure. His hands were as skilled at arousing passion in her body as they were at bringing life to clay and bronze. Everywhere his long, artistic fingers touched set her on fire.

The sensual abrasiveness of his moustache added its own flame as his mouth finally released hers to slowly explore her face, the wildly beating pulse in her throat, and the lush fullness of her breasts. Jaclyn arched when Josh pulled back. She was as eager to feel his passionate mouth plunder her breasts as she had been to experience his kiss.

"Damn!" Josh cursed, filled with bitterness over his lack of sight. "If I thought I could see even a blurred image of your body, I'd tear these bandages off so fast you wouldn't believe it."

"No! No!" Jaclyn cried, reaching out with both hands to cup his face. "That could make you permanently blind."

She didn't care that he might recognize her if his eyes were healed enough to see. Her only fear was the tragedy of his future if he should cause lasting damage from the momentary desire to view her nakedness.

"Please don't." Her eyes were wide with anxiety as she sensed the indecision warring in his mind. "I'm not worth that kind of risk."

"I'll decide that," Josh explained stubbornly. "Right now, for a glimpse of you beneath me, I don't care beyond this one moment."

Jaclyn lay wordlessly, watching his chest rise and fall with each rapid breath as he tried to control his frustration. "God help me," he burst out, lowering his voice to a husky entreaty, "but you have the most enticing silken-skinned body in the world."

His features tightened perceptibly as he raised his hands to rub the taut skin of his forehead. "I can't stand not imprinting your vision in my mind along with your tantalizing scent and the memory of your delicate touch."

"Yes, you can," Jaclyn placated. "If you do, I'll give you another, er . . ."

"Give me?" Josh questioned, throwing his head back in disbelief. "You'd give me a free . . ."

"Anything you want," she interrupted with a husky promise. "But only after you have a medical release and your sight is restored."

"Nothing could give me more incentive to follow doctor's orders," Josh admitted in a thickened voice. He reached out to touch her face with surprising tenderness.

Jaclyn felt a warm glow flow through her when Josh visibly relaxed. For all his arrogance and irritable gruffness nothing he did could ever make her care less. Though her pledge was a lie, the intent was done only with his well-being in mind.

"I'd better warn you now that as soon as I can see again you're mine for the night." The harsh, frustrated admonition seemed torn from his lips.

"I'll be waiting," she pledged softly, wishing she really could have a second night in his arms to look forward to.

Amazed by the depth of his desire, Jaclyn moved her head sideways, placing kiss after kiss on his wrist as his hands reverently touched the silvery strands of hair that spread unseen across his pillow.

"You'd better be readily available or I'll come find you," he threatened in a serious voice. "Wherever you are."

Not when you don't know my true identity or even the country I live in, she reflected silently.

Josh's fingers never stilled while he talked, returning from their lazy journey up and down her side to cup her breasts. He pushed from the sides until her flesh burgeoned upward with the dainty nipples erect and waiting.

"Hmm, that feels delicious," she said with a sigh, thinking how beautiful his hands were for a man. Proportioned like his lithe frame, they were large, though her fullness overflowed each palm.

"Delicious?" he said laughing. "That's a hell of a way to describe how you feel."

"It is delicious," she contradicted in a breathless whisper, squirming as she anticipated even greater pleasure.

She stretched indolently, letting her legs casually rub against his. It took every ounce of control to submit passively, as he had asked, when he kept stroking her skin with his fiery touch.

"It's also delectable and scrumptious," she added when his thumbs rubbed slowly back and forth across her nipples.

"You sound like a thesaurus description for a recipe," he interrupted with impatient ill-humor.

"Luscious too," she pointed out impishly, enjoying his bad temper, since it was sensually induced.

"Damn it, woman, just shut up and enjoy," Josh commanded, lowering his head with a helpless groan. "I want to savor your beauty in silence. There's lots of gift wrapping left to inspect and I don't want to be disturbed."

Jaclyn smiled joyously, welcoming the quiet when his face touched her waiting breast. His caresses were like nothing she had ever dreamed. He didn't leave an area untouched as his mouth sought first one creamy mound then the other while his tanned fingers kneaded the soft flesh with erotic tenderness.

Involuntary tremors caused her fingernails to dig into his hard shoulders when he took one sensitive nipple into the exciting moist interior of his mouth. "That's wonderful. The most . . ." she broke off, remembering his desire for silence.

Jaclyn's deep dove-gray eyes turned charcoal as his mouth moved from breast to breast. Dark lashes lay in a lustrous shadow on her cheek as she unsuccessfully tried to keep them open. She ached to take advantage of being able to view his finely honed features without his knowledge. His volatile lovemaking made it physically impossible to do anything but lie back with her eyes closed and savor each sensation that swept through her body from head to toe.

Josh's tongue rapidly flicking back and forth before

laving a circle around her sensitive nipple brought forth a husky plea for him to stop as she pulled away.

"Oh, Lord, that's . . . that's enough!" Jaclyn gasped. She could no longer think, just feel, and the pleasure was fast becoming unbearable.

"The hell it is," Josh countered, continuing his erotic ministrations to the satiny perfection. "I've barely begun."

When his head trailed from her tender nipples, still damp from his oral stimulation, to the underside of her breasts then down across her clenching abdomen, she knew her knees would have collapsed if she'd been standing.

The hands that kneaded her breasts with such delight were doing the same to the soft skin of her bottom. He easily slid his fingers beneath her when she arched to meet his probing tongue as it mapped her abdomen with detailed precision.

"P-p-please. No more," Jaclyn stammered incoherently long minutes later, completely forgetting her bold claims about being an experienced call girl.

Tossing her head back and forth, she clenched her teeth, writhing sensuously beneath the intimate probing that continued until every inch of her body was imprinted with his practiced touch. "Please stop," Jaclyn implored softly when Josh returned again to the aching warmth between her legs.

Her hands fell helplessly at her sides when she tried and failed to prevent his head lowering to caress that same warmth with his well-defined masculine lips.

"I-I can't stand anymore."

"The hell, you say," Josh exclaimed in a ragged voice. He rose up to take her mouth in a dizzying, hungry kiss before returning to his point of origin.

"I—I really can't," she whispered as repeated tremors shook her body. His tongue sent erotic shock waves wherever it touched, making it impossible to even think.

It was true. She thought she'd lose her mind if he continued, yet her legs rose automatically when his knees parted her thighs. Her motions were instinctive and urgent as she pulled him to her.

Jaclyn quivered expectantly as he kneeled over her with his palms spread flat on the sheets alongside her breasts and his shoulders hovered protectively above. "If you won't stop, then please let me deliver your g-gift now," she beseeched in a throaty entreaty. Her heart ached with tenderness as she stared at his face with shimmering, tear-drenched eyes.

Could that husky pleading actually be her own voice asking Josh to make love to her? It seemed like a dream until she realized no night vision had caused the deep need for fulfillment that made it seem natural to ask Josh to make her his.

Josh rose up, his back straight and the lines of his powerful upper torso sharply defined. Resting on his knees between her legs, his hands cupped her hips, moving them until she was in a perfect position to accept him.

"I think you're confused, woman," Josh pointed out. "You have the gift but I deliver and you receive." His voice was deeper than she had ever heard it and unsteady, matching the trembling of his broad palms.

Jaclyn gripped his biceps, marveling at the taut muscles that bunched beneath her touch. He was as physically fit as any athlete she had ever seen and she couldn't get over the freedom of looking at him without censure. He was so handsome with his sun-bronzed skin glistening in the dim lamplight. Her eyes widened, following the sensual pattern of the dark hair on his chest down to the enticing excitement of his arousal.

She could have looked at him forever if she hadn't been breathless with desire to feel that same aroused portion of his anatomy deep inside her in the final act of love.

"Damn it, witch!" Josh complained impatiently. "I can't sit poised over you all night while you feast your eyes on my state of readiness."

"How can you tell I'm staring?" Jaclyn asked in a breathless query.

"Men's intuition," he informed her in the self-assured manner she admired. "I shall also find it decidedly more pleasurable to be in you than on you."

Without further words Josh leaned over, taking Jaclyn's feverish mouth at the same instant his body eased forward. One hand cradled her face, the other lowering to assist in the unbearably delayed entrance.

"Josh, ooh, Josh," Jaclyn cried out, biting back the urge to confess who she was and that it was her first time with a man. Instead, she moved her hands along his rib cage and held her breath.

"Relax, honey," Josh soothed. "Trust me and relax." Tender concern filled his voice as he spoke against her lips. His hands caressed her as he pushed with steady insistence until she began to accommodate his hardened flesh.

"Don't worry, little one, I'll make certain it's heaven for both of us."

Jaclyn could feel sweat break out on Josh's shoulders and forehead, unaware of the effort it took to control his urge to pillage the thin barrier that kept him from giving them both release. She gave a sigh of relief. Josh didn't have the slightest idea she was a virgin. Her worries were over.

Now, Jaclyn became increasingly impatient to become his in the fullest sense of the word. She curved to meet him, pushing her buttocks upward until her legs were wrapped around his lean hips and they were as close as physically possible.

His mouth took hers in a long, searching kiss, swallowing the sudden cry as he thrust deep into her throbbing body, waited, then began to slowly move.

All vestiges of reality left with the depth of feeling engendered as his thrusting motions alternately stopped and started until she was able to accept his great size with total gratification. Steadily, he gained momentum, increasing until she matched him with her own instinctive rhythm.

Josh released Jaclyn's lips when her brief outcry changed to a continual purr of contentment. He rained kisses across her face as his hips continued their exquisite pounding until she gasped her pleasure over and over with each driving force.

"Oh, Josh, my darling Josh," Jaclyn whispered into his mouth as he possessed her parted lips with unerring accuracy during the final earth-shattering spasms. She thought her heart would burst, it was so filled with love for the gentle man above her.

Tears slipped from her eyes as Josh withdrew to bury his face against her neck. She listened mutely as incoherent murmurs escaped his throat and his warm breath was expelled in her tousled strands of hair.

Jaclyn had never felt more lethargic or complete in her life when Josh rolled over without releasing her body. Cradled in his arms while they regained their breath was a bliss of its own. With his legs still entwined with hers she knew he felt equally satiated. Years of closely guarded desires were all eased in one perfect moment as the seduction was fulfilled.

Two thoughts hazily came to mind. One was, despite her previous shyness, she had a surprising capacity for experiencing passion with uninhibited pleasure. The other was, for her, it was right that she waited to share it with Josh. A fact she had shyly concealed since she was fourteen years old.

In the silence Josh reached out and touched her face with tenderness, stroking the smooth outline from her chin to her throat.

"Was it good for you?" Jaclyn asked in a reticent voice. She gripped his hand to place a kiss in the palm before cradling it to her throbbing breast.

"I think the man is supposed to ask that, little one," Josh answered, laughing huskily as he gently stroked the smoothest skin he'd ever touched.

"Well?" she prompted, still needing assurance in her role as a satisfying feminine partner.

"You were the best." He kissed the tip of her nose and brushed her responsive lips with his mouth. "You are the best." His hand moved to still her motions. "And if you don't stop squirming your sexy bottom back and forth, I'll find out if you're just as good the second time around."

Jaclyn gave a low, nervous laugh. Her entire body still tingled from his touch, and she wasn't certain if her pounding heart could stand another loving so soon.

"Well?" Josh urged, sliding his hand lazily up and down her body in a way that already started shock waves shooting through her bloodstream. "You do owe me another gift. Remember?"

"One for your birthday and one from Santa, wasn't it?" Jaclyn whispered.

"That's right, honey," he declared, rolling her beneath him as his body hardened with the speed of a youth.

Jaclyn flung her arms around Josh's neck, pulling his head down to her mouth. She was as eager now to give as she was to receive. "I said I could easily handle a man like you," she teased, delighting in the feel of his strong body as he gently began to make love to her the second time.

"We'll see about that, woman," he taunted, increasing the tempo of his hips until she clung to his arms, and begged he release her from the fiery coupling that seemed to never stop.

"Had enough?" Josh demanded, bruising her mouth with the same hunger with which he possessed her body.

"Yes, Josh! Aaagh, yes," she cried out, biting his shoulder as his violent shudders matched hers, and they both collapsed satisfied and happy in an exhausted tangle of arms and legs.

"It'll be hard to top this next year," Josh moaned in a thick voice, trying to catch his breath. "Birthday and Christmas gift-giving has reached a new high tonight."

"Shush," Jaclyn groaned, wanting nothing more than to close her eyes, stay curled in his arms, and sleep undisturbed for twenty-four hours. She knew it would take at least that long for her heart to settle down, her heated skin to lose its sensitivity, and her mind to take in all that had happened in the last hour.

"How did you know my name?" Josh asked after long minutes of silence.

"Your name?" Jaclyn gasped, instantly aroused from her sensual lethargy. Had she really called out his name?

"Yes, my name." He cradled her nape, forcing her face up from his chest, where it was burrowed as if she never wanted to leave. "You called me Josh several times."

"The answering service told me," she replied, pleased at her ability to come up with a plausible reason in such a short time.

That was too close. She'd have to be more careful about what she said. As it was, she constantly had to bite back telling him over and over how much she loved him.

When Jaclyn tried to squirm away, Josh lay on his back, pulling her close to rest tight against his side. He lowered his head, letting his lips move across her cushiony mouth in a tender caress.

"Now that I have a name and we've just been as intimate as a man and woman can be, don't you think I should know who you are too?"

She nuzzled his neck, responding with a soft, noncommittal sigh. Still overcome with the indolent feeling of physical satisfaction, she had to force her thoughts away from the overwhelming pleasure of being beside him in the privacy of his room.

"Why don't I call you Jazzy?" Josh said, laughing huskily against her forehead when she didn't answer. He slipped his arms around her in a gentle hug. "This entire situation has been unreal to me and I think I prefer not even knowing your—" he coughed in a suspicious manner—"er . . . working name. It's probably a pseudonym anyway."

Jaclyn stared warily for a moment, wishing she could see Josh's eyes to help determine if he was putting her on or not.

"Why Jazzy?" she insisted, too curious not to ask. She couldn't help but wonder, since it sounded like a nickname for her Christian name. Surely he didn't suspect who she was?

Deciding he had no reason to, she ran an inquisitive finger through the fascinating hair on his chest that contrasted so beautifully when it touched her own skin. This was much more enjoyable than worrying about his remarks.

"Many reasons," Josh answered guilelessly.

"Name them." She laid her head on his chest, content to listen to the steady beat of his strong heart.

"You said you're too nervous to model for me," he told her with an amused smile she didn't see.

"And?" she prompted, continuing her lazy exploration from his chest to his flat abdomen.

"Your body trembled when I first took you into my arms." He reached one hand out to stop her fingers from going lower.

"Any more?" she yawned, closing her eyes as waves of tiredness rushed over her. Worry had disturbed her sleep ever since she'd heard about Josh's accident.

"Yes," he explained patiently. "Your mouth quivers with curious innocence each time I kiss you, and you respond with uninhibited delight when I'm inside you."

"Enough!" she shot back, preferring not to know just how blunt his next words might be. "Nothing you've told me so far indicates why you'd pick the name you did."

"Since you appear to be nervous, or jazzed up, ever since you've been here, I decided Jazzy is very appropriate."

Obviously he didn't know who she was, Jaclyn thought with relief.

"You aren't on drugs, are you?" Josh broke in on her thoughts.

"Of course not!" she countered with vehemence. Of all the nerve. Just because she was nervous over her first seduction and responsive to his touch didn't mean she was a doper.

"Many hustlers use a john's money to support their habit."

"Not me." She raised her face to give him a fierce glare, doubly angered because he couldn't even see it.

"Why do you turn tricks, then?" he urged, enjoying her mood swings as much as the enlightening conversation.

Jaclyn pulled back to check his features. He looked as innocent as a baby, lying with his head propped on the pillow, yet his probing questions seemed intent on tripping her up as much as finding out about her life-style. She was alert now and would make certain not to make him more skeptical than he was.

"Answer me, Jazzy. Why do you sell yourself for a living?"

"I have to support my"—she thought fast—"grand-mother."

Jaclyn could hear Josh's chest rumble. The unsym-pathetic beast was laughing at her, bringing her tem-per to a fine edge. Supporting an aged relative sounded like a good reason to her.

"Why don't you work as a secretary?" he asked with feigned innocence.

"I can't type." Another lie, she thought, since she was an excellent typist and had been hired by the Peace Corps when she was twenty-one and mainly for her secretarial skills.

"A waitress, then." Josh's lips twisted in a grin.

"They don't earn enough."

"Oh, does grandmother have high medical bills, perhaps?"

"Yes." Jaclyn's eyes snapped gray fire. "She's in a nursing home that costs five thousand dollars a month!"

"It must be a nice one. Does she know what you do to keep her there?" Josh insisted.

"No." At least that was the truth. She didn't have a grandmother so naturally didn't have a relative that knew what he thought she was doing.

Josh's refusal to drop the interrogation continued until she ached to reach up and yank a handful of chest hairs that moments ago had enticed her to caress them.

"What time is it?" Darned if she was going to lie in bed with a man determined to learn about a life that she knew nothing about in the first place.

"I can't see," Josh reminded her.

Jaclyn eyed him, embarrassed by her gaffe and hoping he wasn't upset. Apparently nothing bothered him, she thought as he took one hand away from her shoulder and casually pointed to the bedside clock.

"Read that." He turned his face toward her, asking pointedly. "Haven't you been here well over an hour?"

"It's ten o'clock!" she exclaimed. Had it only been two hours since she'd arrived in his house? It seemed like a lifetime. It was certainly the most traumatic two hours she'd ever experienced.

"I thought you had other tricks to entertain tonight."

"I—I do," Jaclyn muttered, thinking that first her lies got her into his bed and now they were the reason she had to leave it.

"Shouldn't you be going, then?"

Though Josh reminded her it was time to leave, his arms didn't release their hold, nor did his fingers stop their gentle stroking, trailing up and down her spine in a way she didn't ever want to end.

"Can't I spend the night?" Jaclyn blurted out impulsively. One full night together would ensure more lasting memories than a two-hour tryst.

"How much would that cost me?"

"Nothing, if you take the phone off the hook and don't answer your door. I'll leave by six in the morning."

Bruce would be curious about what happened but concerned enough about Josh's health that he wouldn't phone before then in case he was asleep. That would also give her time to get to the airport and make certain she was booked on the next day's flight.

"What happens at six?" Josh demanded, shifting his weight so she was tighter to his side and her legs were relaxed alongside his.

"My manager will come looking for me."

"Then what will your pimp do?"

"He'll beat me." Jaclyn closed her eyes. Her lies were getting so out of hand she couldn't stand to look at Josh as she told them. "Again."

"Again?"

"Yes. All of us girls get beat."

"To keep his stable in line?" Josh asked in mock seriousness.

Jaclyn pulled away to stare at Josh. Having a bandage over his eyes ruined everything. She had no idea by listening to his voice what he was thinking. She'd never heard that word connected with hookers before and wasn't the least bit psychic so was forced to ask what he meant just as if she hadn't heard him clearly.

"Did you say stable?"

"Isn't that what a pimp calls the girls who hustle for him?"

"Of course," she swallowed nervously, thinking she'd like to know how that silly expression originated. "That is true."

"Where are you supposed to be now?"

"On my way to"—she tried to think of a city where there were always lots of unattached men about—"San Diego." That was a good choice with the naval base and fancy hotels. "I'm working a convention."

"That should earn you lots of money for, er . . . Grandma's upkeep."

"It will, but I don't always like it," Jaclyn continued, heaping one lie on top of another. *Forgive me, Lord,* she thought as the list of untruths got longer and longer.

"Why?"

"Too many old men. Old, ugly men with"—*this should touch his sympathetic soul if he had one*—"Perverted desires."

"Like Jazam and . . ." Josh went on listing names of exotic sex acts she vaguely remembered from Lerisa's books.

"Yes," Jaclyn admitted beneath her breath, wondering what on earth a Jazam was. Was it one of those centuries-old acrobatic feats that only an Olympic gymnast was limber enough to do?

"All those positions and more," she bragged. There was no need to quit exploiting her capabilities, especially now that she was experienced.

"Don't you like sex?"

"Yes. Right from the start." Fortunately, she was interrupted before she could add, *Which was tonight.*

"I thought you were too responsive to fake it," he pointed out in a husky voice. "In fact, I could have sworn you even had an or—"

"In my business you learn to be a good actress." That was certainly true, she praised herself mutely. She was giving an academy-award-winning performance tonight.

"Be honest with me, Jazzy," Josh insisted, tongue-in-cheek. "Wasn't I any good as a lover?"

Jaclyn hesitated, thought over every delicious moment that still sent tingles through her body, and whispered solemnly, "You were excellent, Josh. I can truthfully say you were the very best I've ever had."

"Now that's"—Josh smiled—"the biggest compliment a man can ever receive. Especially coming from a woman who's had hundreds of lovers."

"Hundreds?" Did hookers service that many men in their young lives?

"Thousands?" he questioned, raising one eyebrow in disbelief, though his mouth twitched in a strange way for a man supposedly expressing shock. "Surely not, since you seem pretty young."

"I never kept track!" Jaclyn cried, wanting to change the subject, and fast. "Can I stay with you tonight or not? It's foggy and cold outside, and I have no place close by to sleep without having to answer to all kinds of questions about where I've been."

"Okay, Jazzy," Josh agreed gently. "You stay here tonight. I'm going to enjoy having your warm, shapely body snuggled up close to me while I try to sleep."

"Thank you, Josh," Jaclyn murmured, stifling a wide yawn. Her eyes closed. Despite the uncomfortable inquiry she had never felt so relaxed or comfortable in her life.

Hearing the yawn, Josh brushed her forehead with his lips and crooned, "Go to sleep, little one. In the morning I have a plan that may keep you free of your current life-style for quite a while."

"Good," Jaclyn agreed with complete trust, not understanding what he meant. She would find out in the morning.

Don't let this night end, she made a silent plea against his chest. *Please, dear God, give me the strength to leave him when morning comes.*

Drifting quickly off to sleep in Josh's arms, Jaclyn knew she'd never be content again sleeping in her lonely bed in her tiny Paris flat.

CHAPTER FIVE

Jaclyn stirred, lifting her eyelids slowly to look at Josh. It seemed the most natural thing in the world to be lying beside him snuggled possessively close. She let her eyes wander from his firm jaw, past the taut line of his throat, and down to his powerful chest, which rose and fell in a steady rhythm.

He looked far less intimidating sound asleep with his mouth relaxed and wavy hair vivid against the rust-colored pillowcase. A smooth cotton top sheet pulled up to their waists prevented her glance from surveying the rest of his body with equal appreciation.

The sight of him was a mixture of torture and love. Torture that she had to seduce him as an unknown woman and love, as always, when she could observe his keen, intelligent features unseen.

He was more than a handsome male with strength showing in his face and hard masculine body. He was the man she loved. It wouldn't have made any difference what his physical features were once his eyes first locked with hers and pierced straight into her innocent soul. No other man had made the slightest impression on her heart since that traumatic moment so long ago.

With great stealth she eased out from under the weight of his arm, making certain not to disturb him, as she scooted to the side of the bed and stood up. It was like a comedy movie, she thought, only this time it was the woman sneaking away in the early morning hours, not a cowardly male lover leaving before an irate husband returned. She glanced at the clock. It wasn't quite five thirty. That would give her plenty of time to shower, dress, and exit by six.

Unperturbed by her state of nudity, she admitted Josh's lack of sight was responsible for a total personality change. A physical change too, she mused, running her hands up and down her sides. She felt like a free spirit who had shed all vestiges of her outer shell. A woman now ready to face the world with a decidedly different outlook.

A smile touched her lips, knowing Josh's attentive lovemaking was such a wonder, she hadn't noticed the bedside light was left on when she fell asleep. Deep pile carpeting felt soft against the bottom of her feet as she glanced around, searching for the most likely door to a bathroom.

Bruce had told her Josh considered the entire upper quarters his private lair, a personal suite no one was allowed to enter. It contained his work studio, a personal collection of bronzes, and private drawings he didn't wish displayed to the general public.

Her brother had only been allowed one short tour when the house was first built, and she recalled he exclaimed it looked like a perfect orgy pad if Josh would just clear out all the art work.

"This should be it," she whispered, pushing open a partially closed door. She reached for a wall switch, knowing Josh wouldn't be disturbed by a flash of light.

Goodness, she enthused silently, admiring all the exquisite green plants along the far wall. This was the most gorgeous bathroom she'd ever seen and the biggest. Imported tiles surrounded twin sinks, covered a vast stall shower, and matched an octagon-shaped tub big enough to hold a man and several feminine companions. Jealousy clouded her mind, picturing Josh lying in the water with a bevy of gorgeous, attentive women, until she remembered him saying he'd been celibate for too many months.

Stained woodwork, shining like the many polished glass mirrors, made up the cabinets, which surrounded three sides of the tub and formed a carved pedestal that contained a bronze nymph with hands outstretched from her fern-covered niche in the corner.

Curiously drawn to the entrancing statue, Jaclyn stepped forward. She ran her fingers over it lovingly, appreciating the talent that formed the perfect figure from a piece of unmolded clay into a work of art. It was beautiful. The young girl had wavy hair flowing down her back and shapely immature breasts thrusting innocently forward as she kneeled on long, coltish limbs.

Jaclyn had never seen this work before and wondered why Josh would keep such an extraordinary example of his talent away from the public eye. She stared at the inscription on the base. It was titled "Innocence Unobserved." What an interesting name for such an exquisite work, she thought, curious to know if it was a figment of his imagination or some young model he had hired.

She had no time to think about that now, Jaclyn thought, as she decided a shower would be much faster than filling the huge tub.

She stepped inside the glass door of the stall, adjusted the water, and felt perfectly at ease rubbing Josh's bar of soap lavishly over her body. A brief shudder ran up her spine as her hands touched areas Josh had possessed with such intimacy, she still tingled from the memory. She carefully avoided getting her hair wet, turning around to rinse off the rich suds before stepping out onto the plush carpet.

Swiftly toweling her skin dry, she wished for her makeup kit. The extras would have to come later. For now being squeaky clean was enough, since she had limited time. Her brother might phone and she intended to be well on her way to Los Angeles when that happened. She had taken a big risk as it was, spending the night here.

She entered the bedroom with glowing skin, tumbled wavy hair, and fingers crossed, hoping that Josh wouldn't wake up before she grabbed her clothes and dressed. Her mind was intent only on rushing downstairs, picking up her purse and coat, and fleeing into the dawn as fast as possible.

Her undoing was turning to stare at Josh for a last, lingering glance. With a heartbroken sob, she found the temptation unbearable. If she could climb out of his bed unnoticed, she should certainly be able to climb back on it for one fleeting kiss over his injured eyes.

Holding her breath, she eased onto the wide bed and moved slowly across. Surely he wouldn't feel her lips if they just touched the bandage. It would help give her the needed courage to leave with her chin held high, knowing she carried his scent with her and had implanted wishes for a complete recovery on his beloved face.

Kneeling over Josh, she placed a feather-light caress over each injured eye as he slept undisturbed. She inhaled his clean masculine fragrance, fighting the urge to bury her face on his chest and stay forever. *I love you, Josh,* she cried inwardly, blinking back tears that were rapidly gathering in the corners of her eyes. *Forever and always, my darling. Until the end of time.*

Biting her lip so she wouldn't sob out loud, she turned away, intent on sliding off the bed and rushing from the room before she burst out crying.

"Where do you think you're going?" Josh demanded, throwing his arms across her naked breast the second she moved. His hold was gentle only because she didn't try to break it.

A temporary paralysis took possession of her vocal cords and legs. Had he been awake and waiting to see what she would do? She paused motionless on the bed for long, uncomfortable moments until he pointed out.

"I asked where you think you're going, Jazzy?"

"B-back to work," she stammered, twisting around so she was fully in his arms.

"The hell you are," he warned in a voice that didn't sound the least bit sleepy.

"I am," she insisted, worried about her brother. "I told you I was leaving by six and it's five minutes before right now." If Bruce found her in Josh's bed, he'd die of shock.

"Tough," Josh threatened. "You're mine. My money's as good as any other man's, and I'm no more satisfied after a one-night stand with you than I was with a single hour."

"You're not?" she questioned, staring with fascination at his dark stubble of heavy beard. Her mind wandered, thinking he must have shaved just before she arrived last night as his face was smooth and sleek when he passionately explored her body.

"You really want me to stay?"

"Yes," he reiterated, bringing her thoughts back to his surprising declaration. "I want more of you. A lot more, and I intend to get it every opportunity I have."

"But how? I—I really have to leave." She glanced nervously at the clock as the minutes went by with amazing speed. She knew her brother too well. He would never relax until he learned every explicit, erotic detail Josh deigned to tell him about his gift.

"In fact, I have to go right now."

"Forget it." Josh wrapped her in his arms, throwing the top sheet aside so she was cradled against the length of his nude body. "I said you're not going and I meant it."

"I am," she argued, desperate to retain a modicum of composure while his hands were sending a message of their own wherever he touched. "I only asked to stay until morning. I have a living to earn, remember?"

"No problem," he told her with exasperating nonchalance. "I'm paying you by the hour but I'm renting you for a month."

"A month!" Jaclyn exclaimed, her eyes wide and her lips parted in shock. Her mind whirled as she tried to figure out how much that would be at two hundred dollars per hour. A fortune by anyone's standard, she thought, giving up after the fifth day's fee.

"No man could afford me for a month."

"I can and I will."

"You won't because I won't be here." She braced her hands on his steel-hard shoulders, trying to break his hold. It was useless until he released her of his own free will. He was amazingly strong and knew it.

"I'm leaving this instant," Jaclyn stormed back, surprised by her own temerity.

"Forget it!" Josh said in a thickened voice. "My mind's made up."

"Too bad! I'm going now and . . . ouch!" she yelped in surprise when she felt a gentle swat on her bottom.

"Shut up, Jazzy," he commanded in a voice that bode ill for her if she disobeyed. "And wrap your silky legs around my hips because I'm eager to see if the third time in you will be even better for us than the first two put together."

"Y-you are?"

Jaclyn's voice was filled with stress when she answered. It was impossible to control the tremors that ran through her body at the thought of making love before driving to Los Angeles. She felt all reason swept away by the desire to be his one more time.

Her dove-gray eyes softened, nearly translucent, as she stared at him with the sudden need to experience the heady satisfaction he gave so generously.

"You're crazy," she moaned, accepting him between her legs without hesitation. His behavior was totally unpredictable. "You're insane! You're a mad artist who's . . ."

Her words were effectively broken off as Josh bent his head and took her mouth with a sensual need so strong it was as if the previous hours had never happened.

Jaclyn responded, clinging to his nape while he played with her mouth, nibbling her lower lip and outlining it with the point of his tongue. In between each drugging caress he rained kisses over her entire face. His touch was so stimulating, deep purrs of excitement bubbled from her throat time and time again.

"You have the most beautiful, the most responsive mouth in the world, Jazzy. I could spend the rest of my life kissing you."

Jaclyn could feel Josh's hands tremble, like the shoulder muscles beneath her fingertips, when he lowered himself to her breasts. He made her feel like the most desirable woman in the world when he reverently pressed his face against the deep cleavage formed by his hands gently pushing in from each side.

"You're so soft and warm." Josh gave a hungry moan. "And you have the smoothest, silkiest skin in existence."

"*You* sure don't," Jaclyn teased, rubbing her hand along his jaw, "when you need a shave as bad as you do now." Unconcerned about his abrasive face when his mouth was doing such delightful things to her nipples, she squirmed in enjoyment.

It seemed impossible she had lived her adult life without his lovemaking. One night and she was insatiable for the man. All he had to do was utter a blunt request, give her several kisses, and she was wild to give him anything he wished.

"You're certainly a hairy monster in the morning," she gasped, clenching his head when he licked her nipples with strokes so exciting she hoped he never stopped.

"Your tongue needs curbing, Jazzy," he scolded, mischievously rubbing his rough face back and forth until she yanked his hair and tugged him away.

"Beast!" Jaclyn gave another sharp pull.

"Beast, am I?" Josh questioned gruffly. "I'll show you just what an animal I can be."

"I can easily handle that," Jaclyn repeated her brave remark one more time, giving him a cocky smile.

His threats sounded rather intriguing, considering how pleasant his lovemaking was. Since they were intimately close with his body as rigid and impatient as it had been the night before, she knew she wouldn't have very long to wait.

Jaclyn giggled softly as deep moans left Josh's throat while he worked his way up and down her body.

"Quit laughing, wench," he commanded gruffly. "You're supposed to be frightened."

"Well, I'm not," she said with another laugh, stroking her fingers along his side. Touching him was already addictive.

"You're not afraid?" he feigned astonishment.

"My only fear is that you'll stop," she admitted,

catching her breath sharply when the firm point of his tongue touched the central warmth of her arched body.

"Good," Josh rasped huskily, "because I'm going to make you on fire for me, Jazzy. As hot as you can be!"

He did, continuing his passionate foray until her joyous whimpers urged him on as he savored each probing, intimate caress. He paused to kiss her silken thighs, hating to bring her sweet-tasting body to the edge of sensual pleasure so soon. Her pleas incited him to resume.

Whether minutes or seconds later, Jaclyn didn't know, but a deep shudder of unbearable intensity caused her to cry out his name over and over in a wondrous plea. "Josh. Oh, Jooosh. Oooh, Jooosh."

When she lay gasping and spent, he raised up to cradle her in his arms until her breathing returned to normal and she was indolently reposed. It was a heady experience to make love to a woman who enjoyed each caress with such uninhibited pleasure.

Jaclyn held him close, placing kisses across his brow in a loving gesture. His unselfish urge to bring her gratification needed returning, and she knew the best way at the moment to say thank you. She moved her legs to cling to his hips and her sensual intentions obvious. "My turn, I believe," she crooned, reaching down to touch his hardened flesh. "My turn to see you feel as satiated as I do."

Josh covered her hand with his fingers, eager to do as she wanted. It had been a long night. He had hugged her close for hours, fighting the desire to take her over and over. As the minutes slowly ticked by toward dawn, it seemed the biggest waste of time in the world to sleep when they could be making love.

The phone rang, interrupting his thoughts just as he thrust deep inside her. He moved slowly without releasing his possession, waiting to see who it was. When she nervously tried to squirm away, he held her body still with his weight and hands.

"Lie still, Jazzy, and listen," Josh demanded. "I'll be damned if a ringing phone will ever stop me when I'm making love to a woman like you."

His hips moved, not missing a stroke, as the phone rang two more times.

Jaclyn started to relax and enjoy the pulsating rhythm of his body when she was nearly startled out of her mind by the sound of her brother's clear voice.

"Who's that?" she cried out, desperately trying to pull away. This was fast becoming a nightmare instead of a dream.

"My answering machine," Josh explained in a soothing voice, keeping her pinned with the pressure of his hips.

"It sounds like the man's right here in the room."

"I leave it on all the time to screen my calls. Now, will you relax? I like your erotic squirming but your mind is obviously not on what I'm doing to your body."

If anything in the world could interfere in her love life, it was her brother's voice teasing Josh in his characteristic way while she lay beneath the man he was calling and listened.

"Josh, this is Bruce. I'm calling to find out how you liked your present. Pretty hot stuff, huh? Call me back and tell me all the wild details, like how many times you got it and what positions you tried. That broad's supposed to be their best, so I hope she gave you something you haven't had before, old buddy?" His deep laughter filled the room as he ended with, "Don't forget you owe me a big one now."

"What's the matter with you?" Josh demanded as Jaclyn writhed helplessly. "The damned machine can't see and it can't hear, so let's continue, since your tight little body has me at the point of no return."

"I—I—" Jaclyn stammered, unable to lie still. She couldn't stand the torment of hearing her brother's awful comments. That was too much to expect of anyone!

"I c-can't," she moaned when he surged against her.

"The hell you can't, you enticing witch," Josh gasped, increasing his pulsating drive until he ground out, "Nothing could make me release your body now."

Jaclyn's heart beat like a wild thing when Josh broke off, repeating his sensual impact until her hips rose and she felt nothing but the force of his manhood thrusting into her with incredible pleasure.

"My God, Jazzy," Josh shuddered in a final surge of excruciating pleasure. "Your response to a man is staggering!"

"It's you, Josh," Jaclyn admitted, her thoughts out of control. "Only to you," she cried, trembling with astonished delight to experience intense satisfaction for the second time that morning.

"Now," he asked, long minutes later, "what is all this bull about not being able to spend a few weeks with me?"

"I can't. This area is filled with men I know, and it would be embarrassing for both of us if I stayed here."

Jaclyn forced herself to sit up. A wistful smile touched her mouth as she gave Josh a loving glance. If she rushed like crazy, she should be in her car in less than twenty minutes with enough memories for a lifetime. She eased off the bed, grabbed her clothes, and called over her shoulder as she returned to his bathroom. "As soon as I freshen up and dress, I'm on my way."

"As soon as *we* freshen up and *we* dress, we'll *both*

be on our way," he warned, swinging his hips around to sit on the edge of his bed. "It might not be a bad idea to take a shower together either. Saves on water if nothing else."

"Absolutely not!" Jaclyn exclaimed. "Besides I showered already before you woke up."

"I know it. I wasn't asleep."

"Were you just lying there listening to me to see what I'd do next?"

"Actually, I was lying here wondering how long I'd have to wait before I made love to you."

"You're acting the mad artist again." She laughed, slamming the bathroom door shut and locking it so she wouldn't be disturbed. When she cautiously opened the door, intent on peaking around the edge to see where Josh was, he grabbed her shoulders and took her mouth in a fierce, hungry kiss.

"Don't even think about leaving without me while I'm in the bathroom, Jazzy," he warned. "We're going to have lots of time together, and since it won't be in the United States, you shouldn't run into any local johns you've serviced in the past."

Jaclyn's eyes widened as she listened carefully to each word. It seemed so right to be with him she kept forgetting he still thought her a call girl. His voice was also so commanding she thought her knees would buckle hearing each forceful admonition.

"I mean it, honey. Stay here while I shower and dress, then I'll explain everything about my plans." With his warning ringing in her ears, and the fiery, lingering kiss still throbbing on her mouth, she listened as he closed the bathroom door between them and locked her out.

"Arrogant beast!" she called out, laughing when the knob clicked. Not the least intimidated with Josh out of sight, Jaclyn knew he'd be busy for quite some time.

With a last glance at the rumpled bed, she rushed down the stairs and across the living room to get her purse and coat.

A sudden desire to leave some memento of her visit made her root through her bag until she found a plain slip of paper and a pen. In large letters she neatly printed "I LOVE YOU," then signed "Jazzy" in flowing script she hoped was completely unlike her normal handwriting.

She placed the note beneath the edge of a lamp beside his armchair. He wouldn't see it or be able to read it for months to come, but it eased her mind to put in words that she had given herself to him with love, not greed.

Just as her fingers reached for the front doorknob, a loud pounding made her pull back. One hand flew to her breast instinctively as she braced herself against the wall wondering what to do next. She bent low, creeping along the floor until she could peek out a side window and see who Josh's early morning visitor was. Her brow beaded with perspiration at her sudden bad luck. Damn it! she cursed in silence, surprised at her temper when the pounding started in again before she even got to the window. Just as she was ready to make good her escape too.

She rested on her knees, raised her head up, and slowly pulled a corner of the drape aside to stare at the unwelcome visitor. "Oh, lord, no," she whispered helplessly. It was the last person in the entire universe she wanted to see.

Her face paled as she watched her brother impatiently waiting for Josh to open the front door. When his hand raised to knock again, she dropped the drape, gathered her purse and coat, and rushed back upstairs to the bedroom.

Josh was waiting freshly shaved and fully dressed in

casual slacks, a knit shirt, and polished loafers. Hearing her enter the room, he looked up. "Who's at the door, Jazzy?"

"I—I don't know," she lied, stuffing her purse and coat out of sight behind a bedroom chair. "I didn't want to answer the door in case it was my pimp."

"Good girl," Josh said, and smiled. "I'll handle it." He strode across the room with more ease than she ever could and walked down the stairs.

"Don't let him come up here," Jaclyn called out. "Whoever it is."

"I won't," Josh agreed.

Jaclyn walked to the edge of the bedroom stairs, scrunching down in order to see as much as possible and not miss a single word exchanged. It was all her fault for being so greedy. If she had been satisfied with just seducing the man once, as planned, she'd be safe in LA and comfortably waiting for the first available seat on an overseas flight.

"Hi, Bruce." Josh greeted her brother pleasantly. "Why the early visit?"

"You know damned well why," Bruce teased, stepping inside. "You didn't return my call so I decided to come over and get my thank you in person."

"Thank you, now get out," Josh told him. He moved away to stand by his chair. "You know I'm leaving this morning, and I've got some unexpected things to take care of before I go."

"It won't take a minute," his best friend said, laughing, looking around as if he expected there would be some change in the house. "As soon as you tell me about last night, I'll cut out."

"The only thing I'll say is, it was the best night of my life."

"Best night?" Bruce questioned, catching on immediately. "Don't tell me she's still here." He glanced quickly upstairs, just missing Jaclyn's frightened face as she pulled back out of sight.

"Yes," Josh answered honestly. "She's with me now."

Bruce wiped his brow with one hand, his eyes glowing with sudden excitement. "Introduce me, Josh, then I'll leave immediately. I don't think I can stand not seeing a woman you think special enough to let spend a night in your cloistered orgy pad."

"You'll leave once you meet her?" Josh inquired, looking up the stairway as if he could sense Jaclyn listening with a pounding heart.

"Hell, yes, man. She must be a knockout, since you haven't even looked at a chick for years. Because you can't see her, I'll be able to describe all of her, er, finer points to you."

"I found all the finer points without your help last night." Josh put his hand on his chin, pondered for a moment, then pointed to a side chair.

"Make yourself comfortable. I'll get her and be right back. It would be a shame to hide all this beauty from the man who paid for the first hour."

"You bet it would," Bruce said, laughing, with his eyes on the stairs as Josh walked up to his private quarters.

Jaclyn scrambled to her feet and dashed into the bathroom. She waited behind the half-closed door, trying desperately to think of a way to avoid her brother.

"Jazzy," Josh called, walking straight toward her. "I have someone who wants to meet you. He'll just say hello then leave."

"I c-can't come out," she gulped inanely, locking the door just before he got to it. "I'm taking a-a shower." The man's ability to find her was uncanny.

"You just took a shower," Josh taunted, knocking for her to let him in.

"I'm taking another one. I always take several a day."

"I don't hear the water running." Josh's voice had a decidedly mischievous tone.

Jaclyn reached inside the stall shower and turned on the faucet. His exceptional hearing was uncanny too.

"Hurry up, then, as we have to get on our way soon."

"Tell the man to come back another time," Jaclyn yelled, secure in the knowledge Josh couldn't get inside. "I—I don't like unannounced visitors."

She heard the doorknob rattle and a pin being inserted in the lock to open it just before she kicked off her shoes and scrambled in the cubicle fully dressed.

"You really are in the shower," Josh said, opening the stall door just as she slammed it shut.

"Of course I am," she snapped. The darned water was freezing cold and felt horrible running down her bare legs as she stood on tiptoes in a vain attempt to get out of the spray.

"That's too bad. I thought it might be interesting to get your opinion of my best friend," he mocked boldly. "And he of you," he added as a taunting afterthought. "He was anxious to give me a full description of you."

"I gave you one last night!" Jaclyn said, fuming. Would Josh never leave?

"Oh, yes," he continued as if he had all the time in the world. "Brown eyes and red hair, wasn't it?"

"Which means I have a temper and you'd better leave before I throw the damned washcloth at your arrogant face!"

Thank heavens, Josh's eyes were bandaged now, Jaclyn thought, squirming around to the far corner so he couldn't touch her without getting his arm wet.

Unfortunately, it was also the direction the direct force of the nozzle was turned, and she felt her arm and the bottom half of her dress get soaking wet as she reached up to aim the spray as low as possible.

"Okay, honey." Josh smiled at her temper. "If you're this determined to get clean, I'll send the man on his way. You two will meet face to face soon enough as it is."

"I'll be waiting," she promised. Overnight she'd become the world's biggest liar and right now she didn't care just as long as he left. "Just go away, please."

Josh shut the door and walked from the bathroom, chuckling out loud as Jaclyn turned off the water and stepped outside in her soggy clothes. She took a towel and vigorously rubbed the material between its heavy nap until the thin nylon was no longer dripping.

Now she'd have to go to her darned car and get a new dress. At least she had left it under a tree at the far side of the parking lot. If Bruce spotted her Ford, that would really be the payoff!

The last few minutes had definitely convinced her she wanted no part of being a super sleuth or leading a life of crime. Both could cause permanent heart damage. This morning's happenings were much too close a call for comfort. She preferred a nice, tranquil existence that was busy and fruitful with her artistic endeavors. The last few minutes had been the most nerve-wracking of her life.

At least her underwear was reasonably dry, she thought gratefully, stepping into her shoes and rushing back to the stairway just in time to hear Josh talk to her brother.

"Jazzy's taking a shower and won't come down," Josh told Bruce without further explanation.

"I guess I'll have to call the answering service and buy my own present," Bruce teased. "What'd you say her name was?"

"Jazzy, but it won't do you any good to call, since I'm taking her with me."

"You're what?" Bruce exclaimed. "Isn't it illegal to transport prostitutes across the border for sexual purposes?"

"If it is"—Josh feigned surprise—"Then I intend to break that law often in the next few weeks."

"Lucky devil," her brother acknowledged with envy. "Be sure and let me know where to pick up the body. After she gets through with you, they'll be flying what's left of your frame back in a casket."

"Good-bye, Bruce."

"So long, Josh." He opened the door to leave.

"By the way . . ." Josh's words stopped him. "Why didn't you use my key and just walk on in like you always do instead of pounding my door down?"

"Because I couldn't find the damned thing. It's always been on my dresser, but I guess the housekeeper moved it."

"Well, find it," Josh told him firmly. "No telling who'll come sneaking into my house if you don't."

"Hell"—Bruce scowled—"with the luck you've had the last few hours it's bound to be some sexy broad intent on seducing you."

CHAPTER SIX

Whoever said you shouldn't eavesdrop was crazy Jaclyn contemplated seriously.

Listening to Josh and Bruce's conversation last night had changed her entire life in one twelve-hour period. This morning it had given her an insight into one mammoth and seemingly insurmountable problem ahead. She knew her tenacious brother would never rest until he met . . . Jazzy.

But there was time enough to worry about that later, she decided, shaking out the hem of her damp dress. She felt miserable in her wet clothes yet was forced to wait until Bruce was completely off the premises before going to her car to get something else to wear. At least she could put makeup on and do her hair, which would make her feel much more presentable even if Josh couldn't see to appreciate each feminine ritual.

She picked up her purse from its hiding spot behind the chair and walked into the bathroom. Studying her reflection in the mirror, she decided her eyes did have a decided shimmer that hadn't been there yesterday. Was it the satisfying night or the early morning tryst? Either way it was Josh who was responsible for her current happiness. He was as marvelous a lover as she had ever dreamed of in the past. Considerate and tender, yet forcefully passionate and unafraid to express all the sensual hunger she had yearned for through the years.

Amazed to find her fingers still shaking over her near escape from running head-on into her brother, she forced herself to settle her nerves before carefully applying mascara and lipstick. With her hair neatly brushed and time to plan, she saw no reason not to get through the rest of the morning free of turmoil.

"What's up, Jazzy?" Josh asked, startling her as she exited the bathroom.

"Nothing," she answered with a quick smile. "I decided to put on makeup while you were talking with your friend."

"I'd better check it over," Josh announced with boyish enthusiasm. He clasped her shoulders and planted a firm, lingering kiss on her soft pink-tinged mouth.

"You taste as delicious as always!" His lips smacked together in exaggerated delight. "Though I thought you'd be taking another shower by now. It's been at least fifteen minutes since the last."

"I'm through until evening," Jaclyn exclaimed with barely concealed pique at his mischievous taunt. She stood perfectly still when his hands began to move, further annoyed by her lack of will power.

Her temper surged as she allowed his inquisitive fingers to run up and down her arms, briefly skim her hips and bottom, then casually clasp her waist in a strong grip. Darned if he didn't act as if he knew she had deliberately jumped in the shower fully clothed to avoid his hauling her down to meet his friend.

"Your dress feels damp in spots," he remarked with such innocence she wanted to smack him. "Did you run out of dry towels to use?"

"No, I did not!" Jaclyn answered smoothly despite the flash of ill-humor sparkling in her eyes. "I stepped outside on your deck and the dripping fog seeped into my clothes in seconds."

Thankfully she remembered Bruce's telling her Josh had a wide deck off his bedroom. She glanced hastily around looking for sliding glass doors. The upper area was vast, and she'd been so busy since she'd gotten up she still wasn't familiar with her surroundings.

"It's funny that the bottom of your dress got wet instead of the top. Except for the one sleeve, of course," Josh added with irritating persistence. "Do you have any idea how that happened?"

Unable to come up with a logical explanation on the spur of the moment, Jaclyn ignored that remark and complained instead about the weather.

"I only stayed outside for a second, and it was so horrible it's a wonder I'm not entirely drenched."

"I hadn't noticed," Josh admitted. "I haven't been out yet."

His hand came up to stroke the lustrous waves of silvery hair brushing her shoulders. "Your hair's not a bit wet. Did you wear a scarf?"

"Yes," Jaclyn lied just to end the interrogation. He was the most presumptuous man she'd ever known. "I always carry a rain scarf in my purse in the winter."

"Glad to hear it. It's not important how you got wet anyway as long as you don't get chilled. I want you in the best of health during the next few weeks." His innuendo was bluntly clear. "Why don't you sit down while I explain our plans."

"I can't," Jaclyn argued, angered again because his concern for her health was only because he wanted her fit enough to stand the upcoming rigors of his planned sexual escapades.

"I have to go to my car and get something else to wear," Jaclyn told him, turning to walk away. "After

I've changed, I'll hear what you have to say, though I'm telling you now I can't go with you."

"The hell you can't!" Josh declared in a voice so firm she knew his temper was tightly controlled. "It's a fact not a question. You're going to be mine for a month if for no other reason than that you can't afford not to be."

"Are you forgetting I get two hundred dollars per hour?" Jaclyn reminded him stubbornly, pausing to stop by the foot of his bed.

"I'm perfectly aware what your fee is," Josh threw back, totally unperturbed. "I also know you can't work twenty-four hours a day or that no pimp's going to give you even half of what you'll earn, and," he ground out bitterly, "usually a hell of a lot less."

Josh faced her with his long fingers clenched along his hips as if amazed she dare argue with his decision to take her with him. "You should jump at the chance to service only one man for the next few weeks."

"I, er, I like variety," Jaclyn blurted out, unable to think of any other reason to give for refusing to go with him. He wasn't the least afraid of her claims of having a mean pimp. "Making out with different men all the time has always turned me on."

"You want diversity?" Josh asked angrily. "I'll give you such varied styles of loving," he taunted passionately. "You'll never need a comparison piece for the rest of your life!"

Josh stormed across the room and cupped Jaclyn's face in both hands before she had time to move. He took possession of her mouth with such fierce intensity she was stunned. Apparently it was unwise to bait a man about your sexual preferences even if they were a lie.

His lips moved over hers so expertly she soon sagged against his chest. Clinging weakly to his arms, she tried to regain some semblance of composure. His power over her senses was staggering, and she ached for the caress to continue. Later was time enough to try and figure out how best to handle his demanding personality.

"I—I really do have to leave," she whispered against his shirt pocket between deep uneven breaths. Each kiss seemed to increase the power he had over her. If she didn't speak up now, she'd be as weak-willed as she had been when she asked to spend the previous night with him.

"I mean it, Josh."

"Forget it!" he reiterated with frightening force. "Starting tonight we'll make love every way physically possible." His warning was mouthed against the wildly beating pulse in her throat. "By the end of the month your body will be so imprinted with the shape of mine you won't be able to think of having sex with another man without my image coming between the two of you."

Jaclyn could picture Josh's injured eyes blazing behind their bandages. At the mention of her supposed sexual interest in numerous men he became incensed. If she didn't know better, she would think his actions were motivated by jealousy, an emotion certainly not aroused from a one-night stand with a stranger or a hooker.

Her mind whirled as she rapidly contemplated if it would be possible to steal a few weeks with Josh undetected. Of course she could, she reflected, recalling the many problems she had successfully overcome just that morning. Whose business was it anyway but her own? She was on a temporary leave from her art school, so why not?

"How can I resist an opportunity like you offer?" she agreed, doing a complete about-face before he could change his mind. "Even if it's only to see if your bold claim proves correct."

"Think you can handle it?" Josh raised his head, warning her he was completely serious.

"I'll look forward to everything you have to offer," Jaclyn said with a nervous laugh. Now she was more worried about making convincing explanations to Lerisa and her brother concerning her absence than meeting Josh's demands.

"Good!" Josh answered. "Tonight I intend to start with a Jazam."

"Great," Jaclyn agreed, wishing he'd quit asking for something she'd never even heard of. "But don't blame me if you're a physical wreck without a bank account when my month is up."

"Do I look concerned, Jazzy?" Josh replied with equal confidence in his wealth and physical stamina.

Jaclyn eyed him warily as he dismissed her with a shrug and walked over to his closet. He slid the door open and traced his fingers over the material of each jacket until he found the one he was looking for.

"Don't worry about my check balance or whether I can handle a hot little hustler like you. Your main concern should be your aged relative," Josh reminded.

"It is," Jaclyn said dryly. Was he ever going to let her forget her masquerade as a call girl?

Throwing his coat across the back of a chair, he turned to face her. "Four weeks with me and my check will cover Grandma's rent for a year with a few bucks left over to buy yourself a trinket or two."

Acting as casual as Josh, Jaclyn answered with throaty indifference, "As you said, one man's money spends as good as another's. Right now my first priority is getting into dry clothes."

"Fine," Josh agreed, suddenly intent on taking care

of his own necessary preparations before they left. "I have some business calls to make now."

Jaclyn left the bedroom without a backward glance. After she changed clothes, she would listen to his plan. She was certainly filled with curiosity to find out where he planned to take her. The reason why and what he planned to do when they got there had never been in doubt! Josh didn't need to know how happy she was at the thought of spending a long time in his company. It was more than she had ever hoped for when she first thought of her scheme for his seduction.

Within minutes Jaclyn had rushed to her car, rooted through her duffel bag for comfortable slacks and a soft cashmere sweater she had purchased in Italy in the fall, and returned to the master bathroom to change. Catching her breath, she thought how lucky she was the fog was still heavy enough to act as camouflage. She knew too many people in Laguna Beach to feel comfortable wandering around outside Josh's home.

Moments later she was dressed and waiting for Josh to return from making his calls. Too nervous to sit and do nothing, she straightened the bed. As she smoothed the spread, she thought of being with Josh. His lovemaking was so perfect, just touching his pillow brought tears of happiness to her eyes.

"Darn it, where is he?" she wondered aloud, picking up her coat to place alongside his jacket.

"Right here," the man in her thoughts interrupted, coming up on her by surprise and taking her in his arms. His hands skimmed her hips and the soft wool sweater with appreciation.

"What color are they?" Josh asked.

"What?" Jaclyn asked, not clear what he meant.

"Your sweater and slacks. I want to picture how you look today."

"Black-and-gray plaid slacks and a gray sweater."

"Good colors for a redhead," he told her, just as if he had a right to question her choice of outfit. "Even better for a blonde."

"Too bad," she answered peevishly. His remarks were undoubtedly brought forth by his artistic nature. Obviously, if he thought her colors weren't pleasing to the eye, he would ask her to change.

"I picked this outfit because it's warm and comfortable to travel in, not in hopes of winning a beauty contest."

"Sensible idea. Now sit down." Josh pointed to the bedside chair like a man giving his favorite hound dog a command. "Since your comfort is assured, I'll tell you what we're going to do."

"Where've you been?" Jaclyn asked, refusing to either listen or be seated. She hadn't realized how outspoken she could be until she confronted Josh's forceful personality.

"I didn't even hear you come up the stairs." She stood braced. "Your sneaking around is unnerving."

"I said I'd be in my office and I never sneak." He moved forward and kissed her brow in exasperation. "Please sit down, Jazzy, while I explain my damned plans before our month is up and it's too late to go!"

"Go where?" Jaclyn questioned, unconsciously doing as he asked by relaxing in his plush bedside chair.

"To LAX to start." Josh stood beside his bed, arms braced across his chest in a dominant male stance.

"We're taking a plane somewhere?" What a stupid thing to ask, she grimaced, thinking how convenient it would be for her if they did. She could return the rented car and contact Pan Am about her return flight too.

"Yes, Jazzy." Josh gave her a wide smile that melted her heart for the umpteenth time. "We're flying to Seattle at one ten. For one night only. Then we go on to Vancouver Island for the holidays."

"British Columbia!" Jaclyn exclaimed. "That's wonderful. I've never been there and I hear it's beautiful in the winter."

"It is. Many people go to Victoria year after year and stay for Christmas, Boxing Day, and New Year's festivities as well."

Pleased at the sudden excitement in Jazzy's voice, Josh continued. "We'll be staying at a new hotel which is extremely elegant, has lots of entertainment, gourmet food, and even a visit from Santa Claus to each guest."

"But what about you? Will you be able to enjoy it not being able to see?" Jaclyn asked with concern for Josh's temporary disability.

"You will be my pleasure, Jazzy. I'll have you by my side all day and in my bed at night. I hope you'll describe the sights to me too. What more could a man want?"

"That sounds heavenly." Jaclyn gave a wistful sigh. "I think I'd like that very much."

"Which? The bed or being my eyes?"

"Both!" She laughed. "You have lots of bragging about your—er—prowess to live up to as I recall."

"Nothing I said was an untruth, as you will see." He looked straight across the room as if he could see the hands on his bedside clock. "Starting in approximately ten hours you'll be *illegitimately* earning the first of your day's fee."

Jaclyn ignored Josh's implication and told him, "If you insist I go with you, then I want to leave now." She was getting more edgy by the minute at the possibility her brother might make another surprise visit.

"A couple more calls from my office then I'll be

ready." He started back toward the stairway. "We'll leave long before your pimp can hunt you down."

"You're probably right," Jaclyn told him with a knowing smile. The only man she was worried about coming around was her brother.

"By the way, Jazzy, if my nurse, Rick, should call on this line, answer it and tell him there will be three going instead of two as planned."

Stopping on the top stair, he turned to glance in her direction. "Don't worry about clothes or personal items. I'll buy you anything you need."

"There's no need," Jaclyn assured him. "I have a couple of bags with me."

"You do?" Josh questioned, raising one eyebrow in surprise. "Why?"

"I told you I was on my way to work a convention," she returned smoothly, bothered because each lie seemed easier to tell and she'd always been a truthful person.

"You're going to be with me a month, not a day or two."

"I packed heavy because I was told there'd be at least two weeks' work."

"The fleet must be in too," Josh mumbled drolly, continuing downstairs without further comment.

Jaclyn ignored him, giving his studio a wistful glance. She was dying to explore his work area and examine all the bronze figures. Unfortunately, she wouldn't have time, nor would he expect her to show an interest in art. All of which was her fault for coming to him as a working girl named Jazzy instead of his best friend's sister, Jaclyn, a fellow artist.

Her thoughts were interrupted by the telephone. She listened to it ring, waiting for the caller to identify himself before answering.

"Mr. Kingman? This is Rick."

"Hello, Rick. This is Josh's friend, Jaclyn. Can I take a message?"

"Hello, Jaclyn," the older man answered in a raspy voice.

"My name is Jazzy," she interrupted. "I guess you misunderstood me." That was much too close!

"Sorry, Jazzy. I wanted to tell Josh that I'll be by to pick him up at nine sharp."

"What are you going to do on the trip, Rick?" Jaclyn inquired, knowing it wasn't really any of her business.

"I'm Josh's official Seeing Eye dog, his valet, and masseur, plus I see he takes the proper medicine at the correct time of day. He's not the best patient I've ever had to work with."

"I can believe that," Jaclyn said, laughing softly and thinking of Josh's demanding arrogance. She waited, hearing Rick cough repeatedly in the background.

"Excuse me," he apologized. "As I was saying, Josh kicked me out of his house as soon as he learned to move around without running into everything. Now I'm only allowed to come over when he needs a chauffeur to his doctor's office, medicine from the pharmacy, or a massage when his migraines become unbearable."

"Does Josh have bad headaches very often?" Jaclyn asked sympathetically.

"More than he should. He also tires easily and is bothered with neck pains," he explained. "But he refuses to admit he's not one-hundred-percent physically fit."

"Thanks for telling me."

"You sound compassionate, Jazzy." Rick coughed several times. "Maybe you can help me keep him in line until his eyes heal. What he needs most is lots of rest and tender loving care."

"I'll only be with him a few weeks," Jaclyn explained, thinking she'd love nothing better than taking care of Josh. "A month at the most."

Another spontaneous idea formed in Jaclyn's mind as she listened to Rick's hoarse voice. The thought of someone else tagging along didn't sound the least bit pleasant. If she could convince Rick to stay home, then she would have Josh completely to herself. It was a much more romantic idea for a holiday trip.

"I bet your family hates you being away over Christmas and New Year, don't they, Rick?"

"Only got a brother down in Florida now."

"Would you like to go see him?"

"Nope. We never did get along," Rick replied, killing that plan in a hurry.

"You don't sound well." Maybe this would work instead. "Are you feeling bad?"

"No, I'm fine," Rick agreed between sneezes.

Darn the man! It would take a clever woman to get rid of him before Josh returned from his business calls.

"If I let you in on a secret, would you promise not to tell a living soul?" She kept her fingers crossed hoping the old man was a romantic at heart.

"Sure, Jazzy," Rick agreed solemnly.

"Well, this is a reconciliation trip, Rick, and I'd like to be alone with my former fiancé. If I paid your air fare to Florida to make up with your brother, would you agree to let me care for Josh by myself?"

"No way. Seeing him don't interest me in the least, nor is it ethical to leave my patient in a lurch, miss," Rick spoke up, blowing his nose loudly.

Good Lord. Jaclyn moaned in silence. *The man needs care more than Josh. He must have a terrible cold.*

"Forget the trip, then, but please let me care for Josh alone. All you have to do is tell me what medications to give him and when, plus all the other ways I can make him comfortable. I had years of private nursing caring for my sick grandmother before the doctor ordered her into a rest home."

Please forgive me for that whopper, Jaclyn pleaded in silence, looking upward just as if she could be heard. "You really sound ill, Rick," she persisted, not about to give up. Darn the stubborn old man! Jaclyn tapped her foot impatiently well aware that Josh's nurse was debating what to do.

"I do feel like I'm coming down with the flu and wasn't quite sure how to handle it. It's really hard to get a last-minute replacement, one that Josh would approve of anyway, during the holidays."

"That's settled, then," Jaclyn blurted out, rushing so he wouldn't change his mind. "Give me directions for Josh's care real fast because I have an awful lot to do before we leave for the airport."

She scribbled notes on a bedside pad, careful to write down the specialist's name in Victoria who would check his eyes each week.

Expecting Josh to come bounding up the stairways any second, Jaclyn rushed through her conversation while stuffing the nursing instructions into her purse.

"Thanks, Rick," she whispered, with both eyes on the doorway. "If all goes well, I'll see you get an invitation to the wedding."

With a sigh of relief she hung up the phone, gathered her coat and purse, and walked downstairs to meet Josh. Her problems were compounding as fast as her lies.

She looked up as Josh exited his office, stepped easily around several large bronze sculptures, and walked straight toward her.

"Did Rick call, Jazzy?"

"Yes." How did the man always know exactly where she was?

"Any problems?"

"No. Everything's taken care of."

"Good. Then he should be here to pick up our luggage and drive us to the airport in about ten minutes."

"Actually," Jaclyn blurted out, "Rick said he was having car trouble, so I said we'd pick him up then come back and get your suitcases."

"Why didn't he just come over in a cab and save you a trip?" Josh pointed out. "It's not your problem to pick up my nurse. I'll call him back."

"No!" Jaclyn grabbed Josh's arm. "I don't mind, since I like to drive."

She'd really be in trouble if Rick told him his . . . fiancee . . . was so eager to spend the holiday without a nurse around, she'd convinced the older man he should stay home.

"Where is your luggage anyway?" Jaclyn asked, looking around. Already she was having problems and they hadn't left the house.

"In the den. He knows where it is, since he packed for me yesterday and put it there when he finished. I have to return to the bedroom to get my electric razor and jacket, then we'll go."

"Take your time." Jaclyn insisted. *Take lots of time, please,* she reflected silently, wanting to move his luggage to her car unseen.

"I'll decide what to do about transportation to the airport after I talk with Rick. Probably have to rent a car, since my Porsche only holds two people."

As soon as Josh started up the stairs, Jaclyn headed for the den. She found Josh's two leather cases easily. Fortunately, she was strong, as they were both heavy.

Returning to the living area, she set them down, opened the door, and scrambled across the deck, down the path and to the Ford. With the speed of a burglar she threw them in the backseat and returned to the house just as Josh appeared.

"We'd better leave, Jazzy," he urged. "I hate to be late, as the airlines are especially busy during the holidays."

"Fine with me, Josh," she agreed quickly, trying to regain her breath before he realized she was up to something.

Her eyes were filled with admiration watching him come down the stairs. He looked so handsome in his casual clothes with the unbuttoned sports jacket exposing his lean abdomen.

"Can I help you to the car?"

"I would appreciate it," Josh grumbled. "My damned lack of sight is a pain in the . . ."

"Eyes," Jaclyn said with a laugh, shutting the door behind them. She placed her fingers on his sleeve, already feeling protective toward her . . . patient.

"That wasn't the area of my anatomy I was going to use. It is irritating having to be led around like a baby in my own yard."

"You certainly know the inside of your house." She pointed out the steps as they walked arm in arm to his gate.

"I should. I bumped into everything in it several times before I was able to walk around in the dark. Now nothing bothers me unless someone misplaces something. Like your shoes on the bathroom rug."

"Oh," Jaclyn looked up after slipping the gate latch aside. "Did you trip over them?"

"No, but I stepped on them when I came to get you to meet my friend."

"I'll have to be more careful," she said, laughing softly. "Here we are." She opened the passenger door and waited for Josh to get inside.

"I can manage to shut the door by myself," Josh explained with obvious annoyance at having to be assisted when Jaclyn prepared to close it.

"Do it, then," she answered brightly, walking around to get in the car.

Jaclyn watched with amusement while he adjusted his long legs in the limited space. She stared at his strong profile a moment, noticing his gritted teeth, then started the car. He was as short-tempered as her brother when it came to allowing someone to help him.

"I'd better warn you that I've never let a woman drive me anywhere before."

"You don't have much choice now," Jaclyn teased. "Why don't you put the seat down a little, lay your head on the high back, and relax?"

"I am tired for some reason," Josh admitted with a wide yawn.

"Too little sleep?" She laughed softly.

"Too much Jazzy," he taunted, facing her with his mouth raised in a mischievous grin. "Just kidding, honey. My tiredness has nothing to do with you. I've had very little sleep since the accident."

"I'd have thought you would have been tired enough to sleep very soundly last night."

"I was much more interested in having your body close. You're so damned exciting to hold I couldn't relax. Instead, I spent the night wanting to make love to you while you slept like a newborn baby."

"Funny about that. I thought I wouldn't be able to rest much either and can't remember ever sleeping better."

"I know," Josh moaned in remembrance. "I was the one forced to endure your lush curves pressed close while you clung to me and murmured little purrs off and on all night."

"Purrs?"

"Closest description I could come up with. You're cuddly as a kitten too."

"Get some rest, Josh," Jaclyn urged, wanting to end the conversation before he noticed they weren't going to his employee's home.

"If you sleep, I can concentrate on my driving. I'll need to pay close attention to the streets, since it's so foggy."

"Are you frightened of the fog?" Josh inquired huskily. He placed his hand on her thigh, squeezing it sympathetically.

"No." Jaclyn felt warmth fill her heart at his concern. "I've driven in much thicker than this lots of times. Does it make you nervous to ride in a car so soon after your accident?"

"Not with a man behind the wheel." He laid his head back, relaxing with hands clasped on his lap.

"You beast," she scolded. "It was a male driver who caused your injury in the first place."

"How did you know that, Jazzy?" Josh demanded in a soft drawl, so casual it belied his interest. He waited, never moving from his indolent posture.

"You just told me you'd never ridden with a woman driver before." That was another close call. She'd have to remember to keep her wits about her at all times or he was sure to trip her up. Josh was intelligent and alertly picked up every mistake she uttered with irritating regularity.

She changed lanes, deciding to continue driving up Highway 101 to Long Beach before getting on the freeway to the airport. Turning on the radio to soft rock, she hoped the music would take his mind off Rick.

"What the hell are you up to, Jazzy?" Josh inquired in the same casual drawl.

No such luck, she moaned inwardly. He knew darned well they should have been at his nurse's house by now.

"What—er, what do you mean, Josh?" Jaclyn asked with all the innocence she could come up with considering his intimidating manner.

"We've been driving for at least twenty minutes now and Rick lives ten minutes at the most from my house."

"Well, there's been a change of plans," she told him boldly.

"Your idea, no doubt?"

"Actually, it was," Jaclyn admitted honestly.

"What is it?"

"Well, since you insisted I spend a month with you, I naturally presumed it would be just the two of us."

"So?" he questioned with a touch of anger.

"So," she snapped back, remembering the redhead's words. "I wasn't getting paid for a three-way swing and decided to get rid of Rick."

"You what?" Josh shot back, sitting up in his seat so fast she almost ran into the car beside her.

"Settle down," she flared with equal determination. "I was looking forward to a holiday with just you and me, so I told him to take a trip."

"And?"

"And he wouldn't." Jaclyn laughed. "So I suggested he stay home and take care of his cold. He sounded awful and I didn't want either of us to get sick and ruin our holiday."

"How thoughtful," Josh said sarcastically.

"It is," Jaclyn explained unperturbed. "Since I'm now in charge of nursing you twenty-four hours a day until this trip's over, and Rick warned me you're not an easy patient."

"And where did you get your nursing degree?"

"I don't have one, but taking care of one grouchy artist shouldn't be too hard, since you can't see to tell me what I'm doing wrong."

"You're too much," Josh said with a laugh, in sudden good humor.

"That's what you told me earlier," Jaclyn reminded him with a giggle.

"Ms. Jazzy . . . ?" Josh broke off.

"Jones." Jaclyn gave him a fictitious last name.

"As I was about to say, Ms. Jazzy Jones, I have a definite feeling my male nurse is easier to control than you will ever be."

He shook his head in disbelief over her actions. "That's why you wanted to know where my luggage was, isn't it?" Before she could answer, he muttered dryly, "No doubt it's now shanghaied to the back of your car."

"Both cases are right behind you."

"From now on, woman, there'll be no more lies and no more schemes. Promise?"

With complete confidence Jaclyn would do as he asked, Josh lay back, completely unconcerned that she hadn't answered his question. "Wake me when we arrive at the United Airlines terminal."

CHAPTER SEVEN

"You're not going to get away with this unscathed, Jazzy," Josh warned between tightly clenched lips. "You've manhandled me ever since we left my house."

"Manhandled?" Jaclyn gave an amused laugh. "I could hardly do that. I'm the wrong sex and you're much too big."

"You know damned well what I mean, woman," he grated, squeezing her fingers in a painful reminder how strong he was as she propelled him nonstop through the crowded airport.

"I could have managed to check in our suitcases with the correct luggage handler."

"How? You couldn't even see the man, much less our luggage?"

"You should have pointed him out and told me where the cases were instead of implying I'm an imbecile and you're my keeper."

"I do make a good nurse, don't I?" Jaclyn teased, chiding him for his bad temper.

"You make a better warden," he blazed back. His shoulders were stiff as he stormed ahead, not looking right or left.

"Slow down and quit acting so stupid, Josh, or you'll run into someone," Jaclyn continued, without losing a step. "Accept my help graciously. It won't make you less of a man to forget your male pride for a few weeks. I'll be glad to take care of everything I can until we get back from Canada."

"From the moment I got in your car things have been going wrong," Josh complained bitterly, refusing to concede she could be in charge of anything. "Now you're leading me around like a toddler and I hate it!"

"I'm certain you do," Jaclyn said with a laugh. "But you'll have to suffer the umbrage a little longer. I'm going to sit you down, check which gate we board from, then see that my car's taken care of."

"Aren't you afraid I'll run away?" he mouthed sarcastically.

"Not today," she announced with a bright smile, refusing to take notice of his caustic attitude. "Here we are. This should do just fine for the next thirty or so minutes."

"What is it? A child-care center?" Josh growled with continued ill-humor.

"No." She laughed softly. "It's an ice cream bar."

"Forget it, witch," he warned, gripping her arm and stopping without thought of anyone behind him. He bent down to exclaim in her ear. "I will not go in there! You can take me to a real bar. One that serves adult drinks to adult men."

"My, you are a grouch, aren't you?" Jaclyn teased. She looked him up and down, noticing his deep scowl and clenched fists. "I guess you would look more at home in the cocktail lounge. Your bitter face is certain to frighten both the little kids and their mothers."

Jaclyn took Josh's hand, leading him reluctantly along beside her. It was best to ignore him and concentrate on what she had to do before they left LA.

"I'll get you for this, Jazzy," he cautioned gruffly. "I mean it. Starting tonight you'll feel my wrath in unexpected ways."

"Sounds good to me," she gave a throaty giggle.

"Let's go this way. I spotted your type of place across the aisle."

"And what is my type of place?" Josh asked, matching her quick steps easily with his long stride.

"Dark, morbid, and filled with a motley-looking group of men."

"Good. Lead on." He tugged on her arm to hurry. He hated waiting around airports at the best of times. Unable to view his surroundings made each minute even more unbearable.

"Prepare to stop and sit down, Josh," she told him, seconds later. "We're about six steps from a padded stool at the end of the counter. Your companion to the right is in his mid-fifties, balding, unfashionably dressed, and holding a briefcase as bulging as his belly. He's drinking Budweiser beer and has a facial expression as morose as yours."

"All I want is a drink," Josh muttered. "You sound like you're setting me up with a blind date."

"It wouldn't work," Jaclyn shot back, unperturbed. "He looks straight to me."

"I'll take your word for it," he retorted grimly. "After all, who should know about a man's sexual preferences better than you?"

Jaclyn kicked Josh's shin. He was acting like a spoiled brat. A foul-minded one to boot.

She surveyed his seat partner through a veil of heavy lashes. He really was a lewd-looking man. It sure didn't take a hooker to know what he wanted when he looked at a woman.

"Bartender!" Josh called, raising his hand once he was seated. He deliberately ignored Jaclyn standing at his left side.

"Yes, sir. What'll it be?"

"Scotch on the rocks."

"Orange juice," Jaclyn corrected in her sweetest voice.

"A Scotch for the man and juice for the lady," the bartender replied in a pleasant voice. His eyes were filled with admiration as he scanned Jaclyn's lovely face and eye-catching hair fanning out over the collar of her coat.

"No, sir," Jaclyn pointed out firmly. "The orange juice is for my, er, patient."

She placed her hands on the young man's white sleeve and gave him a wide smile, completely disregarding Josh's sudden intake of breath.

"Jazzy!" Josh warned in a low hiss.

"This is my patient," she continued without hesitation. "I'm a nurse and his doctor specified no alcohol."

"The hell he did!" Josh contradicted in a clear voice. He turned from her to look toward the man behind the counter. "Make that a double now. Without ice."

"Don't listen to him, please," Jaclyn pleaded. "He's inclined to be cranky when his head hurts."

The bartender looked from one to the other, shrugged his shoulders, and walked away before Josh could protest. He fixed a drink and returned, setting the frosty glass down on a napkin.

"You're a lucky stiff despite your injury," he commented out of the side of his mouth to Josh. He leaned across the counter to confide further. "Where'd you find the lady? I've always been partial to tall, shapely bl—"

"Sorry, sir," Jaclyn stopped him before he could say blondes. "I insist you leave us alone or we'll take our business elsewhere. Conversation worsens my patient's headaches."

Whew! That was a close call, Jaclyn sighed to herself

as the bartender left. She was still shaking in her shoes over his candid remark.

"Why did you send him away before he finished what he was saying?" Josh questioned bitterly. "It was just starting to sound interesting."

The man next to them butted in in a booming voice. He hadn't missed a single word of the interchange and was eager to give his unasked opinion.

"The bartender's mad 'cause he got run off before you answered his questions. Nothing you haven't had to handle in the past, huh, good buddy?"

"What's his problem?" Josh invited in a conspiratorial whisper.

"The kid's got the hots for your nurse. Just tell him to go hire one of his own if he bothers you again."

Josh turned his head, giving the stranger an innocent smile. "I will . . . friend. That's how mine came to me. Right out of the phone book. She was hired for one hour the first night and did such a satisfactory job of healing my aching body, I rented her services for an entire month."

"She gives you twenty-four-hour care!" the man exclaimed enviously. He wiped his perspiring brow with a pink plaid handkerchief. "That must cost a fortune."

"It does," Josh replied matter-of-factly. "But you get what you pay for and she's worth every penny. My nurse knows every . . . *trick* . . . in the book." He turned to give Jaclyn an innocent smile. "Every single *trick*. Right, Jazzy?"

"You talk too much, sir," she snapped, giving his shin another sharp kick. He had a lot of gall to speak about her to a stranger as if she weren't there.

"I guess it's worth all that bread just to have a looker like her around," the florid-faced man probed without embarrassment.

"Unfortunately, I haven't seen her," Josh confessed.

"Is she really a good-looking broad?" he insisted with devilish humor as Jaclyn fumed beside him.

"The best-looking dame I've seen in days."

"Describe her to me." Josh egged him on, ignoring a sudden poke in his back.

"Well, she's . . ." the man started in.

"Will you be quiet?" Jaclyn interrupted, pushing her way between them. She gave the man such a frosty glare, she hoped he'd be speechless for days.

"If you don't leave us alone, we'll have to go. My patient can't stand the stress of trivial gossip."

She was debating what to do if the man ignored her request when he gave her a startled glance, checked his watch, and stood up.

"Take it easy, lady." He peered around Jaclyn's stiffened form to speak to Josh. "She's got a sharp tongue for such a young woman."

"Sharp but sweet," Josh explained with a knowing squeeze on her waist as he moved her aside. "A very sweet tongue in fact," he called out as the man sped away.

"You have an odd sense of humor, Josh," Jaclyn scolded, trying to pry his hands from her back where they were causing delicious tremors to run up and down her spine.

"Me?" Josh asked with such innocence she felt the urge to stomp his elegantly shod toes. "You're the one who ran off my only . . . *good buddy* . . . at the airport."

"That does it!" Jaclyn scolded, expelling her breath. "You be quiet too. Both of you were obnoxious and rude to talk about me as if I weren't here."

"You shouldn't have eavesdropped. No telling what kind of terrible situation it will get you into someday."

"Forget it, Josh. You're impossible to reason with." He was right about eavesdropping. She'd been escaping close calls since last night, caused by her listening to conversations unobserved.

Jaclyn looked around. At least with his seat companion out of the way she felt safer about leaving Josh alone. He was in such a trouble-causing mood it was no telling what he might have said or done.

"I'm going before you say something else outrageous," Jaclyn scolded severely.

"Good," Josh told her. "My ankles and my back need healing now as well as my eyes."

As she turned to leave he grabbed her hand. "Why did you order me orange juice, Ms. Nightingale? When I come to a bar, I don't sit down to drink fruit juice."

"It's better for you."

"I'm not paying you to improve my health, only to increase my sex life."

"Sit here and try to stay out of mischief, Josh. I have business to take care of before our flight leaves."

"Damn it, woman!" He spun around on the tall stool. He pulled her so close her breasts pressed against the front of his jacket and his nostrils were filled with the heady scent of her gardenia shampoo. With his hands clasped behind her back, he held her still in an unbreakable position, forcing her to listen to each commanding statement.

"What the hell do you think you're doing? Did you forget this is my trip? You're my guest. I make all the plans and you just follow them!"

"I know that," Jaclyn returned, unsuccessfully trying to hold her body tense.

She gave up, putting her arms on his shoulders and squirming closer. She found his surprising behavior rather enjoyable. He was really something when he was angry and it didn't frighten her one bit.

"Quit acting like a broody mother hen with one

chick," he continued, "and leave me to enjoy a man's drink in a man's sanctuary."

"Chauvinist!" she chided, pulling away when his grip slackened.

"You bet!"

"Apparently you haven't heard that women can't be excluded from a . . . man's sanctuary . . . anymore."

"I heard and it's a damned fool decision with a woman like you on the loose," he railed. "Now get going or we'll miss the plane. You're a positive menace."

Jaclyn fled the bar and headed straight to her car rental agency. It took several minutes to pay her bill and a few more to phone Lerisa to tell her she was postponing her return to Paris indefinitely. With a sigh of relief that all her business was settled she returned to the lounge.

As expected Josh was sitting by himself drinking a double Scotch without an apparent care in the world. Beside his hand, untouched, was the glass of orange juice she had ordered.

She slid silently onto the stool beside him, glowering at his profile as he raised his head and consumed the remainder of his drink in one swallow.

"What took you so long, Jazzy?" he asked, sitting the glass down with a thump.

"How did you know I was here?" she questioned in surprise. She hadn't said a word to the man.

"I recognized your footsteps as well as the sweet fragrance of your body. No other woman has your scent."

"You're crazy." Did she really smell so sweet and special to him he could tell from the multitude of other females around? How wonderful!

"Settle your bill, Josh, so we can go to the gate and wait for departure."

"It's paid."

"How did you manage that?"

"I handed the bartender my credit card and told him if he overcharged me, I'd return in a couple months and break both his arms."

"I don't believe you one bit."

"I did and I can."

"How do you know? He might be a bull of a man."

"He wasn't. I could tell where his voice came from that I'm six inches taller than he is and when he touched my hand his fingers were soft and smooth. Almost as nice as yours."

"Forget it. You're intoxicated. I knew you shouldn't drink this early. You haven't even had breakfast."

"Nor have you. That's why I bought you this." Josh handed her a huge box of expensive chocolates concealed on his lap. It was brightly wrapped in cellophane with red ribbon and an enormous bow.

"I'll eat some on the plane." Jaclyn gave him a tender smile, overcome by his thoughtfulness.

"We'll both eat some during the flight," Josh reminded. "I happen to have a craving for something sweet, and since I can't start in on you, I'll have to make do with some overpriced chocolates."

"How did you get this?" Overlooking his brazen comments was getting easier all the time.

"Simple. I bribed the man."

"With more threats of violence."

"No," Josh assured her politely. "I used a twenty-dollar bill instead."

Jaclyn took Josh's arm, smiling as she walked proudly beside him to the gate. He was really something. They arrived just in time to board the first-class section.

Sitting in the luxurious comfort of wide seats with lots of leg room, Jaclyn looked around. She hadn't expected this kind of treatment. A flight attendant started waiting on them and serving drinks the moment they sat down.

She relaxed, laying her head back with eyes closed. From now on everything would be perfect. Her brother wouldn't pop in, nor would she see a single soul she knew. One full month with no other company but the man she loved. Bruce didn't realize that in giving Josh a present he gave his sister the best gift of her life too.

An hour later Jaclyn looked at Josh and smiled. They had talked nonstop on varied subjects. Not one mention had been made about her life-style and she felt totally at ease.

Delving into Josh's complex personality was a joy. Though she had a diary crammed with newspaper clippings, and every detail possible gleaned about his life, she knew very few intimate details beyond her startling physical reaction to him. In the next few weeks she intended to learn everything about the man. Right now she had never been happier.

Piercing a tender asparagus tip with her fork, Jaclyn prepared to put the last bite of hors d'oeuvres in her mouth. The meal was delicious, from the cold pink salmon salad to the succulent filet of beef wellington.

"What's your pimp's name?" Josh asked out of the blue, taking her completely off guard.

"Er, B-Bugsy," Jaclyn blurted out, nearly choking on her food. Darn the man! His question took her by surprise and she picked the most stupid name possible. Every cop show on TV used a Bugsy as the villian.

"Is he a good lover?"

"What?" Josh caught her unawares again. She placed the fork down and bowed her head. His erratic probing into her supposed life-style was enough to give her a heart attack.

"I hear pimps always use their stable's services as they wish. In fact, the preferred female is supposed to get the most attention. Am I right?"

"Oh, yes, they, er, we do, er, she does," she stammered foolishly, refusing to look up. She'd have to quit hesitating each time she lied. It made everything she said sound more unbelievable than it was.

"Are you the favorite?" Josh prodded.

"Heavens, no." Jaclyn laughed nervously, playing with the stem of her wineglass. "He likes blondes, and as I said, my hair's a vivid red."

"The man must be crazy. I can't imagine any woman being favored over you."

"Thanks for the compliment, but it's true." She took a sip of wine, wishing it were a double shot of scotch. She'd never been interested in strong alcohol, but Josh apparently thought it a good pacifier, which she needed desperately.

"Let's finish our dinner and then talk," she urged hopefully. "I'm starving."

"I guess we'd better, since you went to so much work buttering my roll, cutting my beef, and pointing out just where everything was on my plate."

"If I hadn't, the flight attendant would have." Jaclyn stared at Josh, trying to control her sudden temper. Her mood had changed as fast as his did.

"Do you really think so?" Josh questioned, cocking one arrogant eyebrow upward in a sudden display of interest.

"Yes," Jaclyn fumed jealously. "She hasn't taken her eyes off you since we sat down. I swear, if she hovers any closer to you than usual when she removes our trays, I'm going to kick her shin too."

"Ms. Jazzy Jones," Josh exclaimed, laughing at her

peevish voice. "If I had the inclination and could afford to fall in love with a hooker, I might pick you."

"I'm not interested," Jaclyn lied. She finished her wine and cast him a dubious glance. "Besides, you don't even know what I look like."

"Not now, but I will." His promise sounded the same as a threat. "I wouldn't think of making a lifetime commitment until I saw the merchandise. Which should be in about three months, if my doctor's diagnosis is right."

"You're talking crazy. I'll be long gone before you see me," Jaclyn reminded boldly.

"Did you already forget the solemn promise you made?" Josh catechized. "When my eyes are healed? I'm going to get a free . . ."

"No, I haven't," Jaclyn cut him off. "But we were talking about the flight attendant's excessive interest in your welfare, not my generous nature. I only brought it up because I thought her constant interrupting us to ask about your comfort in a sickly sweet, feverish drawl might annoy you."

"Sickly sweet, feverish drawl!" Josh repeated, trying hard not to laugh out loud.

"Yes," Jaclyn snapped. "I can hear her panting from here."

"I can't," Josh told her, cocking his head to listen. "Funny too, since my hearing is excellent."

"Forget it. You'll get a headache if you keep straining your neck checking to see if she's coming this way to fondle your shoulder again. Does she irritate you or not?"

It certainly put a damper on her trip every time the sophisticated attendant returned to fawn over the man she loved. Especially when her own comfort was being ignored in the process.

"The only thing that irritates me," Josh whispered

in a voice so sensual Jaclyn quivered in response, "is that it's going to be at least four or five hours more before I can make love to you. Are you ready?"

"Ready for my dessert," she sassed, feeling a hundred percent better knowing he wasn't interested in anyone else.

"Hmm, it looks delicious and sinfully rich." She picked up her fork. "Frozen chocolate mousse with a bitter chocolate leaf and plump red maraschino cherry on top."

"All we need is more chocolate," Josh complained. "I ate enough candy to last me a week."

"If you don't want it, give it to me." Before Josh could agree, Jaclyn reached over to remove his dessert. His hand came down and gripped her wrist in a steel-hard hold. "I didn't say I wasn't going to eat it."

She could feel a tremor run the length of her spine at the touch of his calloused fingertips. Each time it happened a physical awareness passed between them that was impossible to curb.

"You told me you were sick of chocolate, which is the same thing."

"Not to me it isn't. That just meant that cherry pie à la mode would taste better."

"You really are crazy." She tugged her hand free. "Eat the thing, then. I'll ask for another."

"She won't give it to you," Josh confided smugly. "It's me she likes, remember?"

"Go to sleep, Josh. We have forty-five minutes before landing and you're impossible to talk with."

"Er, miss," Josh motioned for the attendant, aware she would be watching. He waited until she arrived then gave her a wide smile. "Would you bring my nurse another dessert. She's off her diet today." He murmured out of the side of his mouth. "I think she suffers from bulimia. Imagine two desserts at one time. Disgraceful, don't you think?"

The tiny raven-haired beauty bent over Josh's shoulder to answer softly, "The poor thing must be sick even to consider eating that much sugar. Being a nurse she should know it's bad for her."

"Can I have another dessert or not?" Jaclyn butted in. It made her feel better to know the woman's fluttering eyelashes were completely wasted on Josh. That was one definite advantage about being in love with a man who couldn't see. His eyes would never linger appreciatively on another female.

"Certainly, miss. Mr. Kingman can have anything he wants." She gave Josh a familiar pat, looked at Jaclyn with sympathy, and rushed to the service area.

"Yes, Mr. Kingman, you can have anything you want," Jaclyn mimicked irritably in a high-pitched squeal. "When it comes, eat it yourself. I just lost my appetite."

Smacking his lips over the last of his piece of mousse, Josh agreed readily. "Great. This stuff's better than I thought."

"Well, you aren't!" Jaclyn grumbled. She couldn't believe her ill-humor. Jealousy must change one's personality completely. She'd always considered herself easygoing and soft-spoken and tried never to say a bad word about anyone. Today she was positively bitchy!

"I aren't what?" Josh asked, using terrible grammar to repeat her statement.

"You aren't any better behaved than I thought you would be. Rick said you were a real . . ."

"Pain." Josh laughed, answering for her. He wasn't the least concerned over what his nurse thought of him.

"What a month this is going to be," Jaclyn suddenly giggled, seeing humor in their situation. A scheming, supposed hooker and an injured man intent on breaking records as a world-class lover. It should be a blast!

"It will be fantastic, honey," Josh assured her. "We'll argue all day and make love all night."

"But that's silly," Jaclyn chided. "What on earth will we find to argue about all the time?"

"How many times we're going to make love at night."

"Be quiet, Josh," Jaclyn scolded. "I want to read a magazine."

Instead she studied his features. Despite the bandage over his eyes, his presence was so commanding he constantly drew the eye of women, young and old. Was there something about dark, brooding men that appealed to a female's primitive instincts?

Jaclyn looked away, thought a moment, then cast Josh another sidelong glance. The man's appeal was obvious. He radiated an aloof sensuality that was impossible to ignore.

"How big a slice of the body works does Bugsy get?"

"What are you talking about now?" Jaclyn gulped. She couldn't even watch him in silence without his mind reverting to her occupation.

"You know damned well what I mean," Josh pointed out gruffly. He finished her piece of mousse and laid his head back on the high seat. "How much of your hustling money do you give your pimp?"

Jaclyn thought fast. Josh had said earlier that pimps rarely gave their girls fifty percent so she compromised.

"Forty percent."

"Not bad," he mused. "When did you get a pimp? Before or after Grandma got sick?"

"After," Jaclyn lied. She was beginning to enjoy the game of putting on a man as sophisticated as Josh.

"Bugsy said I was stupid to give it away when he could sell it for tons more bread than I'd ever make slinging hash."

"Bugsy must be very astute." Josh coughed, barely able to control the urge to laugh out loud.

"He is. Being a professional escort pays better, is more fun, and a heck of a lot less work."

"You seem to have a good business head, Jazzy."

"I do, which brings up a big point. How do I know your check won't bounce or you won't put a stop payment on it?"

"You'll have to trust me."

"I guess if it does I could always rip off a few statues. What I noticed looked kind of cute."

"Cute!" Josh exclaimed. "You think my art is cute?"

"Some of it, anyway."

"That's a hell of a description for art that some people revere."

"I especially like the kid in the bathroom." That should really dent his ego. It was an exquisite work and worth a fortune.

"Keep your hands off her," Josh hissed. "She's mine."

Jaclyn shrugged her shoulders, answering in a bored voice, "Fine with me. One looks much like the other." Each word she uttered was sacrilege to an artist.

"You have a lot to learn about art, Jazzy," Josh informed her between clenched teeth.

"No problem," she assured him. "My only interest in collecting it anyway is that I hear the good stuff appreciates in value fast."

"And you think my . . . stuff . . . will be worth more in the near future?" Josh persisted in an even voice.

"It looked okay to me." She placed her fingers on his thigh, smiling mischievously. "Are you any good?"

"Fair," Josh admitted without conceit. "Some critics think I'm great. A few connoisseurs even collect me."

"Better change your lock when you get back, then," Jaclyn advised tongue-in-cheek.

"I just did. Why?"

"If my check isn't good, I might be tempted to clean out your gallery."

She trailed her fingers up and down the fine cloth of his slacks. The feel of his thigh muscles tightening nearly took her mind off her taunting questions.

"I'll take my chances," Josh replied, placing his palm over her fingers. Instead of removing them he held them in place as if her touch was everything he wanted.

"Just remember I warned you," she continued, trembling as the warmth of his body flowed into her hand. "I may take everything."

She withdrew her hand. It was too dangerous to leave there when she ached to touch him more intimately.

"Except for the kid on the pedestal upstairs," she assured, suddenly filled with remorse over her horrendous lies. "I'll leave her, since she seems special to you in some way."

"Was Bugsy your first lover?" Josh changed the subject, deciding it was time to put Jaclyn on the defensive.

"I don't want to talk about my life-style," Jaclyn shot back, glaring at his relaxed posture.

"Be realistic." Josh ignored her rebuff. "That would be impossible for any man to do." He rested his head indolently on the seat back, reclining as if he didn't have a care in the world. "Now answer me, Jazzy," he persisted. "Was Bugsy your first or not?"

"No. I've been wild about sex since I was sixteen."

"Sixteen?" Josh whispered, drawing his brows together in deep thought. "Very interesting. I knew a girl who at the age of sixteen turned me on like no other older female ever had."

"You did?" Jaclyn asked breathlessly.

"Yes." His lips rose in a contemplative smile. "What a sweet young innocent she was, but so sensual I had fantasies about making love to her for years."

"What happened?"

"Nothing yet," Josh answered matter-of-factly. "I keep her in my dreams, where all special fantasies should remain."

"Sounds like a waste to me," Jaclyn scoffed. "It's better to join the real world and make your fantasies come true like I do."

"Do you have romantic fantasies, Jazzy?"

"Not anymore." She gave Josh a knowing smile at the thought that he had fulfilled all of them last night.

"Well, then." Josh turned and drew her into his arms. "Will you try to make my dreams come true during our trip?"

"You expect me to happily stand in for some teenager who raised your pulse beat years ago?" Jaclyn asked peevishly. "Forget it."

"No, I don't want you to act as a stand in," Josh assured her, bending forward so their lips were almost touching. "I want you to replace her with your own brand of magic. With your experience it should be easy to blot her out of my mind while we're together."

"And when this trip's over?"

"After we part, I'm afraid I'll continue dreaming about my first love."

"The heck you will," Jaclyn promised with a spurt

of temper. "I'll give you so much tender loving care you won't think of making love to another woman without my image coming between you."

"And that, my fiery-tempered beauty, is exactly what I told you earlier I intended to do to you."

Jaclyn let the seat back, sighing with pleasure at the feel of Josh's hands gently cupping her face in both palms. Her eyes fluttered open to observe the Fasten Seat Belt sign flash overhead.

"We have to buckle up, Josh," she whispered against his mouth. Darn it! Of all the times to get air turbulence. Just when he was prepared to kiss her.

"The warning signs are still flashing, Josh," she murmured when he continued to ignore her and started placing gentle kisses on her brow, across her cheekbones, and the tip of her nose.

"Do you think Ms. United Airlines will do it for me?" he teased, taking possession of her mouth in a fierce kiss that left her clinging to his shoulders and trying desperately to act composed.

"If she dares place her hands anywhere near your lap to fasten your seat belt, I'll deck her."

"Hmm," Josh moaned, nipping her on the side of the neck. "Don't you share?"

"Not someone paying me what you are!"

"Mercenary witch."

Jaclyn pushed him away, taking a deep breath. "Fasten up, Josh. I'm going to finish the article I started earlier."

"Good. I'll sit here quiet as a mouse and think of how little time I have left before we get to it."

"Do you always talk so bluntly?" Jaclyn scolded.

"What did you want me to say?" Josh flipped back. "That I'll rest my weary head on the seat while impatiently contemplating the endless passing of time until

I can indulge in a romantic interlude with you next to my pounding heart?"

"That's a little better."

"That's stupid." He took her hand, turned it over, and ran his index finger in slow circles around her soft palm.

"Why?" Jaclyn quizzed breathlessly. His fingers were sending an erotic message impossible to ignore.

"Because you know what I want and I'm learning fast what you enjoy too so why should I ever mince words? Besides"—he smiled tenderly—"I think you want to make love as much as I do. I can hear your heart beating from here."

"You cannot!" Jaclyn denied hotly. Surely no human being's ears were that keen. "Won't you at least behave until we get to the hotel."

"Fair enough," Josh agreed with surprising cheerfulness. He released her fingers, crossed his hands over his lap, and pretended to sleep until the flight was over.

CHAPTER EIGHT

"Have you stayed at a Four Seasons before, Jazzy?" Josh asked as the hired limousine pulled into the curved driveway.

"Not the Olympic."

She looked out the window at her surroundings. She was still awed that a chauffeur had awaited them at the Seattle-Tacoma Airport. He had taken care of their luggage, assisted them into the luxurious rear seat of a gleaming Cadillac, and driven the twenty-mile trip in record time.

Josh reached over, took her untouched glass of champagne, and carefully placed it in the tray of the tiny bar directly in front of him.

"You didn't drink any, did you?"

"No," she admitted in a throaty whisper. "I was too busy looking at the TV set and the scenery. I can't say I expected this kind of holiday."

"Don't you like the good life, Jazzy?" Josh asked curiously.

"Very much," she agreed truthfully. "Though it's a stark contrast with other places I've lived. A sad comparison in many ways."

"Where was that?" Josh asked in a quiet voice, keenly interested in what she would say. "Tell me, Jazzy," he prompted when she didn't reply.

"Here and there," she answered noncommittally.

She had forgotten for a moment he didn't know she'd spent years working in a remote, less developed country. It was a period of her life she would always remember with a mixture of pain and pleasure.

Jaclyn breathed a sigh of relief when her door was opened before Josh had time to demand she be more specific. Taking the young driver's hand, she stepped gracefully from the car and raised her face for a moment.

The weather was overcast with huge dark clouds threatening rain at any moment. She hugged her coat tightly around her waist, pleased for its warmth until Josh exited and they went inside. When he stood beside her, she lifted her eyes to stare at the sky.

"I wish you could see, Josh," she whispered softly. "It's so beautiful. A perfect late afternoon."

"I can smell rain in the air." His nostrils flared as he inhaled the pungent aroma. "Which isn't the least surprising considering the time of year and where we are."

"I guess not," Jaclyn agreed, reaching for his hand. She gave his fingers an affectionate squeeze. It was heaven to be able to touch him any time she wished.

"Do you like rain, Jazzy?"

"I love this kind of weather."

It was going to be a wonderful night to be cloistered inside with Josh. Stormy with a definite chance of precipitation. After years of study and hard work, she deserved this vacation. Nothing could be more enjoyable than sharing it with this man at her side.

"Are you feeling romantic, honey?" Josh quizzed in a deep whisper intended only for her ears.

"Very much so," she admitted honestly. "I've always been emotionally moved by inclement weather."

"I'll see what I can do to make this a special evening for you," Josh promised. He took her hand and raised it to his lips, pressing a gentle kiss on her palm. "How's that for a start?"

"Beautiful." Jaclyn placed her head against his shoulder, partially closing her eyes to contemplate. She thought back to how considerately Josh had always treated her as his best friend's sister, never dreaming the difference it made to receive such courtesies now that he was her lover.

"Let's go to our suite, Jazzy," Josh insisted huskily. "With complete privacy and a Do Not Disturb sign outside the door, I intend to see you have an evening you'll never forget."

"I'll always remember everything that's happened between us since the moment we met," she vowed. He'd never know how many years' worth of memories that was.

Moving on, Jaclyn automatically told Josh when to step up as they walked inside arm in arm. It seemed perfectly natural to assist him when he needed her vision to get around without mishap.

"Have you been here before?" Jaclyn asked when they entered the huge, multileveled foyer with restaurants, lounges, and hallways leading in several directions.

"Yes," Josh admitted, waiting patiently as she stopped to look over the hotel.

"Then I don't need to describe how elegant everything is."

"No. Service and luxury are a guarantee."

They hadn't moved over three steps forward when Jaclyn stopped to exclaim without thinking, "Oh, Josh, you must see this. There's a complete Seward Johnson sculpture exhibition on display. Each work appears so lifelike I had to look twice before I recognized they weren't actually real people but bronze figures."

She continued speaking in an excited voice, totally caught up in the thrill of seeing the Princeton, New Jersey, artist's work she'd previously admired only from photos.

"Come quick!" Jaclyn stepped forward, tugging on Josh's hand to hurry. "Mr. Johnson was a painter until 1968 when he turned sculptor." She looked sideways over her shoulder, laughing. "What a faux pas. Who should know better than you, of course?"

She paused, turning to give the room a cursory glance before walking ahead. "Oh, it's marvelous, Josh! There's a man painting the hotel wall, complete with a real canvas drop cloth and paint buckets, one sitting on a hotel bench reading a newspaper, another . . ."

Josh's voice brought her to a quick stop in front of the first presentation. "And how, my neophyte connoisseur of fine art, did you know it was Seward Johnson's works on display?"

Jaclyn's eagerness to share the appreciation of another sculptor's fine talent with Josh left the second he questioned her recognition of the man's distinctive style. She swallowed nervously, wishing she could vanish into the floor until she had a plausible reason to give the silent man at her side.

"Because"—she gulped—"his name is prominently displayed by each exhibit." Deciding to bluff with a question of her own, she asked, "How else would I know one man's work from another?"

"How else?" Josh repeated dryly.

"No way, that's for sure," she tried to assure him. Her eyes grew smokier at the about-face as she suddenly pretended to be a novice judge of art. "Gosh, Josh, the bronze alone in his big statues makes them worth more than yours. Why don't you do bigger . . . stuff?"

"Maybe I should"—he grimaced at the insult—"since you seem to think the larger a piece of work is, the more valuable it is."

"That would be super great," Jaclyn cooed insipidly, sounding like an unintelligent gold digger. She hated the pretense of ignorance in her field of study, though she admitted it pleased her mischievous side to put Josh on.

"You like large stuff, do you?"

"I always have," Jaclyn admitted, staring upward at his grim face. She leaned contentedly into the comfort of his towering frame.

"You sound like a keen critic already," Josh told her in a flat voice.

"I've always been a fast learner," she bragged with an impish twinkle in her storm-colored eyes.

"I don't doubt it for a moment," he admitted wryly.

"If you did something the size of . . . what's that famous Italian artist?"

"Michelangelo."

"Yes, his . . ." She hesitated as if trying to come up with his statue's proper name.

"David," Josh suggested sardonically.

"That's it," Jaclyn thanked him, barely able to keep from laughing out loud. "If you did another David-type thing but used bronze instead of marble it should really be worth a lot of bread."

"Utterly priceless," Josh commented in a monotone voice, giving her fingers a punishing squeeze.

He stood beside her, marking time for what seemed like endless moments while she remained completely quiet.

"What are you doing now, Jazzy?" Josh hissed through straight teeth as the uncomfortable silence continued and she didn't move a muscle.

She could feel the steel in his grip and knew he was

becoming more irritated by the second. In her most innocent voice she answered, "Nothing."

"Why?" He expelled his breath trying hard to control his rising impatience. "We still have to check in."

"I know," she told him with a saucy smile. "I'm waiting for you to handle everything. I definitely remember being told in LA that"—her voice rose to quote him verbatim—"it's your trip. I'm your guest. You make all the plans and I just follow them. Did you forget your loud threats already?"

"Not a one, you aggravating little devil," Josh scolded, taking her in his arms.

"Nor had I," she taunted mischievously.

He gave her an exasperated smile before covering her mouth in a quick, hard kiss.

"I can just picture your defiant little face staring up at me with all the nerve in the world."

Not clearly, I hope, Jaclyn reflected mutely. He'd get the shock of his life if he could.

She watched Josh with love shimmering in her eyes, silently observing his strong, intelligent face. She wasn't the least worried about his look of scorn for her impertinence. It was deserved for not resisting the urge to jibe back when the opportunity arose.

In a deep voice filled with feigned remorse, he begged, "Please, Ms. Jones, will you take me to the registration desk and help me sign us in?"

"Yes, sir!" Jaclyn agreed jauntily, taking his arm and turning him toward the main desk. "If you'll follow me, it's right this way."

She walked to the counter and waited by Josh's side, interested in seeing how he handled the situation without sight. "I'm impressed by your ability to manage," she whispered when the clerk walked away to answer the phone. "Also by the deference shown you by this man and the chauffeur."

"If you'd give me the same respect for my wishes, it would make for a better vacation," Josh lowered his head to whisper into her ear.

"I'm not getting paid to be reverent," Jaclyn teased softly. "Only to improve your sex life, remember?"

"Knock it off, Jazzy," he scolded in a husky murmur. "Just sign the slip before the clerk returns and you really get in trouble with your sassy mouth." He shoved the forms along the polished counter until they were in front of her.

"Do I sign my name or yours?" she asked, picking up the pen.

"Either one. It's just a formality, since I reserved ahead of time and have an open account on my credit card."

Jaclyn took the pen, signed "J. Kingman" on the papers, followed by her own initials alongside, then gave them back to Josh.

"Here he comes," she warned, nudging his side.

"I know. I can hear him," Josh reminded, beneath his breath.

Pocketing the room key, he turned to her for assistance. "All you have to do now is hold my hand and follow the bellhop to our suite. Our luggage will already be in the room."

Jaclyn was silent on the elevator ride. She had never gone to a hotel room with a man before with the intent of spending the night. A soft, self-conscious flush touched her cheeks when she noticed a covert glance from the hotel employee.

It was unnerving to realize at this late date she was old-fashioned enough to feel a touch of guilt that she and Josh weren't married. It was rather like locking the barn door after the horse had been stolen, she thought sadly, wishing she was his wife instead of a temporary mistress supposedly hired to bring feminine warmth to his lonely bed. She shrugged aside the momentary twinge of remorse. There would never be a man in her life other than Josh. Her fidelity was guaranteed, married or not.

The elegance of the room occupied her mind at once. Each service was courteously pointed out and everything for their comfort explained before the young man accepted Josh's generous tip and left.

"I've never seen rooms any nicer than these," she said enthusiastically. "They're extremely plush."

"I know," Josh agreed, trying to get his bearings as he stood in the unfamiliar living area. "Surely you didn't think I'd bring you to a hovel?"

"No." She watched him shrug out of his sports jacket and walked over to take it from him. "But I didn't expect a fancy three-room suite with a phone in every room, including the bathrooms, either. There're almost as many color televisions too, and all with remote control."

"You approve, then?" Josh asked, cautiously moving forward as he tried to recall the exact number of feet it was to the lounge chair.

"Very much. It's two steps straight ahead," she told him, automatically second-guessing his needs. "You would love the color scheme, since you're artistic and they blend so well. Vivid sapphire and robin's-egg-blue, dusky rose, and creamy ivory for the walls, drapes, and rugs, plus dark polished mahogany furniture."

"How does the bed look?" Josh asked candidly. "I'm not concerned about the rest."

"It's as big as the one you have in Laguna Beach."

"Great. I hate to run out of mattress when I'm making love."

"Hush. You're beginning to sound like you have a one-track mind," she scolded.

"I do when I'm with someone that costs me what you do by the hour," he shot back impersonally.

"Don't worry about overpaying me," Jaclyn returned with equal insouciance.

The beast! If he thought his remarks would put her off, he was very much mistaken. She glared at his face, annoyed her most provocative glance was wasted. "I'll see you get your money's worth every time we make love."

"You're damned right you will," Josh returned, with a wicked smile that emphasized his sensual lips. "With the first payoff starting within an hour or two at the most."

"What about my romantic evening?" Jaclyn reminded pertly.

"That's the major part of it," he answered with arrogant boldness.

"Shush, Josh. You need your rest and I'm going to take a bath."

"I'm not surprised." His mouth rose in a humorous grin. "I presumed you'd want to shower as soon as we checked in."

"What should I wear tonight?" Jaclyn questioned over her shoulder as she entered the hallway toward the bathroom.

"Your birthday suit will do fine."

"Be serious, Josh!" she scolded sharply. "Are we going out, or what?"

"Do you want to eat dinner in the Georgian Room?"

"Do you?"

"Frankly, no," he admitted, kicking off his shoes and placing them out of the way beside his chair. "I hate eating out when I can't even see the damned food. It's the only time I really feel self-conscious about my lack of sight."

"Could we order dinner from room service?" Jazzy asked agreeably. "I would prefer that tonight. We could leave the lights low . . ."

"Turn them off if you want," he teased. "I won't even notice."

"Oh, Josh," Jaclyn apologized. "I'm so sorry. I keep forgetting you can't see."

"I prefer it that way. You'll act more natural with me if you do."

"Anyway," she continued happily, "we could pull the drapes and sheer panels aside and look at the city lights while we dine in complete privacy."

"That sounds perfect to me," he admitted, relaxing with his head leaning on the back of the chair. "Only you'll have to describe everything that looks interesting enough for you to want me to visualize it."

"I'd love to do that. You rest while I unpack and bathe, then I'll get your evening medication and read you what's on the menu."

"I'll drink to that,"Josh told her bluntly. "Speaking of drinks. When you get through, order our bar stocked first thing."

Jaclyn ignored him, too busy studying his clothes to pay attention to his remarks. It was amazing what you could learn about a person by their attire. Everything in his suitcases was of the finest quality and obviously expensive. His shirts and slacks were mostly casual, all fashionable, and expertly color coordinated. He obviously had a keen eye for dressing well as much as he did for sculpturing.

She held up a pair of navy briefs. Her eyes were bright with affection as she imagined how sexy he looked in them. Even more sexy out of them, she thought with an impish smile.

"Did you hear me, Jazzy?" Josh called in. "I said I want you to order our bar stocked after your bath."

"Okay," she murmured, placing his undershorts neatly in the bureau drawer. She turned to her case, deciding to just lay out the things she would wear that night and the next day instead of unpacking as she'd done for Josh.

"No orange juice either!"

"Not for you but I might want some," she reminded him, walking into the bathroom.

"You can have it with your breakfast. Tonight I'm going to ply you with vintage champagne, and after you're replete with a gourmet meal, I'll have my way with you."

"A Jazam no doubt?" she called out over the sound of the water filling the deep tub.

"You're finally learning," he teased in a husky drawl.

Jaclyn ignored him and stepped into deep suds nearly foaming over the edge of the high tub from the bubble bath supplied by the hotel. It felt heavenly to shed her clothes and relax. She intended to spend a full hour with her eyes closed and her body submerged to the shoulders.

Minutes later her lethargy was broken by Josh's voice directly over her.

"Do I get in or do you get out?" he asked in a serious voice.

Jaclyn sat up with a start, staring at his towering figure braced beside the tub. "Do you want to smell like a flower garden tonight?"

"Lord, no," he exclaimed indignantly. "One flowery body in our bed is enough."

"What are you doing in here so soon? I'm not nearly ready to get out."

"Too bad, because your time is up. I intend to take my shower before dinner and I'm getting hungry."

"I noticed a bathroom off the other bedroom," she prompted. "Go take your shower there."

"I will not," Josh explained matter-of-factly. "There's also a bed in the room. Neither will be used unless we use them together."

"Okay, then," Jaclyn protested, climbing out under protest. "I'll leave my warm sanctuary and get dressed."

She stood beside him, dripping water on the rug and glaring at his unconcerned expression. "Don't steam up the bathroom so much I can't see in the mirror to put fresh lipstick on."

"How would I know whether you can see in the mirror or not?"

"Sorry about that," she apologized, not the least uncomfortable standing naked in his presence when he couldn't see. "I guess it would be impossible to tell unless you reached a hand out and felt it for moisture."

"Turn the fan on or leave the door open and there won't be a problem."

"Excellent idea," she agreed, turning to let her bath water out. She reached around him to grab a towel. It was one of the biggest, thickest, softest towels she had ever used. Exactly the same quality as Josh had in his home.

Josh removed the bath sheet from her hand and placed it around her shoulders and back. He gently patted off the drops of water clinging to her smooth skin, taking his time until she was completely dry.

Jaclyn frowned in annoyance at the brevity of his touch. It was disgustingly impersonal, not remaining long enough on any one area to satisfy her sudden desire for his caresses. When he smoothed the soft nap over her breasts and buttocks, then between her thighs, she could hardly keep from begging him to take her right there.

Finished, Josh wrapped the beige terry cloth completely around her before hugging her close. Inhaling her clean scent, he gave a long broken sigh. "I should be congratulated, sweetheart," he pointed out in a deep frustrated moan. "I didn't think I had the willpower to dry your sensuous body without laying you on the soft carpet and making love to you right here in the bathroom."

"Congratulations," Jaclyn muttered peevishly, giving him a stormy-eyed look. "Next time forget about being so saintly self-willed, as I might not have stopped you if you had." At least that was the truth. She was more than ready to experience his exciting lovemaking from its sweet beginning to the wondrous ripples of pleasure during the turbulent climax.

"I'm aware of that," he told her, sweeping her tumbled hair from her brow and replacing it with a tender kiss. Confident in his power to seduce her when he wished, he promised, "Tonight I don't want to rush you. I intend to make our first coming together in Seattle very special."

"Hmm," Jaclyn murmured, nuzzling his chest. So far each one had seemed special to her no matter when or how he had made love. She clung to him, aching to be rushed and definitely displeased by his constraint. After all, she had years of celibacy to overcome in only a few weeks.

"You're a fastidious lady, aren't you, Jazzy?" Josh asked, interrupting her hazy thoughts about their making love. "Does this need for cleanliness have anything to do with your chosen career?"

"Not in the least," she explained calmly, pulling from his arms. "I'm a happy hooker, remember? If you think baths are a Freudian desire to purge my soul of its earthly sins by excessive cleanliness, you're wrong."

She walked to the doorway and faced him. "Surely my actions have demonstrated quite capably how much I enjoy your lovemaking?"

"Yes, Jazzy." He turned, unbuttoning his shirt as he prepared to shower. "You've shown me quite explicitly that you're receptive to everything I've done to you so far. Will that same pleasure be increased by what I intend to ask of you tonight?"

"You'll just have to wait and see," she taunted, reaching for her makeup kit. "Rick told me you need lots of rest, so it's probably best if we don't make love at all." That should raise his temper in a hurry!

"The hell with Rick," Josh scowled, reaching out blindly to hang his shirt on a door hook. "There's not a damned person in the world who could convince me I can't get it on with you whenever I want."

"You really are a terrible patient, aren't you?"

"It's my eyes that don't function, not my . . ."

"That's enough!" Jaclyn scolded, laughing as she walked back to take the shirt from his hands. His outburst was both amusing to watch and hear.

She looked at the awesome appeal of his bare, hair-covered chest. He was lean and fit and so handsomely masculine, she gloried in the ability to stare unobserved.

Her fingers itched to commit his beauty to canvas. She momentarily closed her eyes trying to imagine the most suitable pose in her sudden urge to paint him, making a serious mental commitment to do so the moment she returned to France.

"What should I do with your laundry? Do you want me to wash it each night or leave it until you have a washerful, then take it to the laundromat?" Either way was fine with her, as she enjoyed taking care of his needs.

"Neither," he reproached her. "Put any articles of yours as well as mine that need cleaning or laundering in the hotel bag. They'll be returned in hours, here as well as in Victoria."

Jaclyn did as he asked, unashamedly staring at his lithe hips and strong legs as he stripped down to his underwear.

With complete ease he removed his briefs and dropped them on the rug. Adjusting the temperature of the water, he turned to look over his shoulder.

"Do you want to scrub my back?"

"Not tonight," she lied, drinking in the beauty of his naked body. "Tomorrow morning I'll scrub more than that if you behave."

"I'll act like an angel from now on," Josh teased, stepping inside and pulling the shower curtain shut. "I might even be coerced into returning the favor too."

"We'll see," Jaclyn told him, making her voice sound casual, though the image projected fired her blood with wanton ideas.

With her view completely blocked, she turned around. There wasn't an incentive to linger anyway if she couldn't look at Josh. While he was occupied, she intended to lavishly powder her body, put on her sexiest underwear, then apply makeup fit for the most elegant private dinner.

Undecided what to wear, she finally picked out a long flowing silk robe. It was almost new, low-necked, zipped up the front, and had wide raglan sleeves. The deep violet shade brought out shining highlights in her eyes which unfortunately he couldn't even see.

With her hair brushed loose around her shoulders and her most sensitive pulse points lightly sprayed with France's most expensive perfume, she felt prepared for Josh's promised romantic evening. Uncertain how best to kill time, she walked around the living room, picked up a huge book on local places of interest, then laid it down unread, to pace again. She was looking out the window with her back turned when he appeared.

"Have you ordered liquor sent up yet?" Josh asked, striding into the room wrapped in a heavy terry robe provided for hotel guests.

"No." She faced him, walked to the coffee table, and picked up the room service brochure all in one graceful motion. "What do you want?"

"Dom Perignon."

Jaclyn's eyes ran down the wine list, stopping at the bottom of sparkling wines. "Do you realize it costs ninety-five dollars a bottle plus an additional sixteen percent gratuity for room service?"

"Yes." Josh's expression was totally unconcerned.

"Okay," Jaclyn shrugged. "It's your money."

"You're learning."

"Could we order some juice sent up as well?"

"Why not?" He smiled indulgently.

As they waited for room service, Jaclyn looked at Josh, then down at her hands before blurting out: "I have to confess something to you right now that may make you decide I'm not as much fun as you thought."

"What serious problem do I need to know that might curtail my night's pleasure?" He cocked an eyebrow, curious to hear her disclosure.

"I don't like liquor."

"Is that all you had to tell me?" Josh questioned softly, amused by her statement. He walked forward, cupping her shoulders. "I was worried you suddenly felt ill."

"I feel fine," she assured him. "It's just that you

seem to want someone to drink with you and I've always hated the darned stuff."

"You've probably never been offered the quality coming to our suite tonight."

"Sorry to deflate your ego, but I've been served the best. It all tastes horrid to me."

"Contrary to what you imply I didn't bring you along as a drinking buddy." He laughed softly, taking her in his arms when she slid her hands around his waist.

"I'm glad." She breathed a sigh of relief. She nuzzled her face into the vee opening of his loosely tied robe. "Three glasses of champagne and I'm out like a light."

"I'll see your limit is two and a half," Josh declared in an amused voice. "I want you wide awake when we make love tonight."

"Good idea," Jaclyn answered with head thrown back. "Though don't expect me to be dishonest and tell you I love your prestigious wine despite its cost. I hate lying."

"Don't you ever lie, Jazzy?"

"No." She closed her eyes, praying she wouldn't have to pay for all the untruths she'd told him in just two days.

"Does that mean you've been honest with me all along, Jazzy?" He pinned her down despite his bandaged eyes. Lowering his head, he clasped Jaclyn's body in a firm grip. "Has everything you've told me so far been the truth? Tell me, Jazzy!"

"Y-yes," she stammered, burying her face on his chest. "What could I possibly have to lie to you about?"

"That's what I just asked you," he demanded forcefully.

Jaclyn withdrew from Josh's arms when she heard a

discreet knock on the door. "Let's forget all the heavy conversation and sample your expensive grape juice."

Pleased at the interruption, she hoped it would take Josh's mind off whether she had always told him the truth or not.

Opening the door, she stood aside as a cloth-covered table was wheeled in by the uniformed attendant. A bottle of Dom Perignon lay nestled in an ornate ice bucket.

"Hors d'oeuvres are compliments of the management, sir," the man explained, fussing to see the service was placed in perfect order. He opened the champagne, poured each of them a glass at Josh's request, and added politely, "We hope you enjoy your stay at Four Seasons, Mr. and Mrs. Kingman."

Jaclyn flinched at the man's assumption she was Josh's wife, watching from the side of the room as he bowed toward Josh and started to leave.

"Mrs. Kingman will get your tip," Josh assured him, turning toward Jaclyn. "My wallet's on the bureau, honey."

She took out a five-dollar bill and placed it in the discreetly extended hand before shutting the door and returning to the living room.

"Maybe I will develop a liking for fine wine after all," she told Josh nervously. Being called Mrs. Kingman twice in two minutes had ruined all the composure she had. "I could use a drink now."

She took a glass and placed it in Josh's hand before getting her own and curling up in the corner of the long couch.

"You certainly changed attitudes in a hurry." Josh mocked with one eyebrow raised in inquiry.

"Not surprising, since I adjusted to saving my favors for one man in record time too."

"Good God, wench," Josh exclaimed between

clenched teeth. "It's been less than twenty-four hours since you placed your sexy body in my arms. That's hardly time enough to pat yourself on the back for successfully practicing fidelity."

"I guess you're right," Jaclyn admitted with a cheeky smile. "I'd better save my bragging until our vacation ends."

"I should hope so," Josh agreed in a scornful voice. "If you do feel the desire for other company during this trip, forget it. While I pick up the tab, you're mine, and I'm a very possessive man with my toys."

"Toys!" Jaclyn pouted, annoyed by his ridiculous comparison.

"Does calling you my woman make you happier?" Josh invited, not the least disturbed by her indignation.

"Much," Jaclyn answered jauntily, taking a small swallow of champagne that tickled her nose. "Being called Mrs. Kingman didn't sound too bad either." That should raise his arrogant eyebrows a notch or two.

"Forget that," Josh mocked. "Until I see again you're mine by the hour only." He put the glass to his lips, tilting his head back to swallow the contents in one drink.

Jaclyn sipped her drink, admiring the taut line of his lean throat. His remarks didn't concern her in the least. In fact, she enjoyed hearing his outspoken cynicisms.

"Why don't you relax and let me tell you what's available on their vast menu?"

"Fine." Josh laid his head back, enjoying the sound of her soft throaty voice reading the list of entrees in a flawless French accent.

"Didn't the manager send us some appetizers?" he

interrupted when his keen sense of smell picked up the scent of one of his favorite foods.

"Yes," Jaclyn agreed, glancing at the delicious-looking tray. "There's smoked salmon, French country pâté with cornichons, and northwest oysters."

"I'd better eat the oysters," Josh teased, giving Jaclyn a wide smile.

She returned his smile, teasing boldly, "Excellent idea considering you're disabled and have a night of heavy lovemaking lined up for me later."

"Just serve the oysters and cut out the wisecracks, Jazzy," Josh said with a frown. He took the fluted dish from her, holding it in front of his face to savor the aroma of fresh oysters on the half shell.

"I also think you should limit yoiur alcoholic intake," she pointed out, trying to hide the laughter in her voice. "I've heard it's a terrible depressant for a man sexually."

"Not with me," Josh warned, relishing the salty but delicate flavor of the local seafood as he neatly raised them one by one to his lips. "I always take care to never drink that much when I'm with a sexy lady."

"Good," Jaclyn mocked. "You did warn me you have the libido of several lusty servicemen, and I'm in the mood to see if you were bragging or telling me a provable fact."

"You're taunting me, minx," Josh scolded. He set the unfinished appetizer down on a side table, stood up, and walked straight across to where she was curled up on the end of the couch.

Jaclyn watched him move with admiration. "You set the oysters down without spilling them and made it over to me without stumbling. I'm impressed," she congratulated him.

"I'm only here because it's easier to seduce you when we're on the same couch, and I'm inclined to prove right now that what I told you about my libido is the truth."

He sat down beside her, drew her into his arms, and ran his hands up and down her gown as he imprinted its design in his mind.

"What are you doing?" Jaclyn asked innocently as his fingers continued their thorough exploration.

"Figuring out the easiest way to get you out of this slinky piece of material, then I'm going to kiss you."

"One zip will do it," she urged with a tremor in her voice.

"I know."

Jaclyn began to tremble as Josh drew her gently into his arms. She loved the way his hands rose and cradled her face so possessively as his head descended. Her lips parted as his took them in a hard, urgent kiss.

Josh's lips were warm and sure and shaped perfectly to fit the cushiony shape of her own. With great skill he forced her lips farther apart, seeking the moist interior of her mouth to manipulate her tongue in the wild response he wanted.

Jaclyn's senses came to life the moment he touched her, bursting into flame as she answered each intimate caress with a hunger of her own.

"Are you thirsty?" Josh breathed into her ear long moments later.

"I'm dying to finish my champagne," she lied, barely able to speak as she laid her head back so he could kiss the wildly beating pulse in her throat.

"Are you hungry too?" He caressed the scented hollow in her neck until she arched upward.

"Starved." She was too aroused to utter more than a single word.

"Do you want to drink, eat, or make love first?"

"Make love. First, last, and always," Jaclyn told

him in a voice so sensual she barely recognized it as her own.

"Good, little one." He groaned his pleasure on her lips. "That's just what I wanted to hear."

She clung to his well-shaped head, letting her fingers thread through the vibrant strands of chestnut hair. Feeling the narrow bandage, she stopped and pulled back. "It's time for your medicine," she gasped, inhaling rapidly in a vain attempt to catch her breath.

"Forget the damned pills," Josh hissed, nibbling up and down her sensitive neck. "The only thing I need is you. Not a drink, not dinner, and especially not my pain pills. My ache can be healed inside you and nowhere else."

"I insist," Jaclyn exclaimed, pushing against the hard wall of his chest. "It could be dangerous not to follow your doctor's orders."

"Tough," Josh fumed, ignoring her poignant plea. His only interest was in continuing his sensual exploration of the scented skin beneath his mouth.

Jaclyn shivered, trying desperately to keep her mind alert as he traced the interior of her ear with the point of his tongue. "I mean it, Josh," she whispered, burrowing her head against his chest. It was impossible to think clearly when his fingers continued to stroke her body from head to toe and his mouth relayed an urgent message wherever it touched.

"I insist you behave," she scolded in a husky murmur.

"Tough again," he scorned, lifting her up until she lay across his lap. "The only thing I want you to give me is the direction to our bed and the warmth of your sweet body surrounding my own."

"You c-can't be serious!" Jaclyn broke off as he cradled her in his arms and started to rise. Before her protest was finished, he was standing and had started moving unerringly toward the wide entrance to the master bedroom.

"Watch me and see," he warned violently, stepping forward as if he weren't blind.

"Stop in three steps, Josh, or you'll have two broken legs as well as two injured eyes."

Deep emotion flared in Jaclyn's heart as she clung to his neck. Her darkened eyes revealed complete acquiescence as he laid her tenderly down on the bed.

"Damn it," he cursed, striking his shin when he accidentally moved his legs forward in an effort to rid himself of his robe as quickly as possible.

Jaclyn smiled sympathetically at his clumsiness, knowing it was caused by his haste to take her back in his arms. She watched him come to her, his body taut and ready, and gloried in the naked expanse of tanned flesh visible. Her eyes traced a path from the whorls of dark hair on his chest veeing downward past his flat navel to the hard flesh below.

"You're an impatient lover," she said in a broken whisper, reaching out to bring him close when he bent over her.

"I know," he moaned against her mouth. "When I'm near you, I'm insane with the need to make love to you. Ever since we left Laguna Beach I thought I could curb my desire until later tonight, but it's impossible. You're too desirable to resist any longer."

Josh settled himself comfortably on the mattress and drew her to the full length of his body. "Can you feel what you do to me?" Josh insisted. His hands cupped her hips, pressing his hardened flesh tight against her softer curves.

"Of course," she confessed softly, squirming to get closer. "As before, you're impulsive, insistent, and your male hormones are out of control."

"We'll see whose sensual emotions are out of control," he threw back in an agony of frustration.

One hand reached for the zipper on her gown, working it down before she could raise a hand to help. He lifted it from her body and threw the vivid-colored silk carelessly beside the bed.

"God, honey," he moaned, touching her wispy bra and panties, "why did you bother wearing these tonight? They barely contain your lush curves as it is."

His fingers were deft as he removed the offending garments in seconds. "They're the most sensual set I have," she told him with quivering lips as his hands stroked up and down her body until she found it impossible to remain still.

"You don't need them," he advised, cupping her breasts tenderly. His thumb stroked her nipples in a slow circular motion until they were taut with arousal.

"You don't need any underwear at all, Jazzy. Your breasts are high and full, your skin is taut and"—he groaned, pressing his face into the velvety cleavage—"I think I'm going mad just touching your scented skin."

"You make me feel so sensual and feminine, Josh," she told him softly. "The most wonderful I've ever felt in my life. I've never had a man express his desire as beautifully as you do."

"That's hard to believe, Jazzy, considering your occupation."

"Forget that," she beseeched, squirming beneath the moist insistence of his tongue working magic over her sensitive skin from her throat to her hips. His mouth teased with lips and teeth that knew exactly where she was the most vulnerable and responsive.

"A good idea for tonight," he rasped thickly, entranced by the soft warmth of her abdomen before burying his face in the object of his desire below.

"You're such a possessive man I'm surprised you ageed so readily to forget about my past lovers."

"I never forget," he warned her. "Only set things aside in my mind to ponder later. Right now I don't give a damn about anyone but us."

Jaclyn clenched his shoulders, unaware her nails left marks in his tanned skin when he pressed a kiss in the silky feminine curls. "Why now?" She held her breath, waiting for his answer.

"Because"—he raised his face to warn her seriously—"I'm going to be too busy feasting on your delicious body to be concerned about who did it to you last!"

"You did," Jaclyn cried out truthfully. "You were the last to touch me there."

"Hmm," he nibbled his way from her hip bone down to the delicate skin of her groin, barely able to speak, he wanted to taste the essence of her so bad.

"You're also driving me wild by not continuing your previous erotic nibbling," she pleaded in between tiny gasps of pleasure.

"Shame on me," he rasped, propelled by the desire to linger over her sweet softness forever. "Now, shut up and enjoy being my entree until room service delivers me something better!"

"I called you a mad artist before," Jaclyn cried out in a poignant whimper, tortured by the exquisite pleasure of his eager, searching mouth pressed to the core of her desire.

All the time he was bringing her to a peak of arousal his long fingers kneaded a message of their own on her breasts and buttocks and the sensitive smoothness of her inner thighs.

"Ooh, Josh!" She caught her breath sharply when the familiar trembling began in her legs.

"Just be quiet and enjoy," he commanded without raising his face.

"You were acting mad last night, and it's even more true . . . oh, do that again right there."

"I will."

"Aagh," she crooned, "that feels exquisite . . ."

"It's supposed to."

"It's more true now. You are crazy . . ." she broke off, stopped by his harsh voice.

"If I am mad, it's insanity caused by the desire to make love to you," Josh muttered, rising up to take her mouth with hungry insistence. "Kiss me, Jazzy. Kiss me like you mean it. Only then will you stay quiet."

"Wonderful." Her voice sank to a deep yearning, whispered against his face while he placed a series of kisses all around her mouth. She reached her palms up to cradle his head, desperate to force him to satisfy the hunger of her parted lips.

Jaclyn poured every bit of feeling she had into Josh's kiss. Locked in his arms, she let the point of her tongue enter his mouth, tracing the moist interior until he returned the exploration in a sensual assault that left her weak and reeling.

"An excellent response," he admitted a lifetime later, with a deep shudder that shook his broad shoulders. "Almost too excellent," he muttered hoarsely. "I'm supposed to be keeping track of how long it takes me to make your responsive little body out of control."

"How long did it take you?" Jaclyn prompted, running her fingers through his thick hair. She was so on fire for the man now, she thought she'd die if he didn't satisfy the ache in her lower abdomen for fulfillment soon.

"I don't know. You kiss so damned good I nearly lost mine the moment your tongue passed my teeth.

Kissing a man like that is guaranteed to get you seduced or pregnant and possibly both."

"I'm willing to risk the consequences," Jaclyn admitted breathlessly. "My emotions have been out of control from the moment we met."

"That makes two of us," Josh said, covering her with the length of his body. "It's a good thing you're a professional working girl and protect yourself from man's careless behavior."

"Sure," Jaclyn agreed thoughtfully. That was one monumental consequence that never entered her mind. If she became pregnant, she would be proud to have his child.

Josh parted her thighs, pressing her into the soft comfort of the innerspring mattress and holding her there with his knees and hands.

Her eyes fluttered open, drawn instinctively from his upper torso to his arousal. It was poised rigid above her, ready to thrust into her warmth the moment she arched her hips.

"I'd give up all my worldly possessions to feel my body in yours again, Jazzy," Josh blurted out in rising frustration. "That's how much I want you."

"You'd give up that much for me?"

"Yes." His voice was filled with meaning. "I'd give everything I own just to feel your warmth while I thrust deep inside until we're both insane with the wonder of our loving."

"You don't have to give up a thing," Jaclyn soothed, wondering if he knew she felt the same way.

"Not all of my possessions anyway," he moaned, cupping her hips as she squirmed beneath him. "Just two hundred dollars' worth every hour you're with me."

"Beast!" Jaclyn scolded, nipping his shoulder in retaliation. Feeling incomplete without him inside her, she raised her legs and placed them around his lean hips. With gentle fingers she reached down to assist drawing him into her as he moved forward.

Josh pushed them away. "Put your hands on my back. I'm doing fine on my own."

Jaclyn's lashes fluttered as he began the thrusting motions that drove everything but his scent, touch, and feel from her mind. She felt perspiration dampen his back as his unfaltering motions persisted until she writhed in unbearable ecstasy.

With a poignant cry she dug her nails into his shoulders, quivering helplessly as the first involuntary spasms began to tremble through her body and continued until she knew nothing but the pleasure he gave her so generously.

"Josh. Oooh, my darling, Josh, I can't stand anymore."

"You talk too much, Jazzy," he ground out, not losing a stroke as he took her mouth in a hard possessive kiss that equaled the increasing force of his body.

"Do I really, Josh?" she started to ask, suddenly going rigid beneath him. She was unable to think, much less speak, as she slipped beyond the point of all control.

"Oh, Jazzy," he cried, burying his facc in the softly scented hollow below her ear, "how the hell do you expect me to know now?"

Jaclyn clung tight, vaguely aware Josh's shuddering equaled her own as she lay cradled beneath him in a final joining of flesh and soul that completely surpassed her erotic visions of the past.

CHAPTER NINE

"Don't you dare move," Josh protested, drawing Jac-lyn back into his arms as she started to sit up.

"I have to," she argued in a slow, reluctant whisper. "You still haven't taken your pills."

Slowly emerging from the turbulent possession of the man beside her, she experienced a depletion of all energy. She felt drained and hazy in the wonderful aftermath that left her with a sense of satisfaction she never dreamed possible.

"Will each time be more perfect than the last, Josh?" she asked innocently.

"It's not possible, Jazzy." He captured her hand and raised it to his mouth to reverently kiss the palm. "Nothing on earth could surpass what we just shared, though I intend to equal it every opportunity we have."

"Hmm," she murmured, snuggling her face against the warm flesh of his chest. "What more could any woman ask?"

"You're a constant delight to me, honey. I never expected you to give your affection as generously as you have these past two nights," Josh rasped huskily against her fingers. "Paid for or not."

"You arrogant man," she reprimanded softly, indif-ferent to his comment about her supposed occupation. She felt much too wonderful to get mad.

"Aren't I though?" he agreed without concern, releasing her hand to cradle her face and lift it upward. With great tenderness he placed a long, searing kiss on her mouth. No words were needed. It was a thank you for the recent past and a promise for what lay ahead.

"That's pretty heady stuff for a starving lady," Jaclyn admitted, fighting hard to catch her breath. She reluctantly drew away to sit up in the middle of the bed and watch him with love in her eyes.

Replete for the moment, Josh rolled on his back. With his head propped up on the pillows he faced her, reaching a hand out to rub his fingertips up and down her spine in a slow, continuous caress.

"Why don't you run through the menu again, then we'll order our dinner?"

Jaclyn pulled away when his fingers left her spine to investigate the full curves of her breast. It was too tempting, making her want to cling to him and return each intimate touch with one of her own.

"None of that now," she corrected softly. "You're going to take your medicine and eat dinner before you get ideas about misbehaving again."

"Honey," Josh retorted with complete confidence in his virility, "if what I've been doing to you is your idea of misbehaving, I'm going to be the devil himself during the next few weeks."

"Shush!" she scolded, though her eyes twinkled with mirth. "I'll be back in a flash."

"Hell," he complained, "you could flash all day and I couldn't even enjoy the sight."

"Not that kind of a flash," she called out, entering the living room to pick up the menu.

She returned to the bedroom, smiling at the tumbled sheets on a bed that was impeccably neat only an hour ago. It was a heady experience to be with a man that desired you so much he was unconcerned about anything but taking you in his arms. Whether the bedspread and blankets were laid back before he made love never entered his mind.

"What are you hungry for, Josh?" She opened the room service brochure, glancing up when he spoke.

"You and another glass of champagne," he told her bluntly. "And in that exact order!"

"Be serious," Jaclyn said with a vain attempt at censure.

"I am. Postpone dinner awhile, come to me, then bring the Dom Perignon in here and we'll toast the start of a splendid evening."

"The start!" Jaclyn exclaimed. "If I came to you first, I'd probably be lucky to get out of bed before breakfast!"

"I'm agreeable to that," Josh returned with enthusiasm.

"You're insatiable is what you are," Jaclyn shot back.

She set the brochure down and returned to the living room to get the ice bucket and Josh's glass plus an insulated decanter of freshly squeezed orange juice.

Seeing his shoes by the chair, she made a quick detour with them into the dressing area. Finished with that she entered the bathroom to pick up his medicine and returned with it and the tray to the lavish bedroom.

"What took you so long?" Josh demanded, propping himself against the headboard and carelessly draping the sheet across his lean hips.

"I had to hang your shoes on the door." She set the tray on the nightstand, filled Josh's glass, and leaned carefully across the bed to hand him his drink.

"You did what?" Josh demanded an explanation.

"Take your champagne and calm down." Their fingers touched as she transferred the glass to his hands. "I placed your shoes in the hotel's bag and hung them on the outside doorknob."

"Thanks, honey," Josh apologized. "I forgot about their courtesy shoe-polishing service. Did you leave a tip inside?"

"Yes," Jaclyn acknowledged smugly. "I enjoy removing five-dollar bills from your wallet, since you seem to have a vast sum of money in it."

"Not for long, I won't," he scowled in mock reproach. "That's a pretty big tip for a shoe shine."

"That's the smallest denomination bill you had," she explained.

"And don't get any ideas about ripping me off."

"You should have seen me cautiously opening the door and peeking around the edge before I slipped one bare arm outside holding a shoe bag," she answered, ignoring his put-down.

"I would love to have seen you, since you're obviously undressed."

Jaclyn ignored him, continuing, "I don't imagine many women guests run around naked while they're tending to a man's needs."

"Just when there's a convention in town," Josh remarked dryly.

Jaclyn slanted him a frosty glance for that dig and poured herself a glass of cold juice.

"Does it bother you to wait on me, Jazzy?" Josh asked seriously. "If it does, I'll hire a valet or male nurse when we get to Vancouver Island."

"No. I don't mind helping you." She looked at his fingers, admiring their long, artistic shape and the neatly clipped nails. "In fact," she admitted honestly, "I enjoy it."

"Most women wouldn't. Aren't you a liberated lady?" Josh inquired in a solemn voice.

"Very much so," Jaclyn flung back, knowing he was surprised by the sudden rise of his eyebrows. "But I don't carry it to extremes. I like caring for you and in return enjoy all the things you do for me."

"An unfair exchange of favors, since I'm blind and you're not."

"Not really," she told him truthfully. "You're paying for this marvelous holiday, which I couldn't afford otherwise, plus I'm getting a salary much better than" —she swallowed over the sudden tightness in her throat—"Bugsy pays me."

"If you're pleased with our arrangement as is, we'll leave it," Josh informed her. "Promise, though, to tell me the moment you get tired of the work. I don't want you feeling like a drudge."

"Hush," Jaclyn scolded, picking up her gown and laying it over the end of the bed. "I've never had a grown man to take care of before and find it kind of fun."

"Honey," Josh interrupted boldly, "that's an outright lie. From what I hear you've taken care of hundreds of men in your short but busy past."

"That's different!" she rebuked him. "I'm enjoying practicing total care instead of just sexual care. It makes for a more rounded relationship."

"Speaking of rounded," Josh teased. "Your soft curves continue to entice me despite our recent bout in this bed. Let's see what we can do to put your well-practiced talents to use again."

Jaclyn refused to reply. Josh couldn't be in need of her so soon. No man was that insatiable. Not even him.

"Come back to bed and share my champagne, or do you prefer something else?" Josh prompted when the silence continued. One eyebrow cocked as he reached a hand out toward her.

"Juice will suit me fine."

"That isn't what I had as a second alternative and you know it." He motioned her to come to him.

"Too bad," Jaclyn insisted, obediently slipping back into bed. She scooted close to Josh's side, held close as he pulled the sheet around her waist and saw she was comfortable.

"You're safe for now," Josh agreed with a gentle hug. He faced her, commenting in a calm voice, "Your near abstinence of liquor surprises me. I thought half your life would be spent draped over a bar stool checking out prospective tricks."

"Quit it, Josh," she nudged his chest. "I told you before, let's leave my life-style out of our time together."

"Honey," he leaned over, pinning her down with the force of his greater size. "I told you that's impossible for a man to do. You are what you are and I can't help but think about it often."

"Think about it all you want," she told him, not in the least intimidated by his dominant position above her. "Just don't talk about it."

Josh pulled her up with him, shrugged his tanned shoulders, and refused to commit himself one way or another. "What's for chow, minx? All this conversation has given me an appetite."

"At least it's for food now and not me," Jaclyn mumbled beneath her breath, drawing away to bring the phone on her lap.

"I'll have you again while we're waiting for room service," Josh pointed out with complete seriousness.

Jaclyn ignored him to scan the menu. "You've already eaten an appetizer, so do you want to start with soup or salad?"

"Both."

Jaclyn glanced at his face to see if he was serious,

decided he was, and read what was available from the regular room service menu.

"I'll have clam chowder and the tomato, avocado, and mushroom salad."

She turned the page past the night menu to the more elaborate Georgian and called out her preference in French. "I think I'll order *coulis de homard au dumet d'estragon* and *salade panachée en saison."*

That should fix him! She looked to see if she could tell what he was thinking by his expression. *Nothing! It was absolutely unreadable.*

"Have you decided on a main course?" *Darn the man.* He just sat there completely motionless with his lips raised in a knowing smile. Nothing she said dented his confidence. *Oh, no, I goofed,* she thought. She had just tried to show her superiority by speaking a foreign language as fluently as a native.

"Have you made up your mind?" she insisted, reverting quickly to English.

"No, but I did decide to change my soup and salad order," Josh told her without a muscle moving on his enigmatic face. "I'll have lobster bisque with tarragon and seasonal mixed salad the same as you."

"You speak French?" Jaclyn asked in shock.

"A little," he answered noncommittally. "For my main course I'll try rack of lamb or *aiguillettes d'agneau,* whichever way you wish to order it."

Thoroughly put in her place, Jaclyn decided it best not to comment. "Salmon cutlet with leeks sounds good to me."

"Not the quiche of the day?"

"Contrary to what you believe not all women are satisfied with quiche for a meal." Her eyes ran down the dessert list. "You have a choice of *pâtisserie française, gâteau,* cheesecake with strawberry sauce, chocolate mousse, or ice cream."

"Have them bring some French pastries for me and whatever you wish."

"Cheesecake," Jaclyn decided without hesitation, phoning their order in.

When she placed the phone on the nightstand Josh drew her back into his arms. "There's plenty of time before our entree for a quick appetizer."

Jaclyn clung to him, raised her mouth for a kiss, and hoped he was right. *He was. Very passionately so.*

"I can't believe you," she whispered twenty minutes later.

"Why?" Josh murmured, throwing back the crumpled sheet and searching blindly for his robe.

Jaclyn stood up, taking it off the floor, where it had fallen unnoticed during the recent tumultuous coming together. She handed it to him, smiling broadly.

"Because you're such a sensual man. How did you ever manage to remain celibate for so long?"

"It was simply mind over matter."

"How's that?"

"If I didn't have the woman I wanted to make love to, it didn't matter." His voice was filled with laughter yet the undertone sounded perfectly serious.

"Forget it," she scolded, confused by his statement. She certainly wasn't in the mood to hear about the woman he cared for right after he had made love to her with such expertise she doubted if her body would ever stop tingling.

"I'm going to dress and freshen up before our meal gets here."

"Good idea," Josh told her, pulling the robe on and belting it around his lean waist. "Room service should be here any minute now."

Hours later Jaclyn lay in bed thinking over the long evening. Their dinner had been wonderful. Josh's mood was excellent. Tender and romantic without once bringing up her occupation or the fact he was paying her to be his companion.

They had listened to music, content to sit side by side on the couch and enjoy the satisfaction of each other's company. As her head began to nod, Josh sensed her tiredness and carried her off to bed.

A secretive smile touched her lips, thinking of his actions after they were tucked in and she prepared to go to sleep. He had reached for her, as vigorous and eager to make love as he had been the first time. It was a wondrous feeling to know he needed her with the same urgency she craved him.

With a wide yawn she curved herself comfortably around his warm back with her legs bent forward in the exact shape as his. She was more than ready to get what sleep the few hours until dawn would allow.

Jaclyn awakened to the feel of Josh's fingers softly caressing her breasts. The nipples were still overly sensitive from his passionate lovemaking, causing her to squirm away until she realized Josh seemed to be aware and took care to treat her with extra tenderness.

"Wake up, Jazzy," he whispered into her tangled strands of hair. "I'm going to have a morning dose of medicine, then we have to get ready to leave for Vancouver Island."

"Your pills are on my nightstand," she murmured back in a sleepy voice.

"You're my medicine, honey. Only with you have I found relief from the damned headaches that have kept me awake since the accident."

"In that case," she teased, twisting to press a kiss on his lips, "you'd better have a double dose."

Josh did. One right after the other.

"That serves me right," Jaclyn told him as they finished dressing two hours later.

"What?" Josh asked meaningfully. He knew full

well what she meant, though it had been a long time since they had gotten out of bed.

"For suggesting you needed a double dose. I didn't think I was ever going to get a chance to bathe or get my breakfast."

"You damned near got a triple dose, you teasing witch," he reminded, laughing at the memory. "Your behavior in a shower is certainly something to remember."

"Mine!" she exclaimed, bristling at his misjudgment. "You were the one that let out my bath water . . . bubble bath yet . . . then stood me up and turned on the shower and insisted I keep my promise and scrub your back and, er . . . other places."

"You did a very thorough job," he complimented her, placing his wallet in the pocket of his sports jacket.

"I was doing just fine until you wanted to play adult acrobatics. You're shameless," she chided.

"It was all your fault," Josh pointed out smugly. "You were the one who lingered disgracefully longer than necessary with your soapy hands where they shouldn't be."

"Thank God they're here to get our luggage," Jaclyn snapped, going to the door. "You have a terrible way of misinterpreting my platonic intent to get you clean."

"Platonic!" Josh's deep laughter filled the room. "With the life-style you lead I doubt if you've had a nonsexual relationship with a man in years."

"You're right," she bragged falsely, miffed that he was taunting her again. "For at least eight years that I can remember."

Josh stopped, his brows drawn together in deep concentration. "You must be twenty-three or twenty-four, then."

"How would you know?"

"You told me yesterday that you've been wild about sex since you were sixteen."

"I'm twenty-three." Telling him her real age wouldn't cause any comparison to be made between who he thought she was and who she really was. There were thousands . . . millions probably . . . of girls her age and all undoubtedly involved in sexual relationships since their teens.

"What a difference."

"In what?" She was curious, since he made no further effort to explain himself.

"In women." He moved forward, opened the door, pointed in the correct direction of their luggage, waited until it was removed, and turned to look at her.

"I know a young woman"—his voice softened as if the memory brought him extreme pleasure—"who I'm certain has never even been with a man, and she's the same age you are."

"Don't count on it," Jaclyn snorted, slipping into her coat and checking with a last glance that she hadn't left anything behind. "Most women my age who are still virgins are that way for two reasons. They don't like men or men don't like them."

"Meow, my little cat." Josh scolded her bitchiness. "Maybe I should have ordered you a bowl of cream for breakfast after that uncalled-for remark."

"It's true," she told him, making herself sound as deliberately casual as possible.

"All women can't be as beautiful as you are, Jazzy," Josh reminded softly, accepting her arm as they left the room.

"You don't have any idea what I look like," she pointed out, walking to the elevator.

"I know exactly how you look," Josh interjected, refusing to make any further comment.

The heck you do, Jaclyn assured herself, eyeing him on the smooth ride down in the elevator. He was a complex man who never once said what she expected.

"How are we going to Vancouver Island?"

"By private charter," Josh informed her. "It's faster to fly. If the weather was nicer, and you had approved, we could have rented a car and driven to Vancouver then boarded the Tsawwassen ferry. It's an enjoyable ride across."

"Maybe we can come back that way," she suggested hopefully. Anything to delay the end of her trip with Josh would be appreciated.

"Possibly," he agreed.

Jaclyn remained quiet, watching the efficient way Josh had planned for their comfort. It was always interesting to watch how smooth a path became when money changed hands along the way.

The plane ride was uneventful, since she couldn't see Puget Sound and the many islands below through the downpour that followed them right to their landing.

Trying to wipe raindrops from her coat in the back of the limo on their way to the Victoria hotel, Jaclyn asked curiously, "Why did you stop over in Seattle? Wouldn't it have been easier to fly direct to Vancouver, British Columbia?"

"Much," Josh admitted. "Rick has an old navy buddy he hasn't seen in years who lives there. Since it made no difference to me what we did, I added one night in Seattle as a goodwill gesture for him spending the holidays away from his family."

"Don't worry about that," Jaclyn told him with a smile. "He has only one brother, whom he dislikes intensely."

"Everything did work out for the best, then," Josh grinned. "He told me last week his Navy friend took his wife to Hawaii for Christmas and they wouldn't be home, but I like Seattle so I decided to come anyway."

Jaclyn was relieved to hear that. She would have hated being the cause of Rick's not having a reunion with his only friend.

She looked over the city with interest as they entered Victoria. The rain had stopped and it was beautiful. It was impossible to take in everything in one glance as the driver sped down the highways as fast as traffic would allow.

"Time to prepare to depart your carriage, my queen," Josh teased. "We're nearing Brad's hotel."

"You know the owner?" Jaclyn asked in a startled voice.

"He's one of my best friends."

"But," Jaclyn stammered, suddenly wondering what she had got herself into. "I thought we were going to spend the holidays in a great big"—*and hopefully very impersonal,* she grimaced to herself—"hotel where you didn't know anyone and no one knew you." *And especially me,* she added as an afterthought.

"Where did you ever get that idea?" Josh queried in a surprised tone. "My entire reason for being here is the special invitation from my friends to be their guest at the grand opening of Victoria Point Inn."

"Friends?" Jaclyn gulped, swallowing back the sudden urge to jump out of the car and run away. "Do you mean more than one?"

"Certainly. Let's see," Josh pondered for a moment. "There's Brad, Brandy, Bobby, Betty, the Colonel, James, Logan and . . ."

"Stop!" Jaclyn exclaimed with rising hysteria. "How, pray tell, are you going to introduce me into this family gathering?"

"Easy," Josh told her. "I'll just tell them I rented you for a month."

"Be serious, Josh," Jaclyn continued, her voice rising as she tried to think of all the complications that could result from meeting Josh's acquaintances. Thank heavens, she didn't think she'd met any of them before. That would really be the payoff to her seduction scheme.

"I am serious," Josh told her with a broad smile. "Nobody ever believes the truth anyway."

"Let me out right here," Jaclyn insisted. "I didn't agree to be a part of one big happy family."

"Settle down, Jazzy," Josh soothed, taking her hand to assure she didn't leave. "These are wonderful people. They are also adults and well aware that man cannot live by bread alone."

"Forget the cliche, Josh," Jaclyn scolded nervously. "I'll feel an absolute fool in front of these people. Especially during this particular holiday."

"Would Mother's Day have been better?" he teased. "You've been doing a lot of mothering of me the last couple days."

"Oh, hush," Jaclyn scolded, trying hard to think what was the best thing to do.

Josh squeezed her fingers compassionately. "Don't worry, honey. I wouldn't dream of taking you anywhere that would embarrass you. This is 1985, so relax. Times have changed, you know?"

"Are you certain everyone will understand?" Jaclyn cried out, looking at him with worried eyes.

"I assure you that everything will be taken care of, so you won't be uncomfortable."

"Okay," she murmured beneath her breath, warning in a barely audible voice, "If it isn't, I'm taking the first flight home."

"You'd cut out early on me and give up all the money I owe you?"

"Heavens, no," she tossed back, suddenly seeing

their staying together in a more modern perspective. "I'd see you were so entranced with my lovemaking that you'd follow me and demand I take it."

"Fair enough," he agreed. "Fair enough for sure."

As the limo driver pulled into a bricked circular driveway southwest of town, Jaclyn cried out in delight. "It's gorgeous, Josh. The sun's out now and everything glistens." She hugged his arm to her side. "I feel terrible you can't see all the Christmas decorations."

"Are they pretty?"

"Beautiful. They're not the phony plastic kind but living pine trees with colored lights, and wreaths of dark green holly with bright red berries and tiny pine cones. The landscaped grounds are vast with hundreds of colorful flower blossoms and lawns that slope to the edge of the bay. I never expected so much beauty this far north during December. The grass is even green."

"This is the Mediterranean of the northwest, honey," Josh informed her. "The mild climate, in Victoria in particular, allows blossoming flowers all year long. Bare limbs on deciduous trees are sometimes the only sign of winter."

Jaclyn stared wide-eyed as she stood near the bricked entrance waiting for Josh. The bay was a vivid blue with several spinnakers skimming across the choppy water in full sail.

"It's so picturesque I hope our room faces the water," she whispered when Josh took her hand.

"It will, honey, as most do, since three sides of the hotel are surrounded by the stuff.

"Let's go in," Josh urged, tugging her fingers. "I'm anxious to see what my friends think of you."

"I'm a little anxious myself," she replied, knowing that was the understatement of the year.

As they entered the vast lobby, Jaclyn only had time

to take in the cozy atmosphere of the large logs burning in an open fireplace big enough to roast an ox in, before she was pulled forward and introductions started.

A momentary twinge of jealousy burned in her heart when a lovely, petite, chestnut-brown-haired woman threw herself into Josh's arms. *Some friend,* she grimaced inwardly when Josh drew her up into his arms and kissed her soundly on her soft red lips.

"This gorgeous female must be Brandy. No one"—he turned his head as if looking her straight in the eye—"other than you, of course, kisses quite like she does."

"Cool it, Josh," a handsome man with raven-black hair and eyes the same gray as her own interrupted, pulling the woman from Josh's arms.

"This arrogant man must be Brad. How are you, amigo?"

"Better than you at the moment," Brad told him, looking at Josh's bandaged eyes with concern. "Are you okay, Josh? No complications or setbacks?"

"None," Josh assured him, taking his hand in a strong grip.

"Good, now you can introduce your beautiful Jazzy to us."

"Brandy and Brad, I would like you to meet my . . . fiancee . . . Jazzy Jones."

Jaclyn stood speechless. If she hadn't been clinging to his arm, she would have fallen down. First, his friends already knew her name, and second, he calmly introduced her as his fiancee. Never in her wildest moments did she dream he would cover up their arrangement by telling his friends they were engaged.

"Pleased to meet you, Jazzy, and congratulations, Josh," Brad said enthusiastically as Brandy gave her a sweet, open smile that assured her everything would be fine despite the fact that her intriguing eyes showed she was suspicious that something was going on.

"Where are my two godchildren?" Josh demanded, cocking his head as if listening for tiny, high-pitched voices.

"With their baby-sitter."

"The Colonel or James?" Josh questioned, knowing each man doted on the twins.

"Both. You'll see them before dinner. I know you're tired so I'll have you taken to your suite, then we can talk after you've rested. We're having a hot wine-and-hor-d'oeuvres get-acquainted party at six for all the guests."

"We'll be there. Won't we, Jazzy?" Josh asked, taking her hand and pulling her forward.

"I'd love nothing better," Jaclyn agreed in her most lilting voice.

She raised her chin, pleased her hair was styled equal to any woman's in the lobby and that her coat was new. She'd really look like a frump entering his friend's fancy hotel with a tousled chignon and wearing a five-year-old khaki raincoat with multicolored paint stains on the front and sleeves.

"Where's Logan?" Josh inquired, following his friends through the crowd of guests.

"He'll be here later tonight or tomorrow," Brandy said, laughing softly. "No doubt, he's scouring the country for a fiancee too."

Jaclyn flashed Brandy a quick look, wondering if she meant that as an insult or not. Her kind eyes and soft smile assured her she meant it in playful terms only.

"Logan's a confirmed bachelor, Jazzy, but a virile one," Brandy explained with a humorous smile. "Somewhat like Josh was before you changed his mind and his eligibility as well."

Brad scanned Jaclyn's tall, shapely figure and lovely face crowned with the most beautiful, gleaming blond hair he'd ever seen. "Knowing your love of the aesthetic, I can understand why you became engaged to Jazzy. No single man in his right mind would let her get away once he met her."

"I agree," Josh told him smugly, giving Jazzy's hand a sharp squeeze. "Within a single hour I knew she was the woman I'd been waiting for all my life."

Jaclyn's shoe nudged the side of Josh's foot. Unfortunately, the others were too close for her to kick him in the shin. If he continued to drop double innuendos that brought her temper forth with a vengeance, she'd do it anyway.

With a smile for Brad and Brandy's hospitality, Jaclyn left with Josh and the uniformed bellhop. She was eager to get to their room and away from the awkward questions regarding her relationship with Josh. She had the distinct feeling that neither of his friends dreamed for one moment she was his real fiancee. She hoped the heavy influx of holiday visitors would keep her hosts too busy from prying deeply into her affairs during the next week at least. After that maybe something else would come up that would take their minds off what Josh said for the rest of their stay.

"The rooms are even larger than the Four Seasons'. I'll have plenty of space to move around without hitting anything," Josh observed when they were finally alone after being shown around and handed a huge fruit basket and champagne by a hotel employee. "How do you like it?"

Jaclyn walked to the far wall in the living room area, pulling the drapes aside to stare out the patio doors. "It's quite elegant. We have a beautiful view of the bay from every room except the bathroom and even have our own private fourth-floor balcony in the living room as well as in the bedroom."

She turned away from the entrancing view and walked back to give him an affectionate hug. "I feel sad you can't see, Josh. Our suite is so lovely and the bay such a bright azure blue now."

"Actually the bay you're looking at is Victoria Harbour to the left and the Inner Harbour on your right. The huge hotel covering an entire block to the far right is the Empress. It's world-renowned for it's hospitality, as the Victoria Point Inn will be with Brad's expertise in hotel management."

"How do you know what can be seen from this room?" Jaclyn asked curiously. Josh sounded more like a tour guide than a guest.

"I flew up when Brad first purchased the property. After looking it all over, I picked out the suite I wanted when he had his grand opening after a complete refurbishment."

"Are you serious?" Jaclyn asked, not decided whether to believe him or not.

"Certainly. Brad wanted my expertise on art work throughout the hotel. Did you notice how much each painting adds to the decor?"

"Yes," Jaclyn admitted. Her eyes had been drawn to the excellence of the works first thing. "Do you do that often?"

"Heavens, no. It was strictly a favor for a good friend.

"Don't bother unpacking," he advised. "Brandy will send her private maid up to take care of it the moment you wish. She'll also be here to help during our stay if you need assistance."

"That's very thoughtful." Jaclyn knew Brandy would be a friend. She had liked her the moment their eyes met and her instincts about people were always right.

"Brandy's as thoughtful as she is kind," Josh explained. "She's also the most devoted wife I've ever met. She adores Brad."

"I noticed that on my own," Jazzy told him softly. "Each time she looks at her husband it's as if a light turns on in her heart."

"It does and for him also. Brad worships the ground she walks on."

"Lucky people," Jaclyn murmured beneath her breath, walking in to survey the king-size bedroom and huge bath once again.

"They are and they deserve it," Josh agreed, overhearing her comments no matter how low she spoke.

"Why did you tell them we were engaged?" Jaclyn spoke up, unable to contain her curiosity any longer.

"I didn't want to make you uncomfortable." He removed his jacket and placed it on a side chair, then continued nonchalantly. "Your prudishness constantly surprises me. It's a temporary title to prevent any embarrassment caused by our staying in the same room."

"I see." She pondered his answer, amazed he would care about her feelings so much he would lie.

"Your attitude about our sleeping together is weird, Jazzy, seeing you do it for a profession every day of the year."

"Not with my client's friends and their families around during a holiday celebration."

"That makes a difference to you?"

"Yes," she admitted, deciding to shift the conversation to their evening ahead. "What do you want to do until our wine-tasting party tonight?"

"I'm going to the men's gym and have the masseur give me a good rub down, then go on to the barber shop for a trim and shave. It will give you a little freedom from my company and a chance to rest or check out their beauty parlor if you wish. Brandy told me there's an excellent hairdresser in the hotel."

"How on earth do you know that?"

"I asked Brandy when I called yesterday morning. I knew you'd need personal attention too. There's also an excellent high-fashion ladies' wear shop on the main floor next to the gift shop. Anything you wish, just charge to me."

"I have everything I need," Jaclyn explained, amazed by his constant generosity and the foresight to think of her needs before they even left California.

"If you're okay"—Josh smiled—"then I'll ring for George and be on my way."

"George?" Jaclyn quizzed curiously.

"The masseur."

"Sounds wonderful. I'm going to wash my hair then relax for one full hour, soaking in my bubble bath. It will be heaven knowing you won't come barging in to haul me out before I'm finished."

"If I didn't have George's only open appointment this afternoon, I'd join you for that remark." Josh flexed his broad shoulders, trying to ease the stiffness from his muscles. "For some reason I suddenly feel like an old man."

"That's because you acted like a young man all night," Jaclyn called out from the bathroom just as Josh prepared to open the door at George's knock and leave her alone. "All morning too, come to think of it," she added impishly.

"I'll get you for that remark later this evening, Ms. Jones," he shot back.

"You'd better rest tonight," she teased in a mischievous voice. "You got me at least five times already today. Six is too much even for you to handle on your own."

Her eyes twinkled with devilry as she heard the door slam with a loud bang. For once she had gotten the last word in with Josh, and he deserved every comment she made.

CHAPTER TEN

"You look very handsome tonight," Jaclyn complimented Josh on the way from their suite to the elevator.

"Thank you," he drawled, taking her arm and hugging her close to his side. "And you, Jazzy, are a knockout."

"What makes you think that?" Jaclyn inquired in a pleased voice. She leaned her head into his shoulder with a wide smile that emphasized the beauty of her soft mouth.

"By touching the silky material and cowl neckline of your tightly belted dress, I can imagine exactly how you look. You're without a doubt the most beautiful woman here."

"Hardly," she scoffed aside his flattery. "But I do think my dress is super. It's new and so pretty I couldn't resist buying it right off the model in the boutique's window display.

"We make a good pair then, don't we, honey?" Josh teased, squeezing her hand.

"The very best," Jaclyn returned, wishing they were paired legally and permanently. She was fast realizing that transitory relationships left much to be desired for her. She was too much in love with Josh not to think about the pain of leaving him when their vacation was over.

Shaking off the momentary flicker of depression, she threw back her shoulders and thought instead of the pleasant plans for the evening ahead.

Jaclyn had never felt more proud in her life than she was now, assisting the striking man beside her. Josh was impeccably groomed and so striking in the deep brown suit and matching accessories she had picked out for him to wear. She knew no woman could resist him despite his serious injury.

"I don't know if I'll survive this evening," Josh stated without further explanation.

"Why is that?" Jaclyn asked curiously as they entered the elevator.

"Because of the heady scent assailing my nostrils. I like your sexy perfume, though you don't need it." He lowered his head to whisper in her ear, "Your natural fragrance drives me wild, as you should be well aware by now."

"Hush, Josh," she scolded, glancing to see if the two elegantly gowned women stepping inside had heard his blunt comment. A smile touched her mouth when they left the elevator on the third floor with their chins held aloofly high.

"You know," she reminisced, "I still find it impossible to think you actually thought you could con me into removing my cocktail gown after you returned from the masseur and were dressed yourself."

"I had a perfectly logical reason for wanting to make love. It was a purely scientific urge only, believe me," he lied without a qualm.

"A test comparison to decide how making love on Canadian soil versus that of the United States affects a man's virility is the idea of a pervert and should be treated as such," Jaclyn pointed out with a soft giggle.

"I damned near had you convinced until Brandy

phoned to say the twins couldn't wait any longer to see me."

"No comment," she returned with a wide smile, remembering her eager response to Josh's kisses. He really was a virile man, and it took all her willpower to convince him to wait until they retired that night to pursue his experiment. "No comment at all!"

"Ha!" Josh exclaimed, reaching out to intimately run his hand over her soft buttocks. "No wonder you refuse to speak. You're too embarrassed to admit you were eager to try anything I suggested."

"Thank God we're going to be among civilized people tonight. That should help curb your appetite and your tongue," she retorted. "A little bit anyway."

Jaclyn took his wayward hand as the elevator stopped and gripped his fingers until the door slid open. She was pleased to see the foyer was crowded. No telling what he intended to do next.

"Promise me you'll behave, Josh," she pleaded in a soft whisper as they started out. "You really do say and do outrageous things."

"No comment," he got back at her, striding forward with his head held arrogantly straight and back ramrod stiff. "No comment at all!"

She couldn't help but notice how confident he was in all situations. He stood a full head above most of the men. One hand firmly clasped hers as he moved, calmly ignoring the covert glances at his bandaged eyes, though she knew he sensed every look his way.

Jaclyn couldn't believe it. She was certain if she was the one with her eyes covered she would be horribly self-conscious. Probably even hanging onto his arm for dear life with her head bowed to keep people from seeing her face.

As they exited into the lobby and started toward the main lounge, Josh was called by Brad. Entering the private office, his legs were tackled by two children simultaneously squealing with happiness.

"Uncle Josh! Uncle Josh! We luv you, Uncle Josh!"

Josh smiled, squatting on his heels to gather the squirming bodies into his arms with obvious delight.

"Eyes hurt?" Bobby asked, touching the bandage with a tiny finger.

"Hurt eyes?" Betty mimicked, placing a kiss on Josh's cheek.

Jaclyn looked on, tears coming unbidden to her eyes at the picture of him being kissed and hugged by the darling children in his arms. It was a scene that tore at her heart because she wanted to be a part of it so much.

Brandy walked in from a side room unnoticed, smiling as she observed her son and daughter climbing all over Josh. She looked at Jaclyn's face, took in the expression, and vowed to find out what was going on if the opportunity arose. Neither she nor Brad believed Josh's story about having a fiancee.

Jaclyn felt a hand on her arm and turned, greeting Brandy with enthusiasm, "These two angels must be Betty and Bobby. They're beautiful children. I think you're very, very fortunate."

"Brad and I both realize that," Brandy concurred, "though they're definitely not angels all the time, believe me."

"Agreed," Brad teased. "Sometimes they take after their mother and are ornery as hell. Then it's all I can do to keep them in line despite their age."

"Don't listen to Brad when he's full of mischief, Jaclyn," Brandy warned with a loving smile. "He's a perfect father as well as husband. The most gentle and loving man I've known." She reached out to touch her husband's arm affectionately.

"I have a firm hand when need be," he interrupted,

turning to speak to Josh. "Too bad you can't see Bobby and Betty now. I think they've each grown six inches since you came to Palm Springs last."

"They must have," Josh acknowledged, standing with one child in each arm. There was no worry about his dropping them as two pairs of tiny arms and hands were tightly clenched around his neck. "I swear they've gained at least twenty pounds a piece."

"That's from their mother's excellent cooking." Brad observed the constant pummeling as they vied for Josh's attention. "You'd better sit on the couch or they'll wear you out before dinner." He took his children until Josh sat down, then handed them back.

Brandy stepped forward, bending to introduce them in her soft voice, "Meet Ms. Jones, darlings."

"Could they call me Aunt Jazzy?" Jaclyn asked, looking at her with a tender expression. She ached with the desire to bear and hold Josh's own children close to her breast.

"Sure they can," Josh interrupted, not waiting for Brandy's reply. "Come here, honey." He motioned her over. "I'll gladly share these two imps' company with you."

Jaclyn sat down at his side, imprinting each face with the eyes of an artist. Her glance moved from the dainty raven-haired, curly-mopped Betty with her daddy's identical gray eyes to the masculine image of Brad, except for Brandy's vivid chestnut hair and intriguing brandy-colored eyes. Both children returned her look, studying her intently while clinging to the security of Josh's strong neck.

"Your twins are obviously not identical, yet they are the image of each of you. Only their coloring is crossed," Jaclyn commented with interest.

Smiling indulgently, Jaclyn watched in silence as Bobby lost interest in investigating Josh's bandage and boldy climbed off his lap onto her own. She saw his chubby hand rise and one tiny index finger tentatively touch her gold bracelet, the matching chains around her throat, and the heart-shaped studs in her ears before he decided her bracelet intrigued him most.

"They would be an artistic delight to paint," Jaclyn exclaimed.

"How would you know, Jazzy?" Josh commented in a quiet voice, still holding Betty's waist as she bent over to cautiously touch Jaclyn also.

"Because of their impish faces and the striking color of their hair and eyes. I may not know a thing about art," she lied smoothly, "but I do realize what makes an appealing picture."

"I agree with Jazzy," Brad pointed out with serious thought. "Brandy and I just had a family photo made, but I'd still like to find a competent portrait artist to do an oil for our living room."

"I know one," Josh told him. "My protégée. Unfortunately, she just left California yesterday and should be in France now. If you like, I could phone her."

Jaclyn froze, swallowing back her consternation at hearing Josh's offer to call. She had vaguely worried her brother might try to get in touch with her before the month was up but never dreamed Josh would be the first to attempt it.

One thing for certain, no one would answer!

"No need to bother her until after the holidays." Brad shrugged off the offer. "We won't be home until the first of the year anyway."

"I'm holding her first exhibit at my gallery in April," Josh continued. "Invitations will be mailed in March, and I expect you and your monied friends to attend." His voice became perfectly serious. "And to purchase."

"We'll be there." Brad looked at Brandy for approval. "Okay, darling?"

"Fine. I'd love to see the works of anyone Josh thinks is so special."

"Is she really as capable as you claim?" Brad asked, unaware how awkard Jaclyn felt hearing herself discussed without their knowledge. "I'm very particular, as you know."

"She's very young but the finest portrait artist I know. Her ability to capture the essence of a person's thoughts and personality, then convey it to canvas with a perfect likeness will stun you."

Brad paced the room back and forth, contemplating Josh's words. He was eager to have a lasting memento of Brandy and his twins while the babies were still young. He looked at his friend.

"Who is she?"

"Her name is Jaclyn Howard."

"She's not Bruce's sister, is she? I heard you mention once he had a sister you'd been intrigued with for years."

"Yes, that's her," Josh admitted in a casual voice that drove Jaclyn crazy with curiosity.

Intrigued with her! Is that all the man was? What else? she thought, since he certainly didn't know he'd been making love to that same person for two nights straight and had arranged to continue for another four weeks.

"Why haven't you mentioned her artistic ability before?"

"She's a very serious and private young lady who's served in the Peace Corps in addition to studying art at the best private schools."

"She must be special," Brad commented, sitting on the edge of his desk to contemplate Josh's praise. "I've never heard you speak so highly about another artist like this before."

"I've been jealously guarding her from exploitation until I knew she was ready. I guarantee you she'll be a much acclaimed and busy artist after April."

Jaclyn couldn't have uttered a word if her life depended on it, so stunned was she by Josh's praise of her talent.

"Very noble." Brad watched Josh's expression thoughtfully. "Bruce never told us about her talent when we met him at your house."

"He isn't aware of his sister's exceptional ability. No one was, though I realized it from the moment we met. It was a gut instinct then and her showing will convince you I'm right."

"Set me up an appointment with her after the exhibit. I'll commission her on your say-so alone. If she likes, she can come to our house and do the portrait there."

"Thanks. She'll be pleased, I'm sure." Josh handed Betty to Jaclyn, smiling as he overheard the babies happy chatter while talking with his friend. "I might as well warn you now that she won't be cheap. I won't allow her to charge less than her worth."

"Have I ever quibbled at the astronomical price of your work?"

"No," Josh admitted with a laugh. "You wouldn't dare."

"Then don't worry. I won't expect to get your protégée for nothing."

"You won't get my protégée at all," Josh warned him in a solemn voice. "Only the result of her artistic talent."

"You sound like Logan now, Josh," Brandy interrupted in good humor. "You needn't worry about Brad and your Ms. Howard. My husband is truly snared. Lock, stock, barrel, and physical prowess as well."

"Good for you, Brandy." Jaclyn congratulated her outburst to set Josh straight.

Brandy looked at Jaclyn and gave her a mischievous wink, then reminded Josh seriously, "You should know Brad wouldn't think of getting such a painting cheap."

"I know, Brandy," Josh assured her ruffled feelings. "Brad's as aware as I am that quality goods of all kinds are expensive."

Josh glanced toward Jaclyn with a devilish grin on his well-shaped lips. "Aren't they, Jazzy?" He placed his hand on her thigh in an intimate manner, not the least concerned his friends could observe his bold display.

She moved her leg in a vain attempt to avoid his touch without saying anything.

"Right, honey?" he prodded.

"Yes, they are." Jaclyn spoke through tightly clenched lips that rose to a smile despite the frost in her eyes.

"And usually worth every penny paid!" She knew darn well she was the expensive goods he meant.

She hugged the twins to her breast, trying to calm down over Josh's verbal misbehavior.

"I'm anxious for you to meet my godfather and his companion, James," Brandy intervened in the sudden tense atmosphere. "They live with us in a separate house behind our main home. You'll like them, Jazzy."

"I'll be happy to make their acquaintance," Jaclyn told her sincerely.

"Both men tried to sneak away to play a game of checkers when two single ladies staying here gave chase and persuaded them into having a private tête-à-tête dinner. Brad and I are constantly amused by their popularity with women. We don't know what we'd do without them either."

"That's for certain," Brad agreed. "We're often busy with our hotels, and they assist the babysitter when it's impossible to have Betty and Bobby with us."

"You're very fortunate." Jaclyn sighed with a touch of sadness. "I envy you having a relative."

"What about Grandmother?" Josh asked innocently. "Did you forget her, Jazzy?"

"How could I, Josh? She's such a darling," Jaclyn lied in her sweetest voice. "It's the closeness I envy, since Grandmother doesn't live with me."

"Lucky for her," Josh mumbled beneath his breath for her ears alone. "She'd get the shock of her life if she ever answered your phone."

He ignored Jaclyn's surreptitious poke in the side and smiled toward Brad and Brandy as if he were the most guileless man in the world.

"Bedtime, Betty and Bobby," Brandy announced to the twins. "After they're settled for the night, we've planned to meet you in the main lounge. All the guests are being welcomed there, but we did manage a private dinner table for the four of us."

"That sounds wonderful," Jaclyn said with a smile, giving each child's dimpled cheek a warm kiss. She handed the soft, cuddly bodies back to their mother. "What about the twins dinner?"

"They've already eaten. Bobby accidentally spilled creamed spinach all over the dress I planned to wear tonight and then Betty knocked her milk over trying to wipe the spinach off me." She hugged her children with obvious love and laughed. "A typical mealtime at the Lucas home."

"If you'll excuse us for a few minutes, we'll put our

babies to bed," Brad told them, taking the heavy babies from Brandy's arms.

"I wanna stay wiff Uncle Josh and Aunt Jazzy," Bobby protested, reaching out toward them with chubby arms.

"Me too," Betty mimicked, wanting to do everything her brother did. "Me stay too, Daddy."

"One more hug only," Brad told them firmly. He held them down for Josh and her to comply.

After Josh and Jaclyn had each received prolonged good-byes and sloppy kisses, Brad walked from the office with Brandy following close by his side.

"Do you want to wait here or get acquainted with the crowd?" Josh asked, straightening his tie and jacket after the recent mauling.

"Let's mingle," Jaclyn urged. "I don't trust you alone."

"Why not?" Josh protested innocently. "Mingling sounds like a hell of a good idea."

His words were spoken with such honesty she should have known he had another idea in mind. Before Jaclyn could decipher his intent, she found herself flat on the couch with her body pinned beneath his. He was so quick she didn't know what was happening until it had.

"Let me up, Josh Kingman!" she demanded, unable to prevent him from holding her hands over her head in complete subjugation. He was so close she could see how smooth his cheeks were after the professional shave, and each hair in his eyebrows and mustache.

"I thought you wanted to mingle," she stormed, feeling her temper rise despite the fact her mind was contemplating the pleasure of his hips pushing hers into the soft couch.

"I do." He bent his head and moaned against her throat. "I want to mingle my body with yours."

"Shush," Jaclyn scolded, glaring unseen at his face. "What if Brad or Brandy should return?"

"No problem. I assure you Brad does this to Brandy every chance he gets."

"I'm leaving," Jaclyn persisted, squirming helplessly beneath his hovering frame.

His lips silenced her protest with effective insistence. "Not until you kiss me in return."

"Is that all you want?" Jaclyn whispered against his mouth, reaching to cradle his head with her quivering fingers.

"I suppose it will have to do for now," he complained, toying with her lips between each word he spoke.

"No problem at all," she assured him, parting her teeth to accept his probing tongue and meet it with the pressure of her own.

Jaclyn began to tremble when the assault on her senses continued unabated. It was impossible not to respond to the relentless possession of his hungry mouth. He kissed with too much expertise for any woman to resist.

Josh's exciting lips and restless fingers effectively relayed the sensual message he would never be satisfied with a kiss or two. His hardened flesh pressing tight against her soft form confirmed that message with indisputable proof.

With a deep groan, Josh straightened up, pulling her into his arms. "Feel what happens the moment I touch you?" He placed her hand against him for a fleeting touch before taking it to his lips to kiss her fingers.

Jaclyn shuddered, not wanting to leave the enticing rise. It seemed natural and sweet to want to intimately caress his aroused body as he had hers.

"I must be out of my mind to think I could give you

an innocent kiss, then calmly proceed to the lounge. I want to take you to bed so damned bad now I'll ache until I do."

"You're crazy," she teased, kissing his chin, then drawing away. "And you are not taking me to bed."

"Not now," he grumbled in surprising ill humor. "I'm obliged to introduce you to the colonel and James, taste hot wine, meet a few hotel guests, and eat my dinner. After that it's straight to our suite to hit the sack for a hot . . ."

"Bath!" Jaclyn laughed, rushing into the office restroom to put on fresh lipstick, brush her hair, and straighten her rumpled dress.

"That was not what I had in mind to have a hot one of and you know it," Josh called out, standing up to smooth his jacket and tie as best he could without sight.

Jaclyn returned in seconds, looking beautifully groomed with a decidedly sensual glimmer in her smoke-gray eyes. She circled Josh, checking him over before stopping to take his hand.

"Your appearance is quite marvelous, sir. No one would ever realize just by looking at you that you're a mass of frustrated manhood biding time until you can rid your tense body of its overabundance of male hormones."

"Skip the smart talk, Jazzy, and lead me to the main lounge," Josh chided, "or I'll release all my male hormones right here in Brad's office."

"Not with me, you won't," she said, and laughed, tugging him to the door and walking down the hall.

For the next two hours Jaclyn had a splendid time. The colonel and James were charming and obviously enjoying their popularity with the many single women about. Just watching them could have kept her entertained all night.

The local and out-of-town guests appeared to be in excellent spirits as they sipped hot, cinnamon-flavored wine and nibbled on tasty hors d'oeuvres with a decided English flavor.

Everyone was made to feel welcome by Brad and Brandy plus their excellent manager and his assistants. Christmas music and lavish decorations filled her sentimental heart to bursting.

The only thorn in her side was Josh. He was acting more outrageous by the moment. She had finally spotted a vacant table in the back corner and sat him down with a sigh of relief.

"Damn it, Jazzy," he mumbled in her ear for the umpteenth time. "When are we going to eat dinner so we can go to our suite? Rick told you I need my rest and your interest in everything and everyone but me is harming my health, not to mention keeping me up past my bedtime."

"It's only eight o'clock," Jaclyn scolded, pushing his hand away from its intimate exploration of her thigh. Fortunately, the large circular table had a cloth draped over the side which prevented anyone from seeing what he was doing.

"You know the doctor said I shouldn't stay up late," Josh persisted irritably, unperturbed by her reminder that the evening was young. He put his hand around her waist and drew her closer.

"You didn't take that into consideration last night," she reminded him, drawing back to her own chair. "I don't think you slept thirty minutes."

"Man cannot live by bread alone," Josh whispered, taking her hand and raising it to his mouth. When she tried to withdraw, he cupped her fingers tight and intimately circled the sensitive palm with the point of his tongue.

"You said that once before, Josh, and I'm tired of

hearing such a stupid cliché, especially the way you mean it."

"Damn it, then," he moaned, bending to nibble her earlobe. "I'm paying you to give me sex anytime I want it, and I want it now. That little display in Brad's office has me all worked up."

"Do you want to take a long walk?" she suggested, glad no one was close enough to overhear his blatant words. "I hear that's excellent for cooling off a man."

"No!" he snapped, "And I don't want a cold shower either. The only thing I want tonight is more of you, and you're playing damned hard to get. At what I'm paying you by the hour, each minute you argue costs me a bundle."

"Consider it a lesson in patience."

"Consider yourself in trouble when we get alone," he said with a scowl.

"Shush," Jaclyn murmured, giving his hand a sharp squeeze. She looked around self-consciously, pleased to see her host and hostess finally start easing toward the doorway.

"Let's go mingle with the guests some more," she suggested, hoping for once he would do as she asked without objecting that he needed his rest. "Please?"

"No! I have just spent two hours listening to motherly old ladies in rustling taffeta gowns who wear too much lavender perfume inquire about my poor injured eyes."

"They were being sweet and showing their concern for your health."

"I know. I received different advice and a proven cure from each one."

"Then let's go talk with the recent arrivals. Maybe they'll know a remedy for your other problem."

"You're the only one who can cure that."

"Wait until after dinner."

"I'm not hungry."

"Behave, Josh. You're acting so terrible I was forced to sit you way over here in the corner like a spoiled brat."

"I am spoiled and you did it to me."

"How?"

"You gave me a taste of heaven and I want more."

"The only taste you'll get is of your dinner. Now be good or I'll leave you alone."

"I'd find you, Jazzy," Josh warned, "then you'd really earn your fee."

"Let's go, Josh. Your threats don't bother me in the least." She took his hand and pushed her chair back. "Brad and Brandy are standing in the hall and motioning for us to come."

"Now that statement"—he gave a roguish laugh—"I won't touch with a ten-foot pole."

"I should hope not," Jaclyn scolded, standing up and weaving her way with Josh in tow through the crowd until they were out of the room.

"It's time for dinner," Brandy announced, urging them forward. "I hope we won't be interrupted." She clung to Brad's arm as they walked to the main dining room. "You'd better be hungry, as we're anxious to see what you think of our new chef."

"Josh is starving," Jaclyn told her in an impish voice, following alongside. "In fact, he's been urging me all night to take him to our room for a . . ."

"Piece," Josh retorted in a calm voice. He didn't miss a step when his meaning was changed by Jaclyn's quick coverup.

"Of fruit." She looked at Brandy and smiled. "The basket waiting in our room is absolutely filled with delicious goodies. After I described them to Josh, he kept wanting to return and sample . . ."

"Everything in the room," Josh cut her off with a smug grin.

Jaclyn entered the dimly lit dining room, aware Josh's chin was held arrogantly upward and refused to comment. He was in a devilish mood and it would be best not to aggravate it.

Seated at a rear table beside huge picture windows overlooking the bay, she looked around with awe. It was so elegant—from the finest silver and dinnerware to linen royalty would admire.

Spreading the napkin on her lap, she gazed outside before asking curiously, "What are the brilliant lights across the bay? It looks like the entire city of Victoria is lit up."

"Not quite, though we think the local citizens do a marvelous job of bringing the holiday spirit to the area. What you're seeing is the Empress Hotel straight ahead and to the side, seemingly covered with dazzling lights, the famed Parliament building. It's an outstanding display, isn't it?"

"Like a fairy tale come true." Jaclyn turned to her right. "I'm really sorry you can't share it with me, Josh. The view is gorgeous."

"I've seen it at night," Josh told her. "If you want to play guide tomorrow and feel energetic, we can walk there from here and see downtown as well."

"That sounds perfect." Jaclyn gave Josh a melting smile, unaware the love in her eyes was clearly visible to Brad and Brandy. "I have several last-minute gifts to purchase."

"I do too," Josh admitted. "We'll do them together."

"Cutting it really close, aren't you?" Brad reminded. "Considering tomorrow is Christmas Eve."

"I hope you don't mind," Brandy broke in smoothly, "that tonight's meal has been prepared without our knowledge or choice and the first course is coming now."

"Potluck then," Josh teased, taking the glass of wine Jaclyn handed him and tasting it appreciatively.

"Wait and see." Brandy laughed. "Henri's very French and highly emotional. Since we think so highly of his skill, we rather humor him along just to keep him with us."

"He's the best chef we've ever had," Brad said, the true businessman when he talked about his staff. "We'll introduce you after dinner."

"I'd love to meet him. He sounds like a typical French chef." Jaclyn looked across the table, talking with enthusiasm. "They're very assured of their ability and demand to be treated with the respect they deserve. French food is one of my favorites."

"French fries, no doubt," Josh interjected in a pensive tone.

"Yes and French McDonald's too!" she sassed. He'd never dream how many hamburgers she'd eaten in the Paris McDonald's.

When the appetizer was placed in front of them, Jazzy leaned over to explain in what position everything was on Josh's plate. It had become a habit already to see to his comfort before her own.

"This looks delicious," Jaclyn told them. "It's goose liver pâté with thin triangles of toast, Josh." She took a knife and spread a generous portion on a piece of toast and handed it to Josh.

"Excellent," Josh exclaimed, taking another bite between his even white teeth. "Creamy smooth and delicately flavored without the least bitterness."

After enjoying fresh mushroom soup, which Josh passed over, they started on celery Victor, a deliciously seasoned salad served like a work of art.

Before Jaclyn could take her third bite, she was startled to look up and see a towering, handsome man with vivid copper-colored hair and piercing indigo-blue eyes the same rich color as Josh's.

His eyes were filled with devilry as he looked over the table, nodded to Brandy and Brad, then clasped Josh on the shoulder and greeted him in a deep voice. "Hello, you lucky bastard." He turned to Jaclyn and Brandy and apologized. "Excuse my language, ladies, but I can't believe it. I've been out scouring the woods for weeks to find a halfway presentable female to warm my bed over the holidays, and Josh . . . who can't even see . . . surprises us all by coming to our gathering with one of the sweetest-looking and most stunning blondes I've seen in my life."

Josh sat without greeting his friend or saying a word. One eyebrow raised upward as he moved his head from Logan to Jaclyn, then back again before asking, "Did you say a blonde?" he asked in a dangerously low voice.

"Of course I said blonde." Logan sat in a chair hastily placed at the table. "Who should know better than you, unless you met the lady since your accident?"

The man looked from Josh's curious expression to Jaclyn's stricken face and tried his best to smooth over the sudden awkwardness of his innocent comment.

Deciding it was up to her to ease the tense situation, Jaclyn came up with a hurried explanation and smiled at the stranger. "You must be Logan. I'm Jazzy and the reason Josh sat speechless for a moment is he didn't know I dyed my hair this afternoon. When we met I had red hair."

Brandy and Brad looked at her sympathetically, refusing to comment on the fact she entered the lobby with the most beautiful natural-looking blond hair they'd ever seen.

Brad motioned for the waiter, instructing him to set

a place for Logan, then started conversing with his friend.

While the others were occupied, Jaclyn turned to the silent man at her side and explained in a whisper, "I wanted to surprise you, Josh, since blondes are reputed to be so much more fun."

"You're all the *fun*"—he paused to emphasize the word fun—"I can handle as it is . . . darling . . . whether you have red or blond hair."

"I can believe that, old man," Logan interjected, overhearing every word said as he sat across from Jaclyn. His eyes shone with mischief as he asked, "You don't have a twin sister, do you, Jazzy?"

"No, but I do have a girl friend as bold as you are."

"Where do I meet her and what's her name?" Logan insisted.

"She's out of the country for the holidays, so you can't meet her now. Her name is Lerisa and she'd be a good match for you verbally. She's smart and beautiful with coal-black hair like Brad's and eyes the color of expensive emeralds."

Jaclyn tried to think back, wondering if she had ever mentioned Lerisa's name to her brother. She doubted it, since they had nothing in common. Even if she had, Bruce would have had no reason to pass the information on to Josh.

"If Lerisa is half as nice as Brandy and you appear to be, I want to meet her. If we click, Josh can do a nude bronze of her for my office desk."

"You already have two of my bronzes even if they aren't nudes," Josh reminded soberly.

"I know, and each one cost me a bundle."

"The lot my house and gallery sit on weren't cheap either," Josh pointed out in a monotone voice.

"Good property isn't cheap." Logan's reply was serious.

"Nor is good art."

"Agreed, and you're the best," Logan said. "Right, Brad?"

"Definitely. I have five powerful sculptures by Josh and want to make it an even six. Will you do the twins for me?"

"Yes, and it won't cost you a cent despite the fact they never remained still a second while I sketched them."

"You've already done a bronze of Bobby and Betty?" Brandy asked in an excited voice. "Is that true, Josh?"

"Wait and see what Santa Claus brings." Josh gave her a tender smile. "No telling what he has in his toy bag."

When Jaclyn was beginning to relax and enjoy the tender filet of beef Wellington entree in its flaky pastry, Logan looked across the table and commented: "A beautiful blonde in a dress the color of rich, full-bodied burgundy wine who has the most provocative, sensual mouth I've ever sat across from is a delight to behold."

Logan glanced over at Josh's mutinous expression with amusement, well aware the man was filled with jealousy by his appearance despite their long friendship.

"Thank you, Logan," Jaclyn said politely in her soft, throaty voice. "You're very flattering."

"He wouldn't say it if he didn't mean it," Brandy assured her, enjoying the interplay. Josh was acting exactly like Brad had the night she met Logan. He had been enraged when Logan had offered to drive her home after she became jealous of Logan's girl friend and her attention to Brad during a nightclub show.

"Thanks, Brandy," Logan said, turning back to Jaclyn. "The name Jazzy fascinates me as much as you do. I must find out how you got it."

"Cool it, Logan," Josh threatened between clenched teeth, doing nothing to conceal his rising anger.

"Josh has terrible manners tonight, Jazzy. Would you be receptive if I tried to take you away from him until he settles down a bit?"

Jaclyn gave a soft, appreciative giggle, knowing Josh would be furious if she answered Logan, though she knew he didn't mean a word he said. It was obvious he was baiting Josh for his own amusement.

Hearing Jaclyn's throaty laugh, Josh turned to Brad and urged intently, "Set Logan's plate with the colonel and James. They always seem to be surrounded by women." He faced Logan. "One should suit you even if they are a little long in the tooth."

"Relax, Josh," Logan recommended in a humorous voice. "You're making jealous noises for the first time in your life. I never poach on another man's preserves until the game leaves the compound."

Logan turned to Jaclyn, reached across the table, and grabbed her hand. "Will you fly to Palm Springs with me tonight, Jazzy? We can spend the holidays alone in the desert."

"Well," Jaclyn pondered, giving him a teasing smile. "It sounds nice but I'd better not, since I hear Santa Claus visits every room at the Victoria Point Inn, and I'm wild about gifts."

"I'll shower you with gifts and show you a Christmas you'll never forget," Logan promised, smiling to assure Brandy and Brad he was only teasing.

"I'll show you the door, Logan," Josh shot back, spreading his hand over Jaclyn's in a move that clearly said stay away. "Lay off. Jazzy's mine!"

"Hmm," Logan pondered a moment with his eyes

closed before glancing back at Josh. "That sounds serious. What'd you do, buy her outright?"

"No. I rent her by the hour, which means when you're around every single second of the day, she's mine!" Josh exclaimed, ignoring Jaclyn's quick gasp. "Now shut up and eat, amigo."

"Interesting." Logan pondered a moment then added, "I think if someone like Jazzy was mine I'd close escrow and see the deed was in my name only as soon as possible."

"That's because you're a real-estate man," Josh returned. "I'm an artist, so I signed Jazzy for a month's showing. She's my private exhibit, so to speak."

"Don't believe a word Josh says, anyone," Jaclyn interrupted, trying to explain Josh's unusual mood. "Since he's been on painkillers, his entire personality has changed." She nudged Josh's knee. "For the worse, unfortunately."

"Put your ill-tempered boyfriend to bed right after dinner, then, and we'll go to the bar and have a drink."

"Jazzy doesn't drink."

"We'll dance, then."

"She doesn't dance."

"I do too!" Jaclyn flashed back, eyeing Josh angrily.

"Not with Logan, you don't," Josh informed her.

"Okay, then." Logan laughed agreeably. "We'll sit and talk. Jazzy does sit and talk, doesn't she, Josh?"

"Knock it off, Logan," Brad interrupted. "If you keep teasing Josh and don't eat your dinner, our chef will quit and we can't afford to lose him with the hotel full."

"Sure thing," Logan said, picking up a knife and fork to finish his cooled dinner.

After the conversation returned to normal, dessert was finished and they were relaxing over glasses of wine, Logan continued his interrogation without preamble. "Where've you been all these years, Jazzy? Are you from California or are you a local lady?"

"She's been involved with a man from my area," Josh butted in, not giving Jaclyn time to think of an answer. "I kidnapped her and brought her here to escape his perverted life-style."

"It sounds like you're well rid of the man," Logan sympathized, undecided if Josh was serious or not. "What's your former boyfriend's occupation?"

"He runs a stable," Josh said with a bold smile, despite the sharp kick on the side of his shin.

"He does?" Logan turned to Josh. "He's a racehorse owner then?"

"Hardly." Josh laughed mischievously. "He just has a stable. Not the horses."

"How did you meet the man, Jazzy?" Logan directed his question directly to her. "Did you work in the stable?"

"She sure did." Josh burst out laughing.

"You're an equestrian, then, Jazzy?" Logan asked.

"Actually, I'm not," Jaclyn told him, finally getting a word in.

"You're not a horsewoman yet you work in the stable. I don't understand." Logan persisted like an investigator for the police department. "Hell"—he looked around with a knowing smile—"the only other men who have stables that I know of are . . ."

"I don't work for him," Jaclyn interrupted, cutting Logan off before he could finish. "He works for me. I earn my living as an independent entrepreneur, and he was my business manager when Josh and I met."

"Your friend has many interests, then." Logan thought awhile. "Maybe Brad or I know him. We both have lots of business transactions in the Southern California area where our main offices are situated."

"I'm certain you don't know my manager," Jaclyn interrupted, looking toward Brandy, who had sat quietly during the entire conversation.

"Logan would be more apt to know him than anyone else at the table tonight," Josh intruded again. "They both have the same interests. Women and money."

"My former manager worked through an answering service, so Logan wouldn't have met the man in person," Jaclyn reminded Josh with a sharp nudge for the second time.

"I guess they both do conduct a large share of their business over the telephone, don't they?" Josh took a bite of his filet and chewed slowly. "I think the man's main business is plumbing. I overheard Jaclyn say once that he services *johns* . . . or something like that."

"Why don't I tell you what's planned for the next few days," Brandy mentioned when the silence became uncomfortable.

"Excellent idea," Jaclyn told her, wishing she could wring Josh's arrogant neck. "I'm having too much fun on this vacation to even discuss my former business manager again."

Jaclyn listened enthralled as Brad and Brandy explained the many festivities lined up each day. Before she realized how much time had passed, Josh gripped her arm and said, "Excuse us, please. It must be at least eleven, and as much as I enjoy the company"—he looked at Logan pointedly—"I must get my sleep. Doctor's orders, isn't that right, Jazzy?"

"Not that I recall," she disagreed impertinently.

Josh deserved everything she could dish out after blurting out double innuendos one right after the other. "The only thing I remember is instructions to take your pills three times a day. Did he really advise you to get lots of sleep too?"

"He did!" Josh pushed his chair back, drew Jaclyn up by pulling on her fingers until she stood, and turned toward the door as if he were leading her.

"Good night, everyone." Jaclyn smiled happily. "This has been such a wonderful night that I can hardly wait to meet all of you again in the morning."

"Likewise, Jazzy," Logan called out, adding with a touch of real envy, "and sweet dreams."

"Sweet dreams to you too, Logan," Jaclyn returned in a soft voice.

She fled the dining room with her chin held high and Josh's fingers squeezing hers until they felt numb.

"Sweet dreams to you too, Logan," Josh mimicked when they were in the elevator alone and on the way to the fourth floor.

"I think we're too far away for Logan to hear you, Josh," Jaclyn told the irritated man beside her with an impish laugh.

"You're in big trouble now, Jazzy," Josh declared. He gripped her elbow and pushed her out of the elevator and down the hall as if he were forcing her. "I've just listened to one thousand dollars' worth of insults tonight, and you're going to pay for them starting in five minutes."

"What on earth do you mean?" Jaclyn demanded, standing aside as he unlocked the door to their room and thrust her inside.

"Five hours," Josh slammed the door shut, "at two hundred dollars per hour"—he headed directly toward the bedroom—"equals one thousand dollars." Tearing his tie and jacket off with equal disregard for their expense, he continued, "I want my money's worth now, starting with a Jazam!"

"Fine with me," she agreed in a sassy voice. "But I

guarantee that after the first two hundred dollars' worth I give you"—she kicked off her shoes and started to remove her dress—"you'll be ready to go to sleep and consider the rest a bad debt!"

"Try me, witch," Josh declared, kicking off the rest of his clothes with rising desire. "Try me and see!"

CHAPTER ELEVEN

Jaclyn finished undressing with serene confidence. It was obvious by Josh's raging temper that he was neither calm nor under control. When she attempted to pick up his hastily dropped clothes, he stopped her.

"Forget my damned suit and get your fanny on the mattress. I've had about all the frustration I can stand for one night without easing it right now!"

Jaclyn stopped him with a gentle hand on the tensed muscle of his biceps. "What's the matter with you, Josh? You've acted horrible all evening."

"You of all people should know what the hell's bothering me, Jazzy. Does it take more than a glance at my aroused body to make you aware of my need?"

Jaclyn automatically cast her eyes down. Josh was right. His arousal was evident and as tightly drawn as his lips, which thinned as his anger mounted.

"I realize you want to make love but I still don't understand why you're so upset with me." Her entreaty was soft and unconsciously sensual.

"You know damned well why."

"Other than a few sassy comebacks, which you deserved, I don't warrant one bit of your anger." Jaclyn stood up to him. "You were the ogre tonight, not me. You deliberately detailed everything about my profession but what you're paying me per hour!"

"That was just to throw Logan off. No one believed

a word I said," Josh scoffed. "They wouldn't dream I'd hire a call girl for a month. My reputation is that of a frustrated sculptor who has all the normal desires but ignores them to concentrate on his art."

"I distinctly remember Brandy saying you were a virile bachelor."

"I am. I'm also serious about my work and not interested in casual affairs. Think back and you'll recall that I said if I couldn't make love to the woman I wanted, I wouldn't make love at all."

Jaclyn gave Josh a scathing look. "The woman you want should see you now!" she scoffed. "What's that saying?" She tried to recall her brother's old joke. "Something about an aroused male has no conscience, I think. You, Mr. Kingman, are a perfect example that it's true."

"Explain that barroom comment, and it had better be good," Josh commanded.

"It is. Here you are bragging about your serious dedication to art plus your noble celibacy while standing before me aroused and demanding me . . . *a woman you didn't even know three days ago* . . . have sex with you immediately."

"True," he admitted without concern. "I haven't changed my mind either despite your sharp tongue. Get on the damned bed and do it now. I'm beginning to think you talk too damned much."

"I'd be happy to," Jaclyn agreed with surprising willingness after her verbal blasting. "I want to make love just as much as you do. The last two nights were the most perfect of my life."

"Why aren't you on the bed, then?" Josh demanded curiously. He was stunned she would admit she enjoyed the nights with him more than any others.

"Because you're still mad, and I won't let you spoil it for me tonight with your misplaced anger."

"Well, I'll be damned," he said, and smiled thoughtfully. "My little spitfire has a temper as well as the nerve to tell me what she will and will not do despite the fact I'm paying for one month's subjugation."

"You're paying for four weeks of sex only. There's a big difference," Jaclyn contradicted firmly.

"Not that big, Jazzy. Not that big. Now come here."

When she complied, Josh cradled her upraised face in his broad palms. He slowly lowered his head until his mouth brushed hers with surprising tenderness. Without parting her lips he kissed her until she sagged against him in total capitulation.

"That's wonderful," Jaclyn confessed, trying hard to catch her breath as she leaned into the inviting warmth of his arms. "I can't resist a man who kisses so exquisitely."

"It's easy when I touch lips shaped like yours and have a partner who responds to each caress as if it will be her last."

Jaclyn gave a satisfied sigh and snuggled close. She was hazily aware his callused hands lowered and drew her buttocks tight to his hardened flesh. Raising herself on tiptoe, she automatically responded to the pleasure of flesh against flesh by clinging to his neck as if she would never let go.

They stood naked for a long, long time, joined from breast to thigh in an intimate embrace that proved Josh's anger was verbal only. Jaclyn was continually amazed by his gentleness when he held her. Despite his anger he always took care to see his great size and overpowering strength never caused her physical pain.

"Please don't be mad anymore," she pleaded softly.

"My anger's not really with you," Josh whispered into the scented strands of hair over her brow. "It's directed at that damned bastard, Logan. God, Jazzy, with this bandage over my eyes I can't even see to insist he keep away. It ate at my guts all night to hear him trying to charm you."

Josh's voice was harsh, filled with intense male frustration that gave her insight into his surprising ill humor.

"You had no need to worry," Jaclyn replied softly, trying to soothe his masculine ego.

"I did!" Josh disputed her statement. "The male of the species is supposed to protect his female, yet all night you led me around like a baby. I should take care of you, not the other way around," he continued huskily. "I wanted to be the one who saw that you enjoyed your dinner, to show you around the area, to take you dancing, and to . . ."

"Hush, Josh. No man in the world could damage your male pride tonight or any other night. You're too self-assured and arrogant for that to happen."

"I'm not!"—he contradicted her with chin raised—"I . . ."

Jaclyn stopped his reply with a gentle fingertip over his lips. "Don't say another word. Your lack of sight doesn't inconvenience me at all. It shouldn't bother you so much either, since it's temporary only."

"My lack of sight doesn't bother me as much as knowing Logan's lurking in the background waiting to fly you to Palm Springs."

Jaclyn smiled, trying hard to bite back the urge to laugh at two grown men acting like boys. "As for Logan"—she made a vain attempt to reassure him—"the man has no more interest in me than he has in the Colonel."

"Don't believe it, Jazzy," Josh shot back with conviction in his voice. "Logan's intrigued. The man openly fawned over you all through dinner. He wants you badly. I could feel it across the table."

"You're mistaken," Jaclyn contradicted, shrugging aside Josh's ridiculous statement. "Absolutely wrong."

"I'm not!" Josh protested fiercely. "Even that wimpy little chef, Henri, has the hots for you."

"Don't be absurd!" Jaclyn scoffed. "You're talking insane."

"The hell I am. I heard every phony-accented word he gushed. It wouldn't surprise me a bit if he prepares a feast in your honor tomorrow."

"Not a feast," Jaclyn teased playfully. "Only a dessert. He promised to fix me a special English trifle because I mentioned I'd never tasted it before."

"I knew it," Josh stormed. "I think I should take you back to Laguna Beach and keep you locked in my studio. No one would dare enter it without my permission. Only then will I have peace of mind until my sight returns."

"Quit talking foolishly. Henri is like Logan. They're both just trying to make me feel welcome."

"How the hell would you know how a man feels and thinks around you?"

"I don't," she admitted, "but I do know Henri is only being kind, and Logan is an honorable man who would never attempt anything while I'm committed to you. He assured you of that himself."

"It doesn't make any difference what he said," Josh complained bitterly. "Knowing that good-looking devil is waiting around in the background doesn't help my peace of mind one bit."

"Don't worry about me." Jazzy put her arms around Josh's waist and hugged him affectionately. "One of my good points is that I'm totally faithful to the man I'm with."

"One hour at a time?" Josh brought up bitterly.

"One hour, a month, or a lifetime. It makes no difference," Jaclyn whispered, resting her face contentedly against the warm flesh of his hair-covered chest. "I'll never look at another man as long as I'm with you."

"Is that true?" Josh demanded in a drawl tinged with suspicion.

"Have faith," Jaclyn soothed, forcing her voice to remain cool. "I'll be as devoted as any woman who's really in love with her man could be."

"I couldn't ask for more," Josh moaned, overcome by the soft pressure of her full breasts and smooth abdomen brushing his taut flesh.

Jaclyn snuggled closer, her eyes glowing with love. She had known for years she was as bound to the man holding her as any wife could ever be.

"Look at me, Jazzy," Josh demanded as she buried her face beneath his chin and squirmed to get closer. "Look at me, honey." He was on edge, filled with sensual energy waiting to be expended in the woman he held.

Jaclyn reluctantly withdrew her face from the warmth of his chest, lifting her heavy lashes to glance upward.

"Good," he murmured in a hoarse voice when she obeyed. "Now watch my mouth descend to take your lips as my body will soon possess yours in the act of love."

Jaclyn stared, shutting her eyes only when his features blurred, and she felt the power of his lips ignite the same miraculous response as always.

Seconds after his mouth took hers she was lying on smooth sheets warm and safe beneath him. It happened so fast she wasn't aware who led whom to bed. His lips seared, working up and down her body until tears gathered in her eyes and she whimpered his name.

"Josh. Ooh, Josh!"

He reluctantly tore his mouth from hers, pausing when he heard her plaintive plea. His muscles tightened with the effort of not continuing his intent to singe each inch of her responsive skin.

Jaclyn lifted her luminous gray eyes to look at him, observing his smile broaden as if he shared her feeling.

"It's beautiful, isn't it, Jazzy? This magic we feel each time we touch."

"Yes, Josh. It's the most beautiful magic in the world," Jaclyn agreed in a throaty murmur.

It was heaven to see him in the softly lit room. Not once had they made love in the dark. She needed the sight of him almost as much as she needed his touch.

Josh positioned himself above her and comfortably placed his legs between her thighs before fiercely demanding she answer his intimate probing.

"Do you feel like this with all the men who share your bed, Jazzy?"

"No, Josh," she told him truthfully. She reached to pull his head down, whispering against his mouth. "This special enchantment happens only with you."

All the while they talked Josh's hands never stilled, running from her throat down the length of her legs. He explored the lush fullness of her breasts over and over, cupping them tenderly while teasing the nipples until they were erect, enticing peaks.

He stroked across the softness of her stomach to the blond feminine curls below, where his fingertips lingered and explored. With gentle expertise he probed and circled until she moved against his hand, demanding he fill the throbbing warmth with his rigid arousal.

Josh refused the silent plea of her outstetched arms and silken legs clenching his sides. He stilled the mute demand for satisfaction by deliberately extending her enjoyment. It was as if he were trying to imprint her aroused image in his mind and wanted her to stay that way forever.

When his mouth lowered to encircle a taut nipple, she curved her hips upward, parting her knees with impatient insistence that he fill the void that ached for his deep, deep penetration.

"Please, Josh. Please," she cried out, digging her fingernails into his shoulders.

Finally, when Jaclyn thought she'd die, Josh came down on her. He eased forward until her buttocks lifted to meet him, yet his mouth never stopped the hungry sucking motions on her breast.

"Josh! Ooh, please," she begged. She was out of her mind with the double pleasure of his thrusting body and the moist tip of his tongue stroking her sensitive breasts at the same time. "It's too much!"

"How many men have thrust deep inside you the same way I am, Jazzy?" Josh demanded against her breast in a voice that went straight to her soul.

"None!" Jaclyn cried out, clutching his finely shaped head with fingers that trembled.

"Tell me, witch," he demanded. "Tell me how many men have felt your tight warmth surround their bodies while tasting the heaven of your full breasts?"

"Only you, Josh. No one has ever done it to me like this," Jaclyn whimpered. "Ooh, please!" she begged, unable to continue.

"Please what?" Josh insisted in a guttural voice.

"Please, more . . ." Jaclyn broke off when he moved sensually, filling her with his great size.

Josh raised his head from Jaclyn's swollen breasts, took her wrists, and flattened them on the sheet each side of her face. As he started the rapid driving motions that tested his control to the ultimate, she matched his movements thrust for thrust.

He teased and taunted, bringing her to an ecstatic

peak, then pausing until she calmed down enough for him to begin the same erotic thrusts once more. Again and again he did this until she lay helpless beneath him, calling out his name over and over in a broken plea. "Josh!" she whimpered. "Oh, Josh!"

"Josh what, Jazzy?" he commanded in a voice filled with power as he slowly eased his hips forward. "Tell me what you want!"

"Josh, I—I . . ." She couldn't finish. It was impossible to even think, her senses were so overpowered by the man not only above but inside her as well.

"Tell me what you want!" he demanded again, slowly pulling back to the limit.

As Josh's hips started to move forward, grinding against Jaclyn's once more, shock waves began to flow through her trembling body. Satiny strands of her hair spread in tousled waves across the pillow as her head turned side to side and her softened lips involuntarily parted to speak.

"Tell me what you want, Jazzy," Josh insisted, raising her hips off the bed. "In explicit terms and now!"

Jaclyn told Josh what he wanted to hear, leaving nothing unsaid. With explicit detail she cried out her desires, never dreaming it would be so easy. Once started, all the words she'd only said in her dreams spilled out without concern. Josh was hers and there was no embarrassment. Letting him know how much she cared seemed the most natural thing in the world.

"Beautiful, Jazzy," Josh moaned into the hollow between her shoulder and neck. He gave her what she craved and more. Her erotic sighs of pleasure were so arousing he found it nearly impossible not to release his tightly controlled need for fulfillment but held off. There was more to come. He wasn't finished with her sexual education yet.

"I—I need you, Josh. I always have," she blurted out unconsciously.

"I know it, honey," he whispered huskily, shuddering when she moved beneath him. "It's so damned sensual to hear you express that need in your throaty voice. To realize you're honest enough to declare those wants to me without inhibition will remain in my mind for months to come."

Jaclyn clutched Josh's shoulders, ready to tell him how replete she felt despite the fact he was still hard inside her. She opened her eyes, staring through heavy lashes when he unexpectedly gathered her close and shifted positions.

"What are you doing?" She was so content it seemed too much effort to even speak.

"Hang on tight and see," Josh told her in a rasping voice as tightly controlled as his movements. With their bodies still entwined he rolled her over, settled her buttocks comfortably atop his hips and smiled.

For a moment Jaclyn's senses swam with the intensity of emotion that surged through her veins. Was it possible to feel a reawakening of desire so soon? It seemed incredible that physical need flooded her mind and body once again. She must be insatiable for the man.

To look down at his handsome, intelligent face and study the picture he made with his head pillowed and broad shoulders glistening from the stress of such vigorous lovemaking tore at her heart. She reached out her hand to rest tenderly over his heart. The erratic beating passed through his chest into her palm as her love flowed unknown back to him.

"This position can bring a woman extreme pleasure, Jazzy," Josh explained in a ragged voice as she adjusted her knees along his hips.

"I've already experienced extreme pleasure," Jaclyn

admitted, staring at him with languorous eyes. She moved and in doing so experienced what he meant. "I—I don't think I c-can handle any more," she stammered.

Josh gripped her hips gently and slowly began to ease her up and down as he spoke.

"W-what are you doing now?" Jaclyn stammered foolishly, aware of a mounting urgency returning with each motion. "Oh, Josh, this feels so good!"

"For a high-priced call girl," Josh mocked, stopping his actions, "who has undoubtedly tried every position man's inventive libidinous nature could come up with, you seem surprised by my actions."

Jaclyn refused to answer, wanting to view Josh's face instead as she sat still. She was enthralled by his expression when his hands lifted to cradle both breasts. His mouth softened when she leaned forward, pressing her soft flesh into his palms. He broke into a wide, satisfied grin as she began to slowly squirm above him.

"Why don't you control the motion from now on, honey," he moaned, clutching her buttocks as she moved once more. "I'm afraid our first bout is about to come to an abrupt end."

An apt student, Jaclyn did as Josh suggested until she felt the first spasms of his pulsating flesh deep inside her. That same exquisite pleasure experienced for the first time three days earlier returned, flooding through her body until she collapsed across his chest, spent, fulfilled, and very, very weary.

"I think you're right, Jazzy," Josh murmured into her ear thirty minutes later. He lay curled around her smooth back with her softness curved into his form in a perfect fit. "You really are."

"About what?" Jaclyn murmured softly. She was so tired she felt as if she could sleep forever.

"One ecstatic hour loving you is enough for me tonight."

"I told you so."

"I know," Josh complained, annoyed by his sudden lack of energy. He hugged her close, resting his palm beneath her beautifully shaped breasts. "I must be getting older."

"We all are," she returned, unconcerned. "Every day of our lives."

"Agreed," he mumbled into her hair. "But you aged me more tonight than time ever could. I never dreamed one dainty female could put so much loving into sixty minutes."

"I warned you," she yawned, burrowing deep into the pillow. She was too sleepy to remind him she hadn't done a thing. He had been in charge of their lovemaking from the beginning to end and she was nothing but a willing pupil.

"You did but I didn't believe you," Josh admitted with reluctance.

"Just wait and see what I do to you on Christmas," she warned, yawning again, and pondering that that should keep him quiet until morning.

"Shut up, Jazzy." Josh yawned back. "I've still got plenty of ideas for Christmas Eve."

"It's Christmas Eve now and I'm finished. Go to sleep, Josh," she whispered, barely awake.

"Good idea," Josh conceded, unaware she didn't hear a word he said.

Jaclyn slept soundly for eight hours until a steady knocking on their door awoke her.

"Darn," she moaned, slipping out of bed. She walked to the closet for her robe, smiling at the thought Josh hadn't allowed her to wear a nightgown once during their three nights together.

"I'm coming," she moaned when the pounding persisted. With one hand holding the low neck of her robe closed, she opened the door and peered around the edge.

Standing impeccably dressed and wide awake was a waiter waiting to enter the room with his laden cart. Thinking Josh had arranged for breakfast in their room, she led the man into their bedroom and stood aside as he set their table complete with a fresh red rosebud beside her plate.

"Compliments of Henri, mademoiselle." The waiter bowed, trying hard not to stare at Jaclyn's tousled beauty or the large man sharing her bed in an obvious state of undress. "Henri fixed a special breakfast for you to enjoy in your room."

Jaclyn nodded, too dumbfounded to say anything other than thank you as she let him out the door. She returned to the bedroom to find Josh sitting straight up in bed with his back ramrod-stiff against the headboard.

"What did I tell you last night?" he complained, rubbing his bristled chin thoughtfully. "That damned little banty rooster is hot for you after one short introduction."

"Don't be silly," Jaclyn scoffed, thinking a cup of hot coffee and a hearty breakfast sounded wonderful no matter why it was delivered.

"I'm not." Josh scowled. "What is this fascination men have for you? Do you pass out business cards behind my back?"

"I wouldn't have to," she teased, lifting up the coffeepot lid to inhale the pungent aroma. "I could hand them out right in front of you and you couldn't see what I was doing."

"A good night's sleep didn't curb your tongue any," Josh shot back, smelling the coffee with as much interest as Jaclyn. "What'd Henri send up? I'm starving."

"Just a second," Jaclyn reached for a lid, "I haven't uncovered the dishes yet."

"I hope it's not a poached egg. I hate them."

"You heard the man," she sassed. "It's my special breakfast, so you'll eat what's here or order your own."

Jaclyn set the lids aside and stared. "My gosh, we have two of the largest, fluffiest omelets I've ever seen. Each one is piping hot and stuffed with crab meat, fresh mushrooms, cheddar cheese, and fresh herbs with chives."

"Sounds delicious," Josh exclaimed, leaning forward to inhale the aroma. "Smells good too."

"Swing your legs over the edge of the bed and we can eat side by side," Jaclyn urged, pulling the table in place.

She settled beside him, poured them each a cup of coffee, and handed Josh his first. It was black, the way she knew he liked it.

"There are also fresh fruit cups containing strawberries, sliced kiwi fruit, bananas, and peach slices." Jaclyn plopped the most delicious-looking strawberry into Josh's mouth and smiled.

He looked like a mussed up little boy eating the fruit until you noticed his brawny, masculine upper torso and heavy beard.

"Do you want a hot buttered blueberry muffin, wheat toast and jam, sweet roll, or flaky fresh croissant?"

"One or two of each will do." Josh gave her a wide grin before turning to pierce the fat omelet with his fork. "I'm a mighty hungry man."

"I'm surprisingly hungry too." Jaclyn smiled indulgently, admiring the careful way Josh had mastered eating without dropping a bit of food.

Jaclyn sighed, enjoying each delicious bite. There

was no need to tell Josh about Henri's single red rosebud or he'd be moody again.

"After breakfast we'll both feel better."

"You felt pretty good to me last night," Josh teased, taking the buttered croissant Jaclyn handed him. "I doubt very much if this meal will make you feel one bit better to me at all."

"Don't start that again," Jaclyn scolded. "I think we can get through the day without bedroom hi-jinks to start it."

Josh smiled, sipped his coffee smugly, and refused to comment yes or no.

An hour later Jaclyn stood up and looked with amusement at the messy table with their empty plates and serving dishes, then back to the tumbled bed. The man had been hungry all right! Hungry for her and food with equal enthusiasm.

She turned to Josh, who lay on his back with a satisfied expression on his face.

"Is it normal to make love as often as we do?" she asked softly. Her body still tingled in the aftermath of his last possession. Surely no other man could equal his stamina.

"How the hell would I know?" Josh laughed. "You're the expert, not me."

"I work by the hour. One man right after the other, so I don't know anymore than you do, smarty," Jaclyn sassed, grabbing her robe and heading toward the shower.

She was used to Josh's sudden outbursts now and was getting to be an expert at ignoring his double-edged put-downs.

"Don't go away," he called out, aware the moment she started to leave.

"Why?" She hesitated, glancing over her shoulder to see what he wanted.

"Before we shower and get dressed, I want you to phone my protégée."

"But isn't she in Paris?"

"I don't remember telling you that," he said quietly.

"You mentioned it," she lied in a calm voice. "Otherwise how else would I know?"

"I was wondering that myself," Josh broke in smoothly, rubbing his whiskered chin in deep concentration.

Jaclyn glared at him, resenting his ability to recall everything she said. Surely he didn't have a photographic memory? Was it only three days ago that she thought herself above that kind of deception? Once started, her untruths appeared to have escalated until she couldn't remember what she'd heard, much less what she'd replied in return.

She looked at the bedside clock, hoping to put the call off until she felt a little more composed. "Isn't it the wrong time to phone anyone in France?"

"There's a nine-hour time difference, so it will only be around seven in the evening," Josh pointed out without concern. "I've been thinking about Brad's offer to commission her and think it would make a great Christmas present for the kid."

The kid! Jaclyn fumed inwardly, giving Josh a scathing glance. *Is that what he thought she was? Some darned kid.* For three nights she'd been acting very much the consenting adult female.

"Call her now," Josh insisted.

"Okay," Jaclyn agreed, laughing inwardly when he told her the number. If there was anything she was certain of, it was her own phone number.

Jaclyn dialed carefully, annoyed the call went right through before she had time to think. Her mind reeled as she planned the best thing to say when the phone continued to ring unanswered in her empty Paris apartment.

"Hello. Is this Ms. Howard?" she asked in an innocent voice.

Jaclyn could hardly keep from laughing at the silence on the other end. She ignored Josh's hand slashing through the air trying to get her to give him the phone. While the rings went on without pause, she carried on a one-sided conversation that completely deceived the man on the bed.

"Yes, Lerisa," she continued in her sweetest voice. "You did say you were Ms. Howard's good friend, and she's in Eze for the holidays. Would you please tell her Mr. Kingman called when she returns?"

Jaclyn turned to make certain Josh was listening, then said in French a soft thank you, *"Merci."* She hung up the phone feeling very smug about outwitting Josh once more.

"Your protégée is in Eze," she told him, biting back laughter at his grim face.

"I'm aware of that," Josh grumbled. "I heard every word you said. I also wanted to talk to Lerisa myself, but you refused to hand me the phone."

He threw the sheets back and stood up. "She's in Eze. What a bleak place to spend winter. The Eagles' Nest, they call it. A hilltop fortress where royalty and wealthy authors spend the summer and artists, wealthy and otherwise, flock to paint the sunsets. This is the wrong time of year to see the maximum beauty of the changing light and the reputed unmatched soft colors of dusk."

"Whether it's the wrong season or not, she's there and her girl friend doesn't know when she'll be back."

"You can help me find her a Christmas gift today, then I'll express mail it with a note included about Brad's offer. That will have to suffice for now."

Jaclyn turned away, desperately fighting back the urge to giggle. First she phoned herself and now she had orders to shop for her own Christmas gift. Her scheme for seduction was fast turning into a slapstick comedy.

Before she could beat Josh to the shower, the phone rang and Brandy's happy voice wished her and Josh a Merry Christmas Eve.

"I have an invite for each of you. Brad wants Josh to meet him and Logan in the gym for a massage and workout, and I want you to join me in five minutes for a relaxing hour in my private spa. Okay?"

"That sounds wonderful," Jaclyn returned. After the last three nights' unaccustomed bedroom activity, she could use time alone to relax her muscles and prepare for the day ahead.

"Let me check with Josh first, Brandy, although he did mention something about going down for a shave before we walk to town."

Jaclyn found Josh already finished with his shower and in surprising agreement with the offer. His open eagerness to meet Logan after last night's anger made her extremely wary.

"You're certain Logan will be there?" he asked for the second time after she returned from telling Brandy good-bye and had stepped past him to take her shower.

"Yes, I'm certain," she insisted, soaping her body thoroughly before rinsing under the warm spray. "Why the sudden urge to see a man you were openly rude to last night?"

"I'm in the mood to brag a little."

Jaclyn stepped out of the tiled stall and grabbed a towel, giving him a stormy look. "You wouldn't dare!" she scolded, aghast.

"I would," Josh told her smugly, dressing in the

sweat clothes she had laid out. "I'll relish telling that bastard what he missed last night. I know damned well he's never had a woman as good as you, and he's hired the best."

"He has?" Jaclyn asked in a startled voice. She slipped into bra and panties. "He's such a handsome man I'm amazed he'd ever have to hire a woman to get sex."

"He didn't have to," Josh returned, as if she were stupidly naive. "He wanted to. There's a difference."

"How?"

"Logan's a busy man and occasionally gets tired of the expected dating routine prior to having sex the normal route. When he does, he phones up a service like yours and pays for what he wants. He says it's less bother and cheaper in the long run. Mainly though, it takes less time when he's too involved in his work to want anything more than sexual release."

"How horrible," Jaclyn chided. She was shocked at Logan's attitude, completely forgetting her role with Josh.

"That's a ridiculous statement coming from a hooker," Josh shot back, zipping the front of his navy sweat suit. "I never agreed with Logan until meeting you. Now I'm thinking I missed a hell of a lot of fun. I put up with years of frustration unnecessarily just because I didn't want paid sex."

"I don't want to hear about it!" Jaclyn stormed, pulling on a maroon jogging outfit with stripes on the sleeves and pant legs like Josh's. "Let's go," she urged, taking his arm in a firm grip.

"Hey," he yelped with a deep laugh. "You're hurting my dainty arm."

"You deserve it, you brawny beast," Jaclyn fumed, rushing him from the suite. "I personally think you, Logan, and the entire male race are sick."

"Look who's talking," Josh scolded, pulling the door shut behind them. "Take us, for example. You're a hooker selling and I'm a john who keeps the country's economy on a firm footing by buying the merchandise."

Jaclyn tugged him into the elevator, sorry there wasn't a policeman to witness his illegal discourse.

Not about to be stopped, Josh continued in a clear voice. "I'm really pro-American, too, by not spending my money on a foreign import." He laughed as if he'd told the greatest joke in the world. "You are a product of the good old U.S. of A., aren't you?"

"Shut up, Josh! This is Christmas Eve and I thought you'd show a little reverence today."

"I still think it's funny." He continued to smile. "You just don't have a good sense of humor."

Jaclyn ignored Josh, gave Brad an effusive welcome when he took his arm at the men's gym, and walked on. She was glad to end their conversation. It was good riddance for the next hour, she thought, rushing down the hall to meet Brandy. Josh was acting more like a chauvinistic idiot each day.

"You look like a woman with a glow on, Jazzy," Brandy greeted her when she opened the door to the lavish spa Brad had built for her private comfort.

"Your eyes express a lot of happiness today also, Brandy," Jaclyn teased warmly, looking around with awe. They were completely alone in a gorgeous room with every device to make a woman feel pampered and help her keep fit.

"They should. After three years of marriage Brad still chases me like he did before the wedding. It's a wonderful feeling for a woman to be physically desired and loved by the man she cares for above all others."

"I know what you mean." Jaclyn bowed her head. "At least about being desired physically."

Brandy gave her a thoughtful look. "If it won't embarrass you, I always soak in the Jacuzzi in the nude." She handed Jaclyn a terry robe and showed her a closet to hang her clothes. "There's a swimsuit your size in there if you prefer to be more modest."

"Actually, no," Jaclyn confessed. "Not this time anyway. For some reason these last few days have changed my life-style and my personality. I've shed my shyness along with my inhibitions."

Brandy removed her robe, exposing a sleek, beautifully shaped figure. No one would dream her petite form had given birth to chubby twins.

"The water looks heavenly," Jaclyn exclaimed.

"It is," Brandy answered, walking without embarrassment to the sunken tub and slipping into the foaming water. She relaxed with her buttocks on a seat formed into the pool, running her eyes up and down Jaclyn's voluptuous figure as she stood on the opposite side.

"Consider me nosy, tell me it's none of my business, or say butt out, but I'm dying to know about you and Josh. What's up, Jazzy?"

"It's hard to explain," Jaclyn answered, slipping into the warmth with a contented sigh. She shut her eyes a moment, expecting her former shyness to bind her tongue as it had in the past. Instead, she ached to share her actions with her new friend.

"For one," Brandy continued, "this bit about your hair puzzles me. Obviously seeing you undressed proves you're a true blonde, and I have a feeling you've never been a redhead. Right?"

"True," Jaclyn admitted. "You'll learn why I lied to Josh when I explain our relationship. I don't quite know where to start."

"At the beginning, please." Brandy gave her a reassuring smile. "If it helps, neither Brad nor I mentioned your engagement to Logan because we don't believe it's true. Josh would never commit himself without placing a token of his love on his fiancée's finger. Am I right about that, anyway?"

"You're right. We're not engaged," Jaclyn admitted with surprising ease. "Josh only told you that because I was embarrassed to learn he had friends here, and you would be aware we were sleeping together."

"That's certainly not a rarity these days," Brandy teased, to lighten her mood.

"Yes," Jaclyn agreed, looking at Brandy. "I know that, but it isn't for me." She smiled. "At least it wasn't until three days ago."

"What's the problem, then?" Brandy prompted, swishing her hands back and forth through the bubbling water. "Obviously you love Josh. Each time you look at him it's beautiful to see."

"Josh's lack of sight is the only reason I can let my feelings show."

"For heaven's sake, why? Josh cares for you or he wouldn't have acted like a jealous lover every time Logan spoke to you," Brandy raised her eyes expressively. "I swear, Josh's hackles even rose when Henri complimented your command of the French language and taste for his cooking."

Jaclyn lowered her lashes, trailing her fingertips along the smooth contours of the tub. She held back a moment, then spilled forth everything that happened from how she felt the first time she saw Josh to her abrupt scheme after overhearing her brother's conversation in Laguna Beach.

"Wow!" Brandy exclaimed. Her eyes were bright with mirth. "That's even worse than what I pulled on Brad in Las Vegas."

Before they knew it, an hour was up and each had

shared secrets they never dreamed they would tell another soul. Their friendship was fast and firm.

As they toweled off and dressed in preparation to leave, Jaclyn posed a question in a serious voice. "Brandy, could I ask you something really personal?"

"Sure what?"

"Have you and Brad ever . . ." Jaclyn's lashes fluttered for a moment. "Have you ever, er, had a Jazam?"

"A what?" Brandy questioned, raising one arched brow in amused contemplation.

"A Jazam. Josh says it's his favorite sexual position and I don't know what it is. He's getting more insistent each night, and I'm running out of excuses on why I won't Jazam him."

Brandy looked at Jaclyn's serious expression and giggled. "I never heard of it, and Brad and I have tried most everything. I'll ask him and let you know."

"Could you do it today? Josh acts like everyone but me does it all the time, and I'm supposed to be an experienced call girl."

"Don't worry, honey." Brandy patted her arm. "Brad will know. If he doesn't, Logan will. He's an experienced devil too."

"Thanks, Brandy," Jaclyn gave a sigh of relief. "Every time we make love I have to put off a Jazam. It's getting more awkward all the time since I don't know what the heck I'm protesting against, much less why."

"This has really been an hour, hasn't it?" Brandy smiled.

"Yes. But you're the lucky one. Our situations are so different. Brad followed you after your masquerade as a sexually frustrated woman and you ended up his wife. Your beautiful twins are proof of your happiness."

"They came exactly nine months to the day after we

were married," Brandy confessed with a knowing smile. She'd never forget Brad's virility that night nor the fact it had never lessened in the years since.

"Lucky you," Jaclyn sighed, wishing she could hold Josh's babies to her breast.

"What are you going to do when your month with Josh is up?" Brandy asked with a note of concern.

"Return to Paris, do a few finishing touches for my exhibit, and after that, who knows?" Jaclyn shrugged her shapely shoulders, then teased mischievously, "By then I'll probably be so in need of Josh's loving, I'll return to Laguna Beach and seduce him again. Only this time it will be as Jaclyn, not Jazzy."

"That should be a kick," Brandy tossed back impishly. She glanced at Jaclyn with shimmering eyes filled with laughter. "I don't foresee much problem, though, after you confess you're not only his mistress but his protégée as well. He seems equally intrigued with you both. To learn you're one and the same will blow his mind."

"I'm sure it will," Jaclyn admitted with a wry smile. "I'll also feel the force of his wrath in many ways. That's why I don't intend to tell him I was Jazzy."

"What?" Brandy questioned her decision. "What have you got to lose?"

"A few layers of skin when he tears off my hide!" Jaclyn laughed. "Josh has shown a ferocious temper these last three days."

"So what? He doesn't harm you physically, so let him rant and rave. That's what I do to Brad. If he gets carried away, I just give him a big kiss and we end up in bed making love. Either way I win."

"You're married, Brandy," Jaclyn reminded her softly. "That's the difference. I have no permanent tie to Josh at all and that's what makes this entire arrangement uncomfortable at times. I want it all. Every enduring bind possible to the man. Not just a few weeks in his bed and a hurried good-bye when it's over."

Brandy patted her hand sympathetically. "I think you're in for a big surprise, honey. If you think you fooled Josh into thinking you're a hooker and then come to his bed a virgin, he'd have seen through your scheme the moment he touched you, like Brad did me."

"I'm absolutely certain Josh didn't," Jaclyn told her in total sincerity. "I did everything I could to act the part of a call girl."

"That would be some heavy acting on your part," Brandy pointed out, taking in Jaclyn's wide-eyed innocent expression. "In addition to the obvious physical problem you're much too vulnerable and soft to fool the most inexperienced man, which Josh Kingman is definitely not."

"I swear he couldn't tell," Jaclyn persisted with a deep frown.

"You must be mistaken, Jaclyn," Brandy disagreed. She tilted her head back and laughed. "Now that I know your real name I'll have to be careful not to call you by it or Josh will really wonder what's going on."

"It's been a constant nightmare that I'd slip up myself," Jaclyn confessed. She gathered her things and started to leave when Brandy spoke up thoughtfully.

"Has it occurred to you that Josh might know full well who you are and be playing a game of his own?"

"Lord, no," Jaclyn returned, shaking her head back and forth. "Josh doesn't have the foggiest idea who I really am."

"Maybe. Maybe not," Brandy thought seriously. "Josh is a private man who has an offbeat sense of humor. He could very well be playing you at your own game and enjoying it immensely."

As Jaclyn reached for the doorknob, Brandy called out, "We're quite a pair, aren't we? A virgin wife of five years and a virgin hooker."

"Not anymore we're not," Jaclyn reminded impishly. She closed the door and thought of her active sensual relationship with Josh. How many times she . . . *wasn't anymore* . . . she'd lost track of after the first night.

CHAPTER TWELVE

"Come on, Jazzy," Josh urged, impatiently pacing the living area. "We have a long walk and lots of shopping to do this afternoon."

"I'm almost ready," Jaclyn called in, pulling her coat on over a jade-green angora sweater and trim-fitting slacks of the same vibrant color. She slipped on stylish walking shoes and left the bedroom with a wide smile. "Let's go."

"It's about time," Josh grumbled, acting like a typical male.

"That was really nice of Brad to offer us limo service anywhere we want during our stay," Jaclyn expressed gaily, overlooking his restlessness.

"Yes," Josh agreed. "I'm very lucky to have Brad's friendship." Pleased they were finally on their way, he turned his head toward Jaclyn. "I told him we'd phone from town for a ride back when we're finished."

"Excellent idea," she acknowledged gratefully. "Especially since I have a long list of gifts to buy. We can't be too late either, as I intend to dazzle everyone at tonight's festivities."

"The only person you need worry about dazzling is me," Josh warned her gruffly.

Jaclyn ignored Josh's harsh reply in order to follow his instructions explicitly. With his warm palm gripped tight in her hand, she left the hotel's bricked walkway and headed along Belleville Street. Her eyes were wide as she tried to take in everything each side of the road and still keep Josh from tripping.

"Can we come back after Christmas and go through the Royal London Wax Museum and into the Undersea Gardens as well?"

"Sure," Josh promised, holding her arm close to his side. "Since I've seen both, I'll be curious to hear your opinion of Madame Tussaud's figures plus the downstairs Tower of London display and the torture chambers."

"Are the chambers scary?" Jaclyn asked, turning back to glance at a sailboat skimming across the water.

"I couldn't sleep for weeks," Josh told her enigmatically.

Jaclyn checked his face, noticed a twitch at the corner of his mouth, and refused to comment. There was a sharp wind blowing off the inner harbor and she shivered despite her warm clothes and leather coat.

"Are you cold, honey?" Josh asked when he felt her tremble.

"A little bit," she said with a laugh, shoving her free hand deep in the pocket. "What I need is a long fur coat like the majority of women guests have."

"That sounds nice to you, Jazzy?" Josh asked with a thoughtful expression on his face.

"Gosh, yes," she exclaimed excitedly. "It's really interesting to see the different clothes people wear. The tour from California doesn't have a fur coat among them, yet I think every Canadian here is draped from head to toe.

"One reason is undoubtedly the colder climate in Canada, honey," Josh pointed out wisely.

"True," Jaclyn admitted, "but they look beautifully elegant whatever the reason." Her voice broke off as she thought how wonderful it must be to feel the soft warmth next to her bare skin.

"We should be getting close to the Parliament building," Josh interjected. "It will be on the opposite side of the street."

"We're almost across from it now." Jaclyn stopped to view it's grandeur thoughtfully. "I think I agree with Brandy. It's a remarkable structure, but I was totally entranced by last night's glittering spectacle. How many lights do you think it has on it?"

"Somewhere around four thousand," Josh answered, listening closely to the sound of traffic whizzing by. "Let's cross Government Street and go inside the Empress Hotel. I want to buy my protégée's gift there."

"Follow me," Jaclyn told him, watching for cars as they crossed the busy intersection and walked up the sloped driveway to the side entrance. "There are several stairs, Josh, then we'll be fine." Her hand gripped his arm firmly until they were inside. "My gosh, the place is packed," she whispered out of the side of her mouth.

"Always at this time of year. Some people make reservations years in advance for the holidays. Turn right at the registration desk, look down on the left side, and you should spot the shop I want."

"I see one exclusive-looking store," Jaclyn explained, walking toward it.

"This has to be it," Josh urged when Jaclyn hesitated. "Let's go inside."

"Wait a minute, please," Jaclyn asked in an excited voice. "I just have to stare at the silver-blue fox fur on display in the corner window. Oh, I wish you could see. It's so lovely."

"Describe it to me," Josh requested indulgently.

"First, it's the most gorgeous coat I've ever seen.

Second, it's full length with a wide collar you can pull up around your face and the natural fur shades from silver to dark blue-gray fading to creamy white stripes. And third"—she gave a sad moan—"it costs twenty-five thousand dollars."

"So?" Josh questioned her sudden loss of interest.

"So let's go inside. The price tag has dampened my fervor considerably."

Josh smiled at her lack of enthusiasm for a new coat when she found out how expensive it was. Entering the store, he knew just what he was looking for and didn't hesitate to inform the hovering clerk what he had in mind.

"I want to purchase your finest negligee and gown in black. Medium size should be fine."

Jaclyn stood speechless, overcome that he asked for night wear for her. Josh had never once, other than her sixteenth birthday, indicated he thought of her other than as Bruce's sister. An intimate gift like a sensual negligee was an intriguing change of outlook.

"We have five peignoir sets you might be interested in, sir," the woman told him, returning promptly and placing each on the counter. She glanced at Jaclyn, not quite certain what to do next, since Josh couldn't see.

Josh turned to Jaclyn, obviously not thinking his lack of sight a problem. "Would you please hand them to me one by one, Ms. Jones," he requested in a formal voice.

Jaclyn did as he asked, watching with interest as his hands held the silk. He felt the texture with long, sensitive fingers, carefully noting its style. Tracing across each inch of the skimpy lace bodice he touched the two wispy satin straps that held it up then set it aside.

Josh repeated this four more times in silence until he had completely brailled each gown and negligee.

"This will do fine." He handed the first set to the

clerk without asking the price before facing Jaclyn with a satisfied smile.

As the woman walked away to gift wrap it at his request, Jaclyn whispered, "It's blatantly sexy, Josh. Your protégée sounds like a serious art student more fitted to high-necked flannel."

"Don't you believe it," Josh corrected her. "Under her shy exterior beats a heart as sensuous as yours."

"How do you know?"

"Men's intuition," he told her smugly.

"That's the second time you've said that. Men don't have intuition. Only women."

"Want to bet on it?"

"Why?"

"Because you'd be wrong. Right now I can intuitively tell that you're jealous of my little protégée. You're also peeved because you aren't getting this sexy nightie, and you're even mad that I have the nerve to ask you to mail it for me after it's wrapped."

"I am not!" Jaclyn snapped, smiling inwardly at his error. *How could any woman possibly be jealous of herself?* Besides, she always wore sensual night wear and would love the gift. She hadn't had a flannel nightgown in years, though he didn't know it.

"You know," Josh pondered seriously. "I feel sorry for the poor little kid. All alone over Christmas with no one close to love her. It's sad when you think about it."

Jaclyn gave Josh a frosty glare. She was very tired of hearing him call her a kid! Unconcerned if anyone overheard, she turned to him and hissed through tightly clenched white teeth. "Aren't I the lucky one to have a lover like you?"

"You bet," Josh admitted, chuckling softly at her stormy reaction.

When the clerk returned and handed Jaclyn a sack

holding the lavishly wrapped gift, Josh surprised her again by calmly saying, "I want the identical gown wrapped to take with me."

"Same size and color sir?" the clerk inquired.

"Exactly the same," Josh explained, turning to Jaclyn to say in a precise tone, "This will be for you, Ms. Jones. You've been quite kind to assist me in my time of need."

"You sound like a stuffy butler calling me Ms. Jones," Jaclyn said, and giggled, when the woman walked away. "But I accept your gift, as I adore sensual black gowns." No longer mad, her voice softened as she touched his hand. "Thanks, Josh. I'll model it tonight."

"I can hardly wait." He planted a quick kiss on her soft mouth. "But I'm warning you now it won't be on you long once we get in bed."

"Shush," she scolded, looking around to see if they were being observed. She took him to the far end of the counter. "Wait here a minute while I go check out a sweater that caught my eye."

She left him, rushing into the private back room as if she had every right to be there. No way was she going to have two identical nightgowns.

"Miss," she whispered, when the woman looked up from placing the order on layers of tissue paper. She held her finger over her lips to warn her about speaking loud.

"I want to change this set for the cranberry-red one you have displayed in the window. Since Mr. Kingman can't see, he won't know I switched gowns on him."

The clerk gave Jaclyn a conspiratorial smile and hurried to do as she asked. When Jaclyn returned from the back room, she found Josh in deep conversation with the owner of the shop.

"Find anything you like, Jazzy?" he asked, hearing her approach.

"Everything," she teased, taking his arm. "But what I need to buy isn't here. Shall we grab our packages and leave."

"They'll be delivered and mailed, so we have nothing to do," Josh explained, thanking the owner.

"Actually I have one thing to do," she told him. "I dropped my handkerchief by the sweaters and have to return to pick it up."

Jaclyn rushed into the back room for the second time. "Make certain you mail the red gown and send the black one to our hotel."

Darned if she was going to get caught this time if someone saw her gift and mentioned the color.

Five hours later Jaclyn left the limousine with Josh in tow. They were both exhilarated by the long walk and the fun of shopping together for the first time.

Jaclyn was elated to find Betty a hard-to-get Cabbage Patch doll with red yarn curls, bright brown eyes, real baby clothes, and its own adoption papers. For Bobby she decided on an imported LAPD police car with a screaming siren and flashing red lights as its wheels propelled it across the room in code-three speed.

Unknown to Josh, at the Cowichan Trading Company, she bought everyone, from the babies to James and the colonel, authentic Cowichan Indian Sweaters. They were handmade by the Indians of Vancouver Island from wool carded, blended, and spun by themselves. That order thrilled the clerk and lowered her checking account by an astronomical sum.

For Josh she additionally purchased heavy socks and gloves, fur-lined Indian moccasins, and a symbolic carving she knew he could enjoy despite his lack of sight. At Hudson's Bay Company she couldn't resist buying Josh four soapstone sculptures made by the Eskimos. The true, simplistic lines of the massive walrus bull with ivory tusks, two mature cows, and one young calf she picked were beautiful. Each piece was labeled with the name of its artist and the community where it was made. She knew he would appreciate the skill in their making.

Jaclyn marched into their suite followed by Josh and a luggage carrier filled with gaily wrapped gifts. "It really looks like Santa Claus has arrived." she pointed out when the limo driver had placed the packages on every available table top in the living area and left.

"I can imagine," Josh commented drolly. "I never witnessed a woman buy so many things in my life."

"I do admit to blowing my budget for the entire next year," she said, and laughed, wiggling her sore toes.

"Fortunately," Josh told her, "I paid my housekeeper to shop for Bobby and Betty weeks ago. Brad and Brandy's gift, along with the twins', was shipped ahead as well as a painting for Logan."

"I can hardly wait to see your sculpture of the babies. I know it will be beautiful."

"What makes you so certain, Jazzy?" Josh pinned her down. "You're not familiar with all of my work."

"I looked around the studio a little."

"See anything you like?"

"You know me," she gave a false laugh. "I'm into bigger stuff than you do."

"I almost forgot that insult," he answered angrily.

Jaclyn smiled openly at Josh's temper, kicked off her shoes, and decided it best to change the subject.

"Why don't we relax for the next fifteen minutes, then get ready? I'm suddenly pooped."

"You rest," Josh prompted, forgetting his chagrin.

"I'll get cleaned up and dressed, then you can have the bathroom all to yourself."

"Sounds excellent," Jaclyn agreed with a weary sigh. She removed her coat, lay flat on the couch with her nylon-clad feet placed on a pillow, and shut her eyes. "Let me know when you're finished."

"Lazy wench," Josh scolded in a teasing voice on his way to prepare for their evening ahead.

As soon as Jaclyn heard water running and Josh's loud whistling in the bathroom, she grabbed the phone off the end table and called Brandy. "Tell me quick, Brandy, if Brad's heard of a Jazam. Josh is taking a shower and insists I give him one for his Christmas present."

"Sorry, Jazzy," Brandy sympathized in an amused voice. "When I asked Brad he started laughing and refused to say another word. I've never seen him so close-mouthed."

"Did he ask Logan?" Jaclyn persisted in a low voice when she heard the whistling stop.

"No. He clammed up and said a decent wife wouldn't be curious about such a thing."

"Oh, Lord," Jaclyn moaned, holding her hand over the receiver so Josh couldn't hear. "I wonder what on earth it is?"

"I don't know," Brandy said, and giggled. "But if you like it, tell me. I might surprise my suddenly stuffy husband with a few tricks of my own."

"Don't even say the word trick around me, Brandy." Jaclyn sighed in total exasperation. "I'm sick to death of anything connected with hookers including their language."

"I can see why," Brandy teased. "Hurry and get dressed. The party has already started in a big way."

"See you and thanks." Jaclyn set the receiver down and walked into the bedroom with a thoughtful frown.

An hour later, wearing the most glamorous dress in her wardrobe, she felt like a million dollars with one exception.

Josh's demand that she give him a Jazam the moment they return to their suite would be a constant worry. Darn him and his innovative positions. Why couldn't he be satisfied with regular old-fashioned lovemaking like any normal man would be?

"Will you fasten the tie for me, Jazzy?" Josh asked, coming up to her after she was dressed and had just finished adding a final spray of her favorite Joy perfume.

"Hold still," Jaclyn warned, concentrating on getting it straight.

"How the hell can I?" Josh demanded. "Your scent and the feel of this slinky evening gown you have on is driving me wild."

"You promised not to fool around until after th. party," Jaclyn reminded him in a stern voice.

"Only because you said you'd Jazam me," he reminded her with a devilish grin.

"Forget that and hold still or you'll look lopsided all night. Perfect," she said when his tie was straight.

Standing back, Jaclyn admired Josh in his black evening suit and formal white dress shirt. He looked so appealing and masculine she wanted to cry.

They entered the dining room arm in arm and were seated with a flourish by the attentive waiter.

"Too bad you can't see your woman, Josh," Logan exclaimed when they sat down.

"I'd like to, Logan," Josh told him in an even voice, turning to Jaclyn as if his eyes could see through their bandage. "I'd like to very much."

"She's a knockout, as is Brandy. You and Brad are lucky devils, believe me."

"We're aware of that," Josh and Brad agreed.

"I love your dress, Jazzy." Brandy complimented her. "The vivid red looks beautiful with your coloring."

"It wouldn't have two days ago," Josh interrupted.

"Why not?" Jaclyn asked in a miffed voice. She had always thought her skin tone went well with red.

"Red hair and a red dress would have clashed." Josh paused. "Or did you forget you're now a champagne blonde? I believe that's the name of the hair coloring you told me you used."

"I didn't forget," Jaclyn lied, between clenched teeth. "I just didn't think it was important enough to mention on Christmas Eve."

Well past midnight, Jaclyn entered their suite with Josh right behind her humming as if he had the world in his hands.

When he carefully locked the door and placed both hands on her shoulders, she turned into his arms with a cry, reaching out to draw him close. Her face rose, touching his lips to instigate a kiss of such tenderness it only hinted at the passion to come.

"It was wonderful tonight, Josh." She sighed and in a thoughtful voice said, "From the lavish meal . . ."

"Which you barely tasted," Josh interrupted, releasing her to remove his tie and jacket.

"Why did they have to tell me we were eating filet of reindeer?" Jaclyn shuddered as she kicked off her evening sandals and carefully placed them out of Josh's way. "All I could think of was Rudolph the Red-Nosed Reindeer."

"Reindeer is not uncommon up here, honey," Josh proffered. "Although I do think it's an acquired taste, since it's rather strong flavored."

"I don't care what it tastes like," Jaclyn protested. "I won't eat reindeer. It's almost anti-Christmas." She slipped off her evening sandals and turned back to add, "I did enjoy the carolers and their poignant medley of songs. Most of the women, including me, had tears in their eyes, they sang so beautifully."

"It was nice," Josh concurred. "Why don't you slip into something comfortable now."

"What?" Jaclyn asked, removing her necklace.

"Our bed!"

Jaclyn threw a soft pillow at his back and rushed into the bathroom. With a satisfied click she locked the door to finish undressing without being disturbed.

To her chagrin, after worrying all day and throughout the evening, Josh didn't mention a word about her giving him a Jazam. When she left the bathroom in her black gown, he gathered her into his arms with great tenderness and carried her to the bed.

Before Josh had time to give her gown more than a cursory touch, he had flung it aside and stretched his length beside her. They made love leisurely and with such worship it brought tears to her eyes. Instead of the frenzy of a rapid coupling he was slow and thorough, making her wait until she drew him between her legs with a pleading moan.

Only then did his kiss become demanding, equaling the force of his body joining hers with such exquisite pleasure she pledged her love over and over in silent reverence against his lips.

Time and time again during the night he drew her into his arms. Each time with more hunger than the last. He seemed to need her with a desperation equal to her own.

Christmas morning, Jaclyn and Josh were awakened by a loud, impatient pounding on their door. Jaclyn scrambled out of bed, pulled on the hastily discarded gown and negligee she had briefly worn for Josh earlier, and rushed to see who was there.

She opened it only to be pushed aside as Logan

burst in. He was dressed as Santa Claus complete with a sack of gifts, a long white beard, and flowing mustache. The devilish blue eyes peeking out and copper-colored eyebrows were a dead giveaway.

Logan walked straight to Josh, who sat braced against the headboard with a decided un-Christmas-like expression on his face.

"Ho! Ho! Ho! Santy's here with your gift." Logan scanned Jaclyn's lush figure, clearly outlined in her sensual night wear. He turned back to Josh and laughed suggestively. "By the looks of Jazzy's deshabille in her sexy black nightie and your indecent state of undress, I'd guess you haven't been a good boy this year and therefore don't deserve a gift. I'll keep it myself."

"Beat it, Logan," Josh told his friend gruffly.

Logan ignored him and gave Jaclyn a wicked leer. "I think I'll take Jazzy with me. Your woman looks decidedly better to me than old lady Claus and my group of weirdo elves."

"Get out of here, Logan," Josh ordered in a fierce voice. He turned toward Jaclyn. "Lock yourself in the bathroom until this maniac leaves. I don't trust him in this mood."

"You should see him, Josh." Jaclyn laughed joyfully. "Logan looks like a perfectly safe, nice old man with a fat belly and long white whiskers."

"He sounds like a pervert," Josh complained. "And those types can't be trusted around young women."

"Jazzy's safe," Logan assured him. "Though it's only because you can't see. She's the most delectable bit of feminine flesh to open the door to me yet this morning and I'm a mighty lonely man."

"Out, Logan," Josh commanded for the third time. He pointed his finger toward the door and frowned when he didn't leave.

"Wow! What a grouch." Logan laughed, placing a cellophane-wrapped basket of cookies, fruits, and nuts surrounding a bottle of imported Dom Perignon champagne on the bed next to Josh's hips.

He planted a loud smacking kiss on Jaclyn's forehead to annoy Josh, gave her a mischievous smile, and left as abruptly as he had arrived.

Jaclyn walked into the living room and returned with her arms filled with gifts for Josh. She set them on the bed and started to crawl back under the sheets when Josh stopped her.

"Hidden behind the couch, at my request, you'll find your gifts. Go get them and we'll open our presents together."

Jaclyn rushed in, staring in amazement at the huge box tied with the fanciest bow she had ever seen. Several more boxes were there along with a fuzzy white toy seal with limpid black eyes.

"Oh, Josh," she cried, rushing back into the bedroom. "I love my seal. He's darling."

"I thought you might enjoy him. I saw them when I was up here last year and bought each of the twins one."

As Jaclyn admired a tartan plaid skirt and top, Josh tore off the outer wrappings of his gifts. Within minutes everything had been opened but the large box. She was saving it for the last.

As Josh stroked his sensitive fingers over the smooth texture of the eskimo carvings, he listened to her excited squeals.

"I can't believe it!" Jaclyn exclaimed, pulling the fur she coveted in the display window over her negligee.

Throwing her arms around Josh's neck, she cried, "I love it. Oh, it feels so gorgeous."

"I know," Josh teased, stroking his hands up and

down the soft fur, though enjoying her feminine curves more than the coat.

She plopped the cuffed hat on her tousled hair and paraded around barefooted while chattering nonstop about the pleasure of receiving such a lavish gift.

"When we go down for brunch I'll be the most lavishly fur-coated woman in the hotel."

"Don't all mistresses have fur coats?" Josh teased.

"I don't have the slightest idea," Jaclyn sassed. "Nor does your insulting implication bother me in the least, Mr. Kingman. How or why I received it isn't important!"

"Only that you did, right?" Josh laughed at her surprising attitude.

"You bet!" she chuckled, coming back to bed to check out her other presents again. Wearing her coat, she looked at everything from perfume to jewelry, clothing to toys. Josh was a very generous man.

The rest of the day passed in a haze as they exchanged gifts. She received a dozen more presents and watched tears come to Brandy's eyes when Josh presented her and Brad the bronze of Betty and Bobby. There was no doubt his talent was unequaled in this generation.

A lavish buffet followed a private double-decker sightseeing tour around town. Everyone wore the raw black, gray, and white wool Cowichan sweaters Jaclyn had given them, and laughed at how funny they looked dressed alike.

There was folk dancing, bingo, group singing, music, and a general exchange of goodwill throughout the hotel. It was a wonderful day and Jaclyn couldn't remember being happier.

A week passed with surprising speed. Jaclyn and Josh visited his doctor twice, the Butchart Gardens, ate hot scones with thick cream and jam between sips of steaming tea, and bought souvenirs neither needed. During the day they explored the island, either walking through town or being driven further afield in the limo.

She couldn't believe it when the New Year arrived, and she and Josh once more attended a gala affair in the lounge.

After a late dinner Jaclyn whispered, "Brandy, did you tell Brad about me?" It was the first time they had a second to themselves all day.

"No. I kept my promise to wait until we returned to Palm Springs. Why?" Brandy asked curiously.

"I can't understand it. All three men have acted conciliatory to me for a week now. Even Henri rushed off without a word again after bringing me my own dish of pickled mushrooms. He barely answers now when I compliment him."

"I overheard Brad tell Henri to lay off," she confessed, adding with a touch of humor. "At Josh's instigation."

"Poor Henri," Jaclyn gasped. "Did Josh really do that?"

"Yes." Brandy nodded her head. "Your suspicions about their attitude change could be the effects of drinking too much New Year's Eve cheer," she said with a giggle. "Although now that you mention it I think they have acted strange all week. Why don't we forget them and indulge ourselves this one night of the year?"

"An excellent idea." Jaclyn laughed back, taking Brandy's arm and walking toward the bar, where the men sat huddled in deep conversation.

"We've been getting frowns from Brad and Josh all evening over our actions. Have you noticed, Brandy?"

"Yes." She chuckled unconcerned. "Look at Josh

now. He's more morose by the minute. Logan's the only one in a good mood."

Jaclyn and Brandy smiled at the men and sat down. They ignored Brad and Josh and accepted a glass of champagne from Logan while conversing happily about the twins' latest antics.

Their continued whispers and soft giggles as they persisted in talking privately didn't make either man any more pleasant as the evening progressed.

Hours later Jaclyn held on to Josh's arm with a firm grip as they stood looking at the lights across the harbor. She had matched Brandy drink for drink of expensive champagne until both Brad and Josh were openly disgusted and Logan looked on with amused eyes.

When the band started to play after a brief intermission, Jaclyn sentimentally decided there was no reason she shouldn't dance. "Come on, Josh." She took his hand. "I want to dance. I can lead you on the dance floor as well as I do around town."

"I'm not in the mood," Josh refused in a tight voice.

"I am," she sassed, breaking into a soft giggle. "So let's shake a leg."

"If Josh won't, I will," Logan offered hopefully.

"Okay," Josh concurred reluctantly, giving Logan a grim-faced nod as they left the window.

Jaclyn slipped into Josh's arms gracefully. She laid her face on his lapel and held him so close she could feel each muscle tense with his rigidly controlled anger.

"What the hell's the matter with you tonight, Jazzy?" Josh demanded through thinned lips. He bent to her ear, scolding harshly when she slumped against him.

"I think I'm in the mood for love." Her soft body

trembled with desire as she pressed her legs against his.

"You need to sober up," Josh growled. "You told me you don't drink, yet Brad practically had to hire another bartender just to keep your glass full. I'm damned disgusted by your actions, witch."

"You are?" Jaclyn cooed in a throaty voice. She placed her arms around his neck and snuggled closer. "I don't know why. You feel so big and powerful and warm and cuddly you could easily get any woman in the same mood I'm in. Though I'd scratch her eyes out if you tried it."

Jaclyn kissed Josh's haughty chin when he stopped in the middle of the crowded floor of the dimly lit lounge. Attempting to pull his head close to caress his lips, she hiccuped instead, found it hilariously funny, and started to laugh.

"That does it," Josh admonished in a fierce growl. "We're going to our suite immediately. The way you're acting tonight I have half a mind to take back your Christmas present."

"What's the other half of your mind going to take?" Jaclyn teased, finally succeeding in drawing his head down to give him a long, hungry kiss. Despite his obvious annoyance, she could feel his body harden against her softness in a deep, involuntary sexual response.

"Shame on you, Mr. Kingman," Jaclyn scolded with a knowing smile. "I'm aware now what it is the other half of your mind wants to take." She rubbed his nape and whispered seductively against his neck, "The same thing it's been taking night and day since I walked into your home in Laguna Beach."

"That does it, Jazzy!" Josh stormed for her ears alone while holding her with a punishing grip. "We're leaving if I have to drag you out of here myself."

"Go ahead, but you won't make it," Jaclyn taunted impertinently. "You'd run into a wall before we got out of the lounge."

"Shut up, witch," Josh grumbled, deciding he needed Logan's help. "You've been shameless since you gave me the longest New Year's Eve kiss on record in Canada. When all the male guests started cheering and stomping their feet, I damned near died of embarrassment."

"I doubt if you've been embarrassed by anything in your life," Jaclyn retorted unperturbed. "Besides, it was fun. You kiss better than any man I know."

"You're impossible tonight," Josh seethed. "I'm going to have Logan take both of us upstairs this minute."

"Yummy. Yummy. A three-way swing with you and Logan," Jaclyn purred in her lowest voice. She ran a polished fingernail along the edge of Josh's clenched jaw and up around his ear. "What a way to start the New Year."

"That does it," he stormed back in a fine temper. "I don't care how many walls I run into. We're going to our suite until you sober up and act like a lady."

"But I'm not a lady," Jaclyn giggled. "I'm a . . ."

Josh's palm over her mouth effectively cut off her next words as he spun her around, stood directly behind her, placed his arm around her waist, and marched her off the dance floor like a comedy act.

Jaclyn's eyes twinkled with happiness. She had never had so much fun in her life. She smiled at everyone's amused expression and carefully guided Josh through the crowd of dancers straight to their friends.

"Good night, all, and happy New Year. It's been a blast. See you in the morning, Brandy, for our daily workout."

She nodded good-bye, ignored Josh's angry mutterings, and stalked off with her chin held high and blond hair swinging in loose waves across her bare shoulders. When they were in the hall, she moved aside to take his arm and proceeded to their room without saying a word.

New Year's morning Jaclyn gave a weary sigh. Her temples refused to quit throbbing and she deserved every miserable ache. She lay with her head resting on Josh's warm chest, snuggled in the protection of his strong arms while waiting for the pain to subside.

Unfortunately, she had total recall of her actions the night before. Josh was right. She had been shameless.

Where was the shy art student who wouldn't even talk about men? Gone forever, she thought. She was now an overly confident imbecile with a bold tongue who was stupid enough to tell Josh she'd be pleased to participate in a three-way swing with his friend just for the pleasure of making him jealous.

Hoping Josh had forgotten her disgraceful conduct, Jaclyn pressed a kiss into the hair-covered chest beneath her face. She trailed her hands lovingly down the planes of his body until she reached his hip bones, thinking he had the sexiest torso in the world.

Remembering what she'd done to soothe his anger when they'd reached the room brought a soft flush to her cheeks. She'd been more wild and sensual than she ever dreamed possible. Jaclyn's eyes softened wistfully as her hand started to explore his flat abdomen and sensed his immediate response.

She smiled. There wasn't a place on Josh's body she hadn't caressed with her mouth or lips during the last few weeks and last night had been the most special of all. When they'd finally fallen into an exhausted sleep, she'd noticed a touch of light as dawn started to break from the east.

It hadn't surprised her that Brandy missed their

early-morning exercise routine either. She and Josh both told her Brad was a virile, physical man, and she didn't doubt that they had a wonderful, loving night equal to her own.

"I have to return to Los Angeles today," Josh announced carefully, interrupting her pleasant memories with shocking news.

"Why's that?" she asked, pressing a kiss over his heart. She clung to his waist as a sudden premonition they would soon part entered her mind and wouldn't leave.

"I didn't want to say anything before, but I'm beginning to see flashes of light, and both the doctor I saw here and my specialist warned me to return the moment this happened."

Tears glistened in Jaclyn's eyes, spilling unseen down her cheeks until Josh raised her face to his lips. With great tenderness he kissed each salty drop away.

She sat up before Josh could speak, looking at him with concern. "Does this mean anything is wrong?" Her voice was filled with worry as tears of anxiety continued to trickle from her eyes.

"No, Jazzy." Josh soothed her. "It probably means I'm going to regain my vision before the doctors thought. It's the best thing that could happen. After this morning I don't think I could continue making love to you without knowing I'd soon see your beauty beneath me."

Jaclyn gathered him to her breast, overcome with happiness that he would be all right. She hadn't realized until now how concerned she was in the back of her mind that he might never recover his full vision.

"Oh, Josh," she cried poignantly. "I'm so happy for you. W-When do we leave?"

"I talked with Brad and Logan last night. Logan has a business meeting in Century City tomorrow morning, and he offered to let us ride down with him in his jet."

"What happens after that?" Jaclyn asked, holding her breath until he answered.

Josh withdrew from her hold and cradled her in his arms. "I'll be in the hospital for two or three days, and when I check out, the first thing I intend to do is . . ."

"What?" Jaclyn asked, waiting with bated breath.

"Everything I've done since we met," Josh teased. "All over again." He gave her a long tender kiss. "Only this time I'll be enjoying the sight of you while I'm doing it."

"I couldn't be happier for you," Jaclyn murmured truthfully. She thought ahead to her own change of plans. "I'll go visit Grandmother while you're in the hospital."

"Sure, Jazzy," Josh told her thoughtfully. He stroked her shoulder as if he would never tire of touching her silky skin. "Do what you want, honey, only make certain to be there when I come walking out of the hospital on my own."

"I'll be waiting," she lied. "Wherever and whenever you want."

Jaclyn couldn't believe how swiftly time passed after Josh told her he had to return to Los Angeles to see his specialist.

She stood alone, sipping her uncounted cup of black coffee in the hospital waiting room while waiting for the results of Josh's tests. The bandages were being removed for the final time, and the moment she was certain his sight was not impaired she would leave.

It had been a horrendous three days. She had bid Josh a hurried good-bye, not wanting him to know she was going to wait around. Instead of going to visit her make-believe grandmother as she told him, she had paced the hospital waiting room, haunted the nurses' desk anonymously, and pestered the staff about his condition.

Pledged to silence about her presence they sympathized and made no objection when she waited alone eighteen hours a day. She left only to go to a close-by motel for a few hours of exhausted sleep, a hot bath, and a change of clothes.

When the head nurse rushed up to tell her Josh was fine, his vision was clear, and there was no permanent damage, she bowed her head and thanked God for the answer to her prayers. Jaclyn praised the nurse and walked away, biting back tears of happiness that threatened to flood her eyes. Josh's total recovery was the most wonderful news in the world. Only one thing was left to do before returning to France.

Walking to a pay phone at the end of the corridor, she phoned the hospital she was standing in, asked to be connected with Josh's room, and forced herself to speak in a normal voice.

"Josh?"

"Hello, Jazzy," he answered in the throaty voice she thought the sexiest in the world. "I was waiting for your call. I'm well now, honey, and free to check out of the hospital tomorrow morning. I have a surprise for you."

"Let me tell you my surprise before you say anything more, Josh," Jaclyn interrupted, deliberately making her voice sound flippant. "While you've been on your back, so have I. Bugsy and I are together again and you know how it is?"

"I guess I should have answered with . . . *how's tricks?* . . . rather than hello," Josh remarked smoothly.

"Yeh. S-Sure," Jaclyn stammered, desperately fighting to keep her emotions under control.

"See you around sometime, Jazzy. Okay?"

She was too stunned even to answer. Josh didn't sound the least surprised over her betrayal or unhappy they wouldn't be getting together as planned.

"What about the money I owe you?" he asked calmly. "Where do I mail the check?"

"I'll send you my address once I get settled in a new pad," she lied. The last thing she wanted from the man was his money.

Jaclyn wiped tears from her cheeks with the back of her hand. Darn him anyway! She loved him until she was ill from worry and lack of rest, yet he was acting so unconcerned she could smack him. It was almost as if he expected her to leave and couldn't care less.

"B-bye now, Josh." She fought back the urge to rush to his room and confess who she was and beg forgiveness for her terrible deception. "It was a blast!"

"Yes, it was, honey," he agreed in a quiet whisper. "A real blast. Have a safe trip, Jazzy."

Jaclyn heard the phone click off as Josh hung up the receiver. She dialed Logan's hotel number knowing he would be waiting. He had promised to hang around and fly them from LA to San Diego before driving them up to Josh's home.

"Logan," she started without preamble. "Could you pick up Josh at ten tomorrow morning and fly him home without me along? I-I have to get back to work."

"Sure thing, Jazzy. Josh will be fine until you meet again."

"Good." Jaclyn bit her lip to keep from bawling her eyes out. "Thanks, Logan."

She hung up the phone with shaking fingers and rushed outside to a waiting cab. During the long overseas flight she wondered why on earth Josh would care if she had a safe trip when he wasn't even sad she left.

CHAPTER THIRTEEN

"I'm still flabbergasted about your painting," Lerisa told Jaclyn in a laughing voice as they entered a busy McDonald's in Paris. "When you break out of your shell, you do it in a big . . . and I do mean *BIG* . . . way!"

"Shush," Jaclyn chuckled. "Someone might hear you."

"They won't," Lerisa shrugged. "It's much too noisy in here." She fanned her breast as if overcome with desire. "Where on earth did your innocent mind fantasize up that hunk of manhood you shipped to California last week?"

"What makes you think the man's not real?" Jaclyn asked, carrying their hastily filled order to the front of the eating place.

"Easy." Lerisa lifted her eyes to smile at Jaclyn. "I specialize in nudes, not you." She leaned back with a mischievous smile. "Not one naked male has even resembled the looks of your hunk."

"You must meet Logan," Jaclyn told her friend. "You both have an outrageous way of getting your point across and the same outlook on life. In fact, his words to me when I mentioned you were, No virgins, please."

"Why'd he say that?" Lerisa inquired.

"He's of the mind that he couldn't handle the trauma of dating an inexperienced female."

"Sounds like my kind of man," Lerisa told her. "It should be a challenge meeting someone with my same views on the subject."

Waiting until Lerisa found two seats facing the sidewalk so they could people-watch through the large glass windows while eating, Jaclyn set the tray down. She divided the cheeseburgers, fries, and cokes between them without further comment.

"If Logan poses half as well as your fantasy man, I'll cover my apartment walls with nudes of him."

"I think he just might," Jaclyn said mysteriously.

"Phooey," Lerisa protested. "Believe me, no model I've ever seen, much less painted, is as big or as impressive a sight as your masterpiece."

"He is tall, isn't he?" Jaclyn admitted with a knowing smile before biting into her juicy sandwich.

"I wasn't talking about his height, Jaclyn, and you know it," her friend giggled between munching piping hot french fries. "Nor his breadth of shoulder or the size of his feet. God, he's a beautiful prototype of the male sex."

"He is that," Jaclyn admitted without further comment, aware she was driving Lerisa crazy with curiosity.

"I felt like I was invading his bedroom to see him sprawled across rumpled sheets in a semiaroused state."

"You weren't supposed to see him at all," Jaclyn reminded her. "If you hadn't barged in before I could drape him, he'd have been on his way to Bruce's house unseen. He'll stay there until after my exhibit and until I decide where I'm going to study next and get settled in a new place. He's my private fantasy and I have no intention of ever sharing him with anyone."

"I know and I don't blame you," Lerisa admitted without apology. "It's just that he's so gorgeous, Jaclyn. I think it's the best oil you've done. Even the title for it is super." She looked on wistfully. "If I had a Stolen Idyll like yours, I'd probably want to keep him to myself too."

"You would." Jaclyn smiled affectionately. "I guarantee it. Now hurry up and eat."

"I can't." Lerisa paused between bites to close her eyes. "I keep thinking of the virile male you depicted. He's handsome, erotic, sexy as hell, and his vivid blue eyes practically beckon a woman straight into his bed."

"Eat!" Jaclyn scolded, amused by her friend's comments.

"Since this school session is finished and there's no telling when we'll meet again," Lerisa shot a haughty glance. "I thought you'd have at least taken me to the best-known outdoor cafe in Paris for our farewell luncheon."

"In April with rain threatening any minute? Forget it. Besides, Cafe de la Paix is out until after my exhibit. I spent a fortune on gifts and plane fare last December plus all the unexpected shopping I've done the last few days. It left me nearly broke."

"A normal state of affairs for me despite an excellent monthly inheritance," Lerisa admitted unhappily.

Jaclyn sipped the last of her coke, grabbed her purse, and started out the door. "If you promise not to tell anyone about my painting, I will take you to Fauchon's for some chocolates."

"Okay." Lerisa laughed at being blackmailed. "Walking through the most famous, not to mention most expensive, food store in town won't be too bad an ending to our day as long as I get to pick out what I want."

"Fine," Jaclyn agreed with a smile. "First I want to cut over on Rue Meyerbeer to Belligne's. I intend to buy some very sensual underwear."

"I thought you were going to an art exhibit not an orgy," Lerisa spoke up, noticing a soft rose color tinge Jaclyn's cheek.

"I want to be prepared." Jaclyn laughed. "Who knows what other offers I might get if my paintings don't sell?"

The rest of the day and the following morning passed in a flurry as Jaclyn closed her apartment, grabbed her bags, and rushed to the airport. She arrived at Orly in plenty of time for her noon flight, giving a sigh of relief that she was on her way at last.

With the seat back and her eyes closed, she thought of the coming meeting with Josh. It was going to be awkward to act reserved around a man she had been intimately involved with only four months ago.

Thinking of the long, restless nights of frustration when she couldn't sleep, tears came to her eyes. Josh's lovemaking had become addictive and she needed him now that they had become lovers more than she ever had when he was her secret fantasy. The yearning was deep and strong and one that only he could fulfill, and she couldn't help wonder if he ever thought of Jazzy in the same way.

Hours later Jaclyn's thoughts of Josh were replaced with dismay. The two-hour layover at New York's Kennedy Airport had been extended to six. When she finally arrived in Los Angeles, her baggage had been rerouted by mistake and shipped to LAX on a later plane, forcing her to spend the night in a nearby hotel.

Instead of getting there the evening before her exhibit and staying with her brother, she ended up a nervous wreck, driving a rented car dressed in a new dress purchased especially for her debut, and arriving a short time before the exhibit was due to start.

She parked the car, rushed past the vast number of luxury cars, and straight through Josh's partially opened front door into his living room.

It was a nightmare and she had never been so upset in her life. Trying desperately to regain a semblance of composure, she took several deep breaths and prayed. "Lord, please help me handle the trauma of seeing Josh without breaking down completely."

"You're finally here," Josh exclaimed in a relieved voice, descending the stairway from his studio.

Jaclyn spun around, startled by his appearance. Her eyes were wide with anxiety as she stared, drawing in the beauty of his deep indigo-blue eyes. It was the most wonderful feeling in the world to know they were healed and could return her look glance for glance.

"I just got off the phone trying to locate you."

"Hello, Josh," Jaclyn whispered in a throaty voice when he stopped before her. She reached up to kiss his cheek, trying hard to curb the involuntary flush that tinged her face when she thought of their previous intimacy.

Josh gave her a long, intense stare. He cupped her face in his palms, slowly scanning each feature with clear eyes that looked straight into her soul. He inhaled her heady fragrance before placing a tender kiss on her trembling lips.

"Only God knows how much I've missed you, Jazzy," he moaned, folding her close in his arms.

"Jazzy?" Jaclyn questioned in a soft mumur against his jacket lapel. "You knew it was me all the time?"

"From the very first, darling."

"I can't believe it." She bowed her head, pleased her hair spilled in shimmering waves about her flushed cheeks. "How did you ever guess?"

"Other than by your using a key only your brother had a duplicate of right after my lock was changed," Josh told her with an indulgent smile, "your wearing the heart-shaped earrings I gave you; the feel of your quivering lips when I kissed you; the gardenia scent of the shampoo you always use; your voice, which didn't fool me for a moment; your flawless French; your touch, size and shape; your obvious virginity; your lack of concern about getting pregnant."

"I'm not. Continue."

"Your complete lack of knowledge about a hooker's life, including their language, occasional spurts of prudishness, your initial embarrassment in being with my friends during the holidays, your willingness to service me without being paid up front or even to demand my check afterwards, your own familiar handwriting on my hotel receipt, and the note you left by my chair . . ."

"All circumstantial evidence," she informed him in an innocent voice.

"Not to me it wasn't," Josh rebutted, nuzzling the silky blond strands aside to kiss her tender nape. "It's not important how I knew anyway." He gave her a tender kiss. "Your coming to me is the only thing that matters. My God, darling"—he drew her face up for a kiss—"those were the most wonderful days of my life."

"Mine too," she confessed, returning his caress with enthusiasm.

"Come upstairs before we go into the gallery. I want to show you something."

Jaclyn looked up, her eyes wide with apprehension. "Good. I'm so nervous about my first exhibit I appreciate the chance to gather my composure a little. The last few days have really been traumatic."

"Why didn't you phone me as I asked?" Josh scolded. "You know I planned to pick you up."

"I c-couldn't," Jaclyn stammered. "I needed the time alone to prepare myself for our meeting."

Jaclyn touched Josh's arm, looking into his eyes with anxious pleading as her thoughts returned to her first showing. "What if no one likes my paintings?"

"They will." Josh understood exactly the way she felt and how important it was to make a good impression the first time one's art was displayed for public view.

"Trust me," he assured her gently.

"You're prejudiced." She smiled into his eyes.

"About you always," he admitted. "About your work, no. Contrary to your belief, I'm not about to praise any art that's not worthy. Your exhibit far surpasses my expectations. François was overcome with excitement each time I contacted him to check on your progress."

"You checked with my teacher?" Jaclyn asked in amazement.

"Yes," Josh admitted without remorse. "I've kept track of you constantly since I first saw you at the age of fourteen."

Jaclyn stared into Josh's eyes to see if he was telling the truth. He was. The honesty reflected could not be misread. "I think we have a lot to discuss."

"Yes," Josh answered smoothly. "A lifetime at least. But not now."

Jaclyn checked her watch and moaned, "Oh, Josh, I'm almost late. Do I look all right?" She glanced down at her flowing knee-length black dress with its tightly cuffed long sleeves and beautifully draped bodice. Touching the single strand of pearls Josh had given her at Christmas, she asked his opinion.

"I'm not too dowdy-looking, am I? I do have on a dreadfully expensive pair of sexy sandals."

"You're gorgeous," Josh assured her. "You look like a very sophisticated young lady."

"Good," Jaclyn said, and sighed, visibly relieved by his praise.

"That is, until you take time to view the open vulnerability visible in your eyes. Their stunning gray color circled by an ebony ring around the iris has intrigued me since we met."

"I look that bad, huh?" Jaclyn asked with a frown.

"No, Jazzy. You're the most beautiful artist I've ever known, and I've been introduced to too many to remember."

"What if the critics give me a terrible review?"

"They won't."

"But what if they do?" she persisted.

"You'll survive. It happens to the best. Everyone suffers through the agony sometime in their career."

"I think I'd die."

"You won't," he assured her, pulling her into his arms for comfort. "And who cares if they do?"

"I do," she cried in a plaintive voice.

"As long as people come to see your work, I assure you they'll buy. Believe me, I know what I'm talking about."

"I realize you're an expert." She turned her eyes up to him, pleading. "But I've never felt this insecure before and now I'm going to be late as well."

"Don't worry," Josh teased. "All artists are reputed to be eccentric, and it's expected the more noteworthy of them will arrive late or not at all."

"That would be unforgivably rude," Jaclyn replied with a spark of sensitivity.

"Some guests never notice. I always provide plenty of champagne and enough hors d'oeuvres to keep everyone happy. You have ample time left before you need to make your grand entrance. This will allow each person the opportunity to evaluate your work in a leisurely fashion."

"I hope the critics don't drink too much." She looked at Josh with twinkling eyes. "You know what happened when I overconsumed on New Year's?"

"Don't remind me," Josh frowned. "I'll make certain we arrive before they're kissing each other or trying to dance when they can't even stand."

"I was terrible, wasn't I?"

"The worst," Josh agreed readily. "Now shush. I have something to show you. It's a lasting memento of the love we shared."

"We have so much to talk about," Jaclyn proffered again. "I won't even know where to begin."

"We'll discuss everything later. Now I want to show you your first birthday gift. After the exhibit I have a little . . . *bigger stuff* . . . waiting for you in my garage. A silver-gray Porsche with a license plate that reads JAZZY."

Jaclyn was speechless. Was there no end to Josh's generosity? She had always thought he looked a dream driving around in his black sports car. Now they each had their own.

Accepting Jaclyn's tearful thank you, Josh smiled as if it were nothing, then groaned. *"Bigger stuff!"*

"Will you ever forgive me for that insult?" Jaclyn inquired, meeting his eyes with a pleading look.

"Never!" Josh insisted, holding her glance with a look of arrogance that would have brought strangers to their knees.

"I didn't think you would appreciate that remark." She laughed, ignoring his glare.

"As I was saying, Jazzy, I don't want any outside

intrusions after we close the gallery and return to our bedroom. I might even throw away the key."

"Don't even mention the word key," Jaclyn moaned, aware that was how her scheme originally started.

"I already have," Josh gave a deep, knowing laugh.

"What will Bruce say?" she asked, suddenly worried about her brother's opinion. "I haven't said a thing to him about my awful escapade."

"Bruce won't say a word. I've told him everything and he couldn't be happier, though he nearly died of shock to know I seduced his baby sister."

"I seduced you," Jaclyn corrected, adding in an honest quandary, "Josh I—I don't know about later with you. I want you but I don't want that kind of a relationship. Do you understand?"

"Yes," Josh added quietly. "Later tonight I'll prove you want me whatever the relationship, just as I want you however I can get you."

"I'm not talking about a sexual relationship. You know I want you that way. I mean a permanent one."

"I agree with you, sweetheart. Is flying to Las Vegas tomorrow afternoon soon enough to make it permanent for you?"

"Is that a proposal?" Jaclyn cried in a breathless voice.

"The only decent one you'll get tonight," Josh teased. "Logan is flying all our group to Nevada, where we'll be married in the same chapel as Brad and Brandy."

"That's the perfect ending to my lifelong dream," Jaclyn confessed.

"Mine too." Josh folded her into his arms for a tender kiss. "No more conversation now or you don't get to see your present," he warned, rushing her up the stairs to his studio.

What Josh showed her brought a gasp from her throat she was so overcome with shock.

"How did you get that?" Jaclyn exclaimed, turning to stare at Josh's amused face then back to the wall.

Carefully mounted in a heavy frame and displayed alone was her painting, "Stolen Idyll." The soft lighting detailed each sensitive brush stroke that depicted a perfect image of the man beside her. From her angle across the room her love was clearly represented in the intimate, personal work.

"I don't understand. I mailed it to Bruce."

"A Freudian slip on your part, darling." Josh gave her a teasing smile. "You put your brother's name on the address label but used my street number as the place to send it."

"Oh, my gosh," she cried with embarrassment. "How could I do such a stupid thing?"

"Easy," Josh explained. "My man's intuition tells me that I was on your mind at the time. Needless to say, I was shocked when I opened the crate and found my own face staring back at me."

"Only your face?" Jaclyn teased.

"Hardly," he added with a devilish grin. "Your boldness surprised me. Flattered me as well."

"I can see why you think that," Jaclyn scoffed. "You are decidedly near a state of full arousal in the darned thing."

"I thought it was part of your exhibit and damned near flipped out when I saw what you had painted. It's definitely the work of a woman who's been loved by the man in question."

"True," Jaclyn agreed softly, giving him an unshielded glance for the first time since his sight returned. "My loving tribute to you."

"As this is mine," Josh told her, removing the draping over a bronze that brought emotional tears to Jaclyn's eyes the moment she saw what it was. "I sculpted this just for you, my lovely wife-to-be."

Her eyes scrutinized the sculpted figure resting on a marble pedestal beside Josh's bed. It was a perfect miniature of her in the same half-sitting languorous state she had painted Josh.

She was posed with her head thrown back and her thick wavy hair loose about her shoulders. Her breasts were full and upthrust as if waiting for her lover to caress them. One long leg was outstretched, the other drawn up at the knee as she relaxed her hips on the marble base. It was a masterpiece and, like her oil, executed with love.

Jaclyn exchanged an intimate glance with Josh. In his arms she had learned from the first touch the power in his sensitive, artistic fingers made every inch of her body come alive. Tonight proved he had the gift to imprint that response in bronze was well.

The most amazing phenomenon was the title. Etched into the base was "Stolen Idyll." Somehow across the ocean a reaching-out of minds and hearts joined as she and Josh each titled their work. A psychic empathy, possibly. Unexplained but beautiful.

Jaclyn rushed into his arms, eager to express her appreciation in the sweetest way she knew. With a soft cry she flung her arms around his neck and kissed him until they both were weak with the need to carry their passion to its climax.

"The little nymph in your bathroom is me, isn't it?"

"Yes." Josh hugged her close. "I sculpted her right after our first meeting when you were only fourteen years old."

"I'm stunned," Jaclyn whispered, pressing her face against his lapel. "Each bronze is exquisite. Thank you, darling."

"Let's miss the exhibit entirely?" Josh insisted in a hoarse voice against the scented skin behind her ear.

"I c-can't," Jaclyn hesitated, wanting nothing more. "I haven't said hello to my brother or Brad and Brandy or even Logan."

"Okay, honey," Josh said, pushing her away and straightening his jacket. "It isn't the best timing, is it?"

"Unfortunately, I have to agree." Jaclyn smiled, giving him a wistful, starry-eyed glance.

"Let's go, then, Ms. Jaclyn Howard." Josh put his arm out for her to take. "This time I'm escorting you as I've wanted to for years."

"I appreciate it, Mr. Josh Kingman." She chuckled, placing her arm in his and following him down the stairs and out the side door to a private, connecting entrance into his gallery.

"I'm so proud of you tonight I could die," Josh told her. "I want to announce our relationship to everyone and praise your work until all the world knows about it."

"Well," she said, and laughed nervously, "I could use a little backup support during the next few hours."

"You need nothing from me, darling," Josh assured her. "Your exhibit is the most forceful I've shown. The realism of your poignant faces will stun your audience. Your time in the Peace Corps was well spent. There's not a superficial work in the group. Just deep, moving, emotional oils that hold a person spellbound with interest."

"Have Brad and Brandy seen their portrait yet?"

"Yes. They're both overcome by your talent. Neither dreamed you would paint the four of them together in such a natural pose. It's on display tonight."

"I'm glad they like it. Their loving expressions were

a challenge to recapture while Bobby and Betty's impish little faces were unexpectedly easy."

"Would you like a Janet and Jason of your own to paint in a year or so?" Josh asked in a serious tone.

"I'd love it" Jaclyn exlaimed, giving him an encouraging smile.

"Good. We'll work on it tonight, my sensual, gifted wife-to-be."

"That"—Jaclyn gave him a wide smile—"is all the flattery I can stand for now." She stood back as he entered before her.

"Give 'em hell, honey," he whispered into her ear. "No one has the slightest idea you're a gorgeous young woman in addition to being a talented one."

Jaclyn raised her chin and followed Josh into the gallery with her hand firmly clasped in his strong fingers. She smiled when necessary, looked serious at appropriate moments, and all the time wished she was up in his studio.

Despite hours of heady praise for her forceful style of painting, she felt the beginning of a headache. The glitter and excessive promises of fame emphasized more than anything that she really was a serious, intense art student more at home with brush and pallet in her hand than being the center of attention.

Josh handled everyone like the professional he was. He looked aloof and elegant in this black tuxedo and obviously felt at east promoting art in an elegant manner to a monied crowd. Jaclyn observed him with interest, wondering if she would ever have his poise and sophistication in a similar situation.

She cast her eyes down, checking the rounded edges of her perfectly manicured nails. Right now she'd much prefer paint stains and privacy. It was too much to assimilate at once when Josh told her the astronomical fees her collection was bringing.

She wasn't so naive she didn't realize much of her popularity was due to Josh. Unknown artists rarely received such prices. It took a name and track record to command an enormous fee. Her one helpful requirement for success was rapport with a gallery owner. On that point she was definitely a winner!

"Come on, honey," Josh whispered into her ear. "We're sneaking away."

"Who will close the gallery?"

"Logan," Josh told her, easing his way past the crowd and through his private door.

"I didn't even get to say good-bye to Brandy," Jaclyn objected, looking back as the door was slammed shut behind her.

"You can say it tomorrow during our flight to Vegas."

"Impatient, aren't you?"

"You're damned right." Before Josh finished speaking, she was upstairs, had been rushed into the bathroom and told to put on the black negligee he had given her for Christmas.

Jaclyn took her time before walking out, freshly showered, perfumed, and feeling beautiful in her sensual nightgown. Her heart beat like a wild thing, thinking about being in Josh's arms again.

"I'm ready," Jaclyn whispered softly, moving across the room.

"I'm more than ready," Josh returned, beckoning her to come to him.

She stared with luminous gray eyes. She wanted him so bad it was an ache deep inside the pit of her abdomen. Her breathing was shallow, her mouth curved into a seductive smile, her lips trembling yet warm and moist in anticipation of his possession.

Josh lay stretched out in the middle of his massive bed watching the beauty of Jaclyn's shapely figure displayed beneath the flowing silk as she moved gracefully to him. His eyes narrowed, willing to wait for what lay ahead.

"Take it off," he commanded without moving a muscle.

"I just put it on," she protested, clutching it around her waist.

"Off, Jazzy," he warned, starting to rise. "I want to see the beauty of your nude body."

Jaclyn slipped her gown off, letting it slide to the carpet. She stood before him, proud to let his piercing eyes absorb her form as hers had so often done his.

"My God!" he exclaimed hoarsely. "How much love you."

Unable to stand the torment of not being in his arms any longer, she went to him with a rapturous cry.

"Likewise, darling. Forever and ever."

The fine sensitive artist's hands that could shape a piece of clay into a thing of beauty gathered her close and brought her fulfillment with the same keen expertise.

It was beautiful. A hungry coupling where neither could bring the other to break the silence with words of love. Their bodies said it for them as they clung together for a long, long time.

After Jaclyn lay replete and cuddled close in Josh's arms she was brought back to reality from the hazy aftermath of his exquisite lovemaking by his generous praise.

"You have a rare gift, Jazzy," Josh whispered into her ear.

"What's that?" Jaclyn asked, relaxing in her favorite position, snuggled beneath his arm with her face resting on his warm chest.

"You always make me feel welcome to your body, yet you also give me comfort in your arms without sex. You're quiet when it's important, talk with me when I want. You're an excellent cook . . ."

"How do you know that?" Jaclyn asked. "I haven't had the opportunity to cook a meal for us yet."

"Bruce told me. He said you were much better than your mother or any of his wives."

"How nice." Jaclyn smiled proudly. "I think it ties in with my artistic nature. I really am good."

"You can prove it in the morning," Josh allowed, "Now don't interrupt. I wasn't finished praising you."

"Continue," she teased impishly. "I love it."

"You also have soft, healing hands that eased the tension from my neck and brow when I was wracked with headaches in Seattle and Victoria."

"You make me sound perfect." Jaclyn laughed softly, twining one inquisitive finger in a whorl of dark chest hair, then doing the same with another.

"Hardly perfect," he teased, drawing her up for a fierce kiss. "You have a quick temper, which I never knew about before, and a damned sassy tongue that often needs curbing."

"Those bad traits are your fault," Jaclyn pointed out with her chin raised haughtily. "You're the only person who made me mad enough for either to surface." She placed a gentle kiss over his heart. "Other than that, I'm perfect, then?"

"Not hardly, witch," Josh disagreed, swatting her on the soft buttocks. "Your former occupation left an awful lot to be desired to a possessive, frustrated sculptor who couldn't see. Whatever made you decide to come to me pretending to be a call girl?"

"I wasn't about to let Bruce send you anyone else," Jaclyn insisted jealously. "It was also the only scheme I could come up with on the spur of the moment to assure I was first in line!" she shot back as an afterthought.

Annoyed by Josh's deep laughter at her temper, she also admitted in a peeved voice, "I've loved you for years and you never even looked at me."

"Oh, Jazzy, how mistaken you are. I've watched, wanted, and waited for you since you were sixteen years old. Sometimes the wanting got so damned bad my guts hurt."

Josh closed his eyes for a moment. "I hate to admit it, but when you were only fourteen, I desired you until I ached with frustration. That caused me many nights of agony because I was a grown man and you were only a child."

"Yes, I was," Jaclyn answered softly. "What you don't seem to realize, though, is girls at that age can also have long nights of unchildish thoughts."

"Show me what they were," Josh insisted, pulling her up for a hard kiss.

"Fine with me," Jaclyn agreed, cupping his strong jaw to return his kiss then replace it with another even more passionate.

"Your true personality has really surfaced the last few months, hasn't it, you wanton female?" Josh commented with a self-satisfied smile on his smug lips.

"Abruptly. I remember the exact day," Jaclyn teased. "It was December . . ."

"Don't remind me," Josh cut her off. "You impetuous, scheming little devil."

Jaclyn shot him a scathing glance and continued, "Before then I wouldn't tell my closest friend how I felt about you. Loving openly and having that love returned has changed my stuffy outlook considerably."

She reached over to kiss him tenderly. "Now I want to shout to the world. *Look, I'm Josh's woman. We're lovers and he's the best in the world.* The hardest thing was not telling you who I was and how much I loved you."

"I had to bite my tongue every night too," Josh admitted, kissing her again. "How the hell did you think you'd ever fool me coming to my bed a virgin?" he scolded gently.

"Good acting."

"No one's that good, honey," Josh teased boldly.

"Well, I had hoped my yearly checkups had solved the obvious physical problem." Jaclyn sat up, staring at Josh's smug expression highlighted by the laughter in his keen eyes. "You never said anything."

"I'm no fool," he insisted, drawing her down for a lengthy kiss. "I wanted you and did everything possible to keep you with me."

"You did?" Jaclyn gave him a scathing glance. "It was *my* scheme!" she told him. *"I* seduced *you,* not the other way around."

"No woman in the world could have seduced me but you, darling. A virgin hooker, yet!" He laughed, doubling up as she became furious over the knowledge she hadn't fooled him for a second.

"Maybe I wouldn't still have been a virgin, Mr. Know-it-all, if you hadn't spoiled me for other men from the innocent age of fourteen. I could never think of another man after that, thanks to you."

"You're welcome," Josh returned with a satisfied laugh. His eyes twinkled, as it was the greatest news he'd ever heard. "See you stay that way too."

"If you cared for me, why didn't you say anything or call me after I left you in the hospital?" Jaclyn asked curiously, ignoring his masculine gloating.

"I didn't want to intrude on your time because I knew how important this opening was to you and how busy you would be," Josh told her. "So I bided my time until your twenty-fourth birthday."

"Okay, that explains your not calling, but what about all those intervening years?"

"I wanted you to have a full life before I entered it. You seemed content attending college, working for the Peace Corps, studying art and painting."

"I was satisfied," she admitted, adding impishly, "other than physically."

"You?" Josh scoffed. *"I* was the one forced to put my sexual energy into my work rather than easing it in you."

"Look how successful you are now because of that dedication."

"The years passed awfully slow, Jazzy," Josh told her seriously.

"It was time well spent," she assured him with an impish look in her eyes. "I have a twenty-five-thousand-dollar coat to prove it."

"Greedy brat!" he scolded, kissing her hard on the lips.

"After my birthday what were you going to do?"

"I was going to entice you up to my bedroom, then seduce you. Twenty-four is long enough for any woman to remain innocent."

"How did you know I still was?" she taunted with a raised chin.

"I paid François to make certain no young art student or old, lascivious patron of the arts bothered you. He had orders to call me the moment they did."

"What then?"

"I was going to fly over and start my seduction scene ahead of time."

"You're crazy!" Jaclyn scoffed at his statement. "A mad artist for certain."

"I don't deny I'm mad about you. I never intended you would leave my side after your exhibit even if I had to kidnap you."

"Really?" Jaclyn asked, feeling rather pleased by Josh's forceful, possessive confession.

"Really," Josh insisted gruffly. "I intended to fly you to my private hideaway in Hawaii, and if necessary, keep you there until you learned to love me or I accomplished a hell of a lot of work."

"You're talking crazier all the time," Jaclyn chuckled, slanting him a sassy glance. "I do admit it sounds rather intriguing. Is the option still open?"

"Anytime you want or misbehave. Either way we head away from here."

"Interesting concept for wife control." She kissed each eye closed and laid her head on his chest. "It just might catch on and be a winner."

"You won't believe how many times, despite the luxury and amidst all the festivities, I yearned to be alone with you in Victoria, Jazzy."

"I felt the same," she admitted. "I wanted to be the one to prepare your meals and take care of you all by myself."

"I would have enjoyed that," Josh admitted. "Especially with Logan around."

"Even being pampered began to pall toward the end. I really am a private person, Josh. I've had it with all the hoopla. Could we go away to your island home and work together or even cloister ourselves up here?"

"How about Eze?" Josh brought up with a quick laugh. "We could go there and paint sunsets."

"I'd love it."

"You brat. I could hear the phone keep on ringing as you . . . *talked* . . . with your friend, Lerisa. You really were a menace in your hooker days."

"Me?" Jaclyn looked astonished. "You were always interrogating me and asking me things I didn't know."

"Yes," Josh admitted easily. "And I enjoyed every

minute of listening to you stammer around, then come up with one preposterous lie after another."

"I thought I did quite well considering I knew nothing about a call girl's life-style."

"As I said, in speech you were a disaster. In bed," Josh put his hand on his chin to think, "you topped them all."

"I think it's because I had an excellent teacher."

"Of course it was," he teased, ducking the pillow hastily thrown at his head.

"You're becoming obnoxious again and I was being honest about my need to be alone much of the time."

"I'm the same way, darling. That's why I purchased my island retreat several years ago. I built an ocean front home overlooking the sands that I think you'll love as much as I do."

"If you built it, I know I will," Jaclyn promised.

"We can escape to it whenever the influx of visitors gets too heavy in Laguna Beach. When you begin to feel hemmed in, away we'll go."

"Josh, would you really have had an exhibit in your gallery if my paintings were bad?" she asked, changing the subject.

"No, I wouldn't," he told her honestly. "I couldn't ruin my reputation as a critic and as an artist. But I would have let you fill a room with them though."

"Which one?" Jaclyn asked, impressed by his integrity despite the fact she knew he loved her.

"The bathroom." He ducked to avoid the hastily thrown bed pillow.

"You beast!"

"Not a beast, you bad-tempered witch. Just a good businessman."

"Only a businessman?" Jazzy questioned with one arched brow raised in disbelief.

"No. A good lover too," he bragged, rolling her

over on her back. He placed his hands on her hips to position her beneath him. "Now, prepare to be had again, woman. I'm in the mood to inspire us both to create another Stolen Idyll starting right now."

"Fine with me," she agreed, pushing against his shoulders to ask, "Josh, just what is a Jazam?"

Jaclyn's eyes filled with frost as Josh burst out laughing. "What's so darned funny? I'm perfectly serious and want to know what it is."

"A Jazam is nothing as any professional hooker would have known. Instead you hemmed and hawed for a week and kept coming up with the craziest excuses I've heard in my life on why you weren't in the mood to do it that night. I've never had such fun."

"Why, you—you beast!" Jaclyn spluttered furiously, squirming out from under him. "I worried every day and night we were together and it was only a joke!"

"Of course. My own at first." Josh laughed uproariously. "Until Brandy started quizzing Brad about it, then we all three had a good laugh."

"All three? You dared tell Brad and Logan about me?"

"You're damned right!" Josh exclaimed without remorse, lying on his back to watch her. "The way Logan came on to you the first night I had to do something, since I couldn't see to rearrange his jaw bone."

"You're terrible," Jaclyn fumed, sitting beside him with hands on her hips. "Each of you are for having the nerve to put me on for an entire week."

"We loved it," Josh admitted. "Though that damned Logan still got carried away when he saw you in your negligee on Christmas morning."

"I wish he had!" Jaclyn glared down at Josh with flashing eyes filled with temper.

"What?" Josh kissed the warm, sensitive hollow of

her palm, unconcerned she was shooting daggers into him with her eyes.

"Carried me away to replace old Lady Claus."

"Oh, that," Josh said casually. "He'd never have made it out of the bedroom with you. By then I was very familiar with our suite and would have took him on rather than let you leave."

"Beast!"

"Just protecting my own." He laughed. "Now, hold still while I make love to you."

"You expect me to hold still for that?" Jaclyn asked in disbelief.

"No," Josh growled, pulling her into his arms. "I expect you to wiggle and squirm, pant and purr and generally act a wanton witch from beginning to end."

"You're even worse than I thought." Jaclyn giggled, pushing Josh away when he tried to draw her back into his arms.

"I'm not," he protested. "I'm just . . ."

"Just about to get your first Jazam." Jaclyn checked his words.

"There isn't any such position, I told you. It was a joke just to see how you'd react. Strictly a spur of the moment figment of my imagination and nothing more."

"Not anymore it isn't," Jaclyn vowed, pressing him into the mattress with determined hands.

"What the hell are you talking about, woman?" Josh quizzed, reaching out to draw her down with him.

"Lie still and I'll show you."

"I don't believe this," Josh groaned, resting his head on the pillow. "I told you there's no sexual position called Jazam."

"There is now," Jaclyn assured him as her fingers began to roam over his taut body.

"There is?" Josh questioned with rising interest. He clasped her hands to still their intimate movements when they reached, then held him in her grip.

"There certainly is," Jaclyn assured him with an impish smile while watching his reaction with interest.

A flame seemed to leap out of Josh's beautiful eyes as he lay back, intently scrutinizing each of her features. It was a fire of the deepest blue she'd ever seen in her life.

"Prove there's a Jazam, if you dare," he warned sensuously as she lowered her face to caress him.

Jaclyn did. More than once.